BALTIC
APPROACH

ALSO BY MAX HERTZBERG

The East Berlin Series
Stealing The Future (2015)
Thoughts Are Free (2016)
Spectre At The Feast (2017)

Reim Series
Stasi Vice (2018)
Operation Oskar (2019)
Berlin Centre (2019)
Baltic Approach (2020)
Rostock Connection (2021)

Other Fiction
Cold Island (2018)

Non-fiction
with Seeds For Change
How To Set Up A Workers' Co-op (2012)
A Consensus Handbook (2013)

After the experience of the East German political upheaval in 1989/90, Max Hertzberg became a Stasi files researcher. Since then he has been a book seller and a social change trainer before writing his debut novel, *Stealing The Future* (2015).
Visit the author's website for background information on the GDR, and guides to walking tours around the East Berlin in which many of his books are set.

www.maxhertzberg.co.uk

BALTIC APPROACH

MAX HERTZBERG

OV Press

P 1 2 3 4 5 6 7 8 9 10

Published in 2020 by Max Hertzberg
www.maxhertzberg.co.uk

c/o Wolf Press, 22 Hartley Crescent, LS6 2LL

A CIP record for this title is available from the British Library
ISBN: 9781913125080 (paperback), 9781913125103 (large print paperback),
9781913125097 (epub)

Set in 10½ on 12pt Libertinus Serif

FEBRUARY 1984

A list of main characters and a glossary of GDR and German terms are available at the end of this book.

Denmark
• Gedser

0   50km

Heiligen-
damm • • Warnemünde
Bad   • Rostock
Doberan
• Border Crossing
Point Herrnburg

Federal
Republic
of Germany

(West Germany)

Malchow •

Lärz •

Gransee •

PR
Poland

West   Berlin, Capital
Berlin   of the GDR

• Königs
Wusterhausen
Wünsdorf •

German
Democratic
Republic

(East Germany)

ČSSR

1
BERLIN LICHTENBERG

"Know this man?" asked Major Kühn. He didn't bother looking round as I entered the conference room, he was too interested in the television screen. Same as the rest of the brass assembled around the wide table.

"No, Comrade Major." I didn't have a good view, and the picture was jumping around—the way it does when the videotape is paused—but I was certain I'd never seen the grey-haired pensioner before.

"Carry on," ordered Kühn, and a man in a blue dust coat bent to press the play button.

We all watched as the subject flickered across the monitor. He was facing a hidden camera in a narrow Sprelacart-lined cabin: one of the entry control booths at Friedrichstrasse railway station border crossing point. At the bottom edge of the screen we could see the back of the passport controller's head bobbing around as he examined paperwork, checked lists and kept a discreet eye open for any instructions that might come through on the screen below the shelf. The subject didn't fidget, but observed the proceedings closely, his eyes darting regularly up to the camera in the corner.

There was no soundtrack, but my mind provided the buzz as the door to the booth opened. The subject stretched his arm out to collect his passport and exited stage right.

"Any further footage of the subject?" asked a stout lieutenant colonel, his mouth moving around an unlit cigar.

In answer, Kühn passed him a folder of still photographs documenting the subject's progress down the steps from the platform and then along the windowless passageway that connects the platforms with passport control. The final still showed him leaving the station by the south exit on Georgenstrasse.

The lieutenant colonel flicked through the pictures, took the cigar out of his mouth long enough to grunt and passed the folder to the next man along, a major general.

They were all in uniform, those men at the table, and they all wore silver or gold caterpillars of braid on their shoulders to show how important they were.

"That'll do." Kühn waved at the man still hovering near the video player, and with a click-click-clunk the tape stopped and ejected. The technician left it jutting out of the machine, and I followed him out of the room, shutting the door behind us.

"Want one?" I offered the man in the dust coat a nail and he took it, his hand reaching into his pocket for matches.

We smoked, but we didn't talk—there was nothing to talk about. The material on the tape and in the photographs was classified, even the tape itself was not a safe topic for conversation—I'd glimpsed the colourful label, JVC, as it ejected—doubtless confiscated from a Western parcel that had never quite made its destination.

We leaned against the wall, ears flapping, wary of footsteps approaching or doors opening. We were on the brass's corridor, didn't do to be found lounging around smoking.

It was a quarter of an hour before the door behind us opened. The caterpillar carriers filed out, none of them acknowledging our presence, preferring small talk amongst themselves: wives and imported cars, weekend homes and Western domestic appliances they'd acquired.

Once the officers had reached a safe distance, I looked around the door frame. The head of my section, Major Kühn, was still sitting at the table, photographs of the subject spread out before him.

"Come in and shut the door, Comrade Heym," he ordered. For some reason, when I'd been posted to ZAIG, Major Kühn had decided my name was Heym, and it wasn't my job to put him right.

So I came in, shut the door behind myself and stood by the table, thumbs along the seams of my trousers, shoulders back and eyes pointing dead ahead.

He left me like that while he shuffled through the photographs again. When he finally looked up, his eyebrows were raised, as if surprised to see me still there.

"Sit down, take a look at these—I want to hear your thoughts." He gathered the pictures together, tapped them square and pushed the pile across the table.

I remained standing, bending over to examine the fuzzy pictures—stills from the video cameras at the border, too grainy to see much—and I still didn't recognise the grey-haired man. That was all there was to it—what other thoughts did the major expect me to have?

"Codename Merkur," said the major, ripping the cellophane from a brand-new red and white packet of Marlboro. He lit up without offering me one, filling the conference room with the scent of Western tobacco. "Came through Friedrichstrasse Station crossing point at midday, headed straight for the police registration desk in the *Haus des Reisens* on Alexanderplatz. Asked to speak to a Gisela Bauer." He took another sip of his cigarette and checked to see whether I was impressed.

I wasn't. So far, I hadn't heard anything to make my ears stick up. A Western tourist goes to register at the police desk—but sooner or later, almost every foreigner who plans to stay for more than a day in our half of Berlin ends up at the registration desk of the central travel agency.

I played around with the photographs a bit longer, just for the sake of appearances. The man had a name now—Codename Merkur—but he looked the same as he had a moment before.

Who dreamt up these ridiculous names? When an informant is recruited, they get to choose their own handle, but in these cases, when potentially negative-hostile individuals are identified, the naming is done by whoever has the honour of opening the case file.

"Gisela Bauer is the legend used by Lieutenant Ruth Gericke. You knew her as Sanderling," my superior continued. "As you know, Sanderling is deceased."

I kept my eyes on the photographs, even managing to finger through them a bit, but with that brief statement, Kühn had caught my interest.

Of course I knew Sanderling was deceased—I was the one who found her body. It was the end of last year, I'd been working with her for just a day or two, and until now I hadn't even known her real name. But I'd liked her—that's something that doesn't happen too often in this business.

I stopped fiddling with the photographs and looked directly at the major, hoping he'd tell me more.

"The police officer at the desk sent Merkur away, he was gone before anyone thought to do anything about him." Kühn tapped his cigarette on the cut glass ashtray in front of him, his eyes large and blurry behind thick glasses.

"Are Main Department II showing any interest, Comrade Major?" I wanted to know why we were talking about Sanderling when she'd been an operative in HA II, the counter-intelligence department. I'd been in this situation before—covering the preliminaries for a case only for another department to take over as soon as I'd done the groundwork. But this time was different, I'd be happy to do the boring research—I wanted to know more about Sanderling, about the work she'd done in the West. And why someone on our side had wanted her dead.

Call it a debt if you want. It was something I owed her, and this could be my chance to pay it off.

2
BERLIN LICHTENBERG

When I got back to my office, I stood by the window, thinking and smoking. Lights from the building opposite shone across the void of the courtyard. How plausible was it that Merkur, the grey-haired gent from West Germany had really crossed the Wall just to ask after Sanderling?

People often do things you'll never understand unless you can find a way into their heads. And since Merkur wasn't here to ask, I poured myself a drink and opened his file. The facts, such as we knew them, were all in there.

The head of Passport Control at Friedrichstrasse Station reported Merkur's entry into the GDR as being logged at 1151.

Just half an hour later, the policeman at the travel bureau was giving Merkur the brush off. The Westerner had disappeared into the wind and sleet and not been seen again. We were still waiting for an exit time, assuming he had left the territory of the GDR.

I went back to the window, drawing on my cigarette until it burnt my fingers. Merkur's trip over here, asking for Sanderling ... was he leaving us a message in a bottle?

If so, what did his message say?

Considering the case was only a few hours old, the paperwork was admirably comprehensive. In the reports, the grey haired man from the photographs was referred to only by his assigned codename, but the copies of his West German passport, the day visa and the compulsory money change receipt all showed his real name: *Werner Seiffert*.

I stared at that name. It wasn't a coincidence—the grey haired gent was Source Bruno's father.

I first met Sanderling during an operation in West Germany, right at the end of 1983. Back then, she'd been in position in Bonn, observing Source Bruno, real name: Arnold Seiffert.

Source Bruno had asked to come over to the East. He was an employee of the BKA, the West German Federal Crime Agency, so the Ministry had been more interested in turning him around and sending him back to spy for us. No doubt there had been the usual promises: stay in place for a year, maybe two, definitely no more than that. A year of uncovering secrets and passing them back to us, then we'll set you up, a hero, a new life over here.

But things had gone wrong from the moment Bruno had offered his services, and the operation had ended with him lying dead on his living room floor in Bonn, and Sanderling and myself needing emergency exfiltration.

After my return to the GDR, I'd been informed that Bruno had been murdered by First Lieutenant Sachse, an officer of our foreign intelligence department, HV A.

That was a surprise, but I could cope with it. Yet about the same time, I found Sanderling's body under the ice of the River Spree, and her death was something I had still to come to terms with.

I lit a cigarette to distract myself from thoughts of my dead colleague, and once the room was dense with smoke, I turned back to the file.

At this stage of any case, we don't bother ourselves with questions like *why?* We focus first on the *who?* the *when?* and the *what?* My first task was to establish Merkur's background, such as it was already known to us, which meant fetching his son's files and dusting them down.

Even now, six weeks after I'd sent those files to the archive,

I could remember practically every detail in the notes: I'd spent days reading and rereading the reports, questioning as many of those who had any contact with Bruno as I could find. I knew the paperwork didn't have much to say about Bruno's father: Werner Seiffert was a postman who'd left the GDR with his wife sometime before the Wall was built and had never returned. Until now.

Nevertheless, I dutifully took the stairs to the basement and started the search for Bruno's files. It took a while to find the F16 card. It wasn't just that his index card was hiding somewhere in the midst of four million others, but that the whole collection had been split between various cellars because somebody at the very top had decided it was a good idea to build a bunker under the archive.

I tracked down Bruno's F16, but my work was far from done. The index card only gave me the information I needed to go on to the next card in the paper trail: the F22.

Until you have the F22 in your fist, you don't know the accession number, and without the accession number you won't find the actual file you started the process to see.

Convoluted? Sure, but it kept us out of trouble.

When I had all the necessaries, I collected the files and sat at the small reading table. A strip light buzzed above me, the archivist flitted between shadows, eyeing me with enthusiastic suspicion.

I ignored the distractions and reacquainted myself with the contents of Bruno's file, flicking through until I found the pages I wanted. Here it was: familial background. Reports on his parents and those members of his extended family who still lived in the GDR. I turned the sheet, revealing a photograph of the father, a mugshot for an *Ausweis* he'd applied for over thirty years ago. I looked at this photo of Werner Seiffert, and he winked back in the wavering light. Pulling out the copy of his up-to-date West German passport, I compared the documents.

Merkur's recent paperwork stated clearly that we were dealing with one Werner Seiffert, the details of his age and place of birth tallying with the information here in the old file.

For any other organ of the state, an *Ausweis* or passport is enough to prove identity. But the Ministry isn't just any organ. We always want more.

The photograph in our files had yellowed and deteriorated over the years, but the outline of Seiffert's features were clear enough. Thirty years can change a person—hair goes grey, recedes, is cut and oiled into different styles; skin sags around the eyes and jowls. Moustaches and beards come and go. Even noses can change if you survive long enough or show sufficient dedication to the bottle. But ears retain their shape, even when they grow with advancing age.

In the recent passport picture of Merkur, his pomaded hair was combed over the top of his ears—no positive identification possible with available material.

I returned the file to the trolley and, since the appearance of Merkur meant the Bruno case had become active again, I went to the main desk to fill in a requisition slip for the file to be sent to my office. The archivist wasn't anywhere to be seen, probably lurking in the stacks, waiting for fresh victims to stare at. I left the slip on his desk and returned to my office.

The day was over, the brass had long since been driven home in their Chaikas, Volgas and Citroëns, leaving us apparatchiki to finish the day's business.

But I was in no rush to leave the office. I locked away the Merkur dossier and found a few other files to revise. There was nobody and nothing waiting for me back at my flat, and since the turn of the year I'd been having trouble sleeping. It was a new thing—I used to be able to sleep anytime, anywhere, untroubled by the workings of conscience. But 1984 was turning out to be different.

Closing my eyes and drifting off wasn't the problem, it was what was waiting for me when I got there.

3
BERLIN FRIEDRICHSHAIN

The sun didn't bother to report for duty the next morning—wasn't even due to return from winter leave for a few more months—but the fading street lamps told me it was time to put the restless night behind me and to start a new day.

I parted the curtains and looked out—the featureless grey clouds were still there, pressing even lower than usual. They matched my mood.

Three weeks and one day since I'd watched a crematorium worker shove Sanderling's plain coffin into the oven. The same day I buried my friend Holger Fritsch. Twenty-one nights of fractured sleep, waiting for one or the other to creep into my bedroom, but it was always her, never him.

Despite the frosty temperature, the bins next to the entrance to my block stank of damp brown-coal ash and rotting cabbage. A passing Trabant added to the stringent brew already scratching at my throat.

But I didn't care about smells or sub-zero temperatures, I'm not the type for phenomenological or meteorological philosophy. What I did care about was getting to my office before the brass had a chance to trundle in. As a rule, the bigwigs enjoy catching us underlings out, even if they have to get up early to do so. I hadn't been in this department long enough to get the measure of the head of my section, Major Kühn, so, for the time being, it was safer to make sure I was present and ready when he came calling first thing in the morning.

I'd had more contact with Captain Dupski, my immediate superior, and I felt I understood him a little. After much observation and consideration of the matter, I decided Dupski really didn't care much about anything other than *Kegeln*. And since I hadn't made the section's bowling team, I could rely on his lack of interest in me and my cases.

I climbed the steps of the U-Bahn station and walked up the hill. A light fog wavered in the air, coating pavement and walls with greasy ice. Magdalenenstrasse is buried deep between tall walls, the blank windows of the MfS Central Headquarters to one side, the barbed wire of the Magda prison on the other. Opposite the gap between spiked prison walls and courthouse, that's where you'll find the back gate I use to enter Berlin Centre. I opened my clapperboard for the sentry, waiting for him to check my mugshot and the coloured stamps that show me to be a fully paid-up employee of the Ministry.

Through the courtyard, stepping over fingers of ice that trace cracks in the concrete, down the side of the Ministry's own supermarket until I arrive at Entrance 1 of House 4.

I wasn't planning on staying long in the office this morning, a brief skim of Bruno's dossier. But when I checked the secretariat, there were no signs that the file had been released from the archive, nor of a report from Friedrichstrasse Station Border Crossing. I was still waiting for an exit time for Merkur.

Back in my office, I leafed through Merkur's thin folder, reaching into the drawer for a lemon-flavoured mint, letting the acid stickiness smother a tongue still thick from a broken night's sleep. I stopped when I got to the reports on Merkur's entry into the GDR and read the short statements twice, making notes as I went.

The next page was a statement from *Hauptwachtmeister* Fries, the cop from the foreigner registration desk at the central travel bureau on Alexanderplatz. I read his statement twice too before reaching into the drawer to pull out a Berlin phone directory.

Flicking through until I found *Reisebüro der DDR*, I dialled 2150, the number listed for the Alexanderplatz office, and asked for the police desk. The line purred as the extension rang, then a click as the receiver was lifted:

"*Deutsche Volkspolizei, Ausländermeldung im Reisebüro der DDR. Hauptwachtmeister Fries am Apparat.*" A deep voice, Berlin accent. Slow but steady.

I hung up on him. He'd already told me what I wanted to know: Sergeant Fries was on duty, I'd find him at his post if I left now.

No need to give advance notice, I find it better that way.

4
BERLIN ALEXANDERPLATZ

Police Sergeant Fries was just how I'd imagined him. He filled his green uniform nicely, his tunic buttons pulled tight over a proud belly. Four chevrons on his lower sleeve showed he'd been a cop for over twenty years, and the Kaiser moustache pinned above his thin mouth told me everything I needed to know about this character.

I was sitting in the waiting area, between a draughty door and a dusty rubber plant. From here I had a good view of the sergeant while I pretended to leaf through a travel brochure advertising the touristic highlights of our little Republic.

An American couple were eyeing the stack of forms Fries had shunted over the desk towards them, they were beginning to wonder whether a visit to Frederick the Great's palace and gardens in Potsdam was worth the paperwork.

The policeman wasn't being unfriendly, he was just doing his job by refusing to respond to any of the pleasantries the couple were trying to share with him. In the end they gave up their attempts at small-talk in broken German and filled in the forms with an industriousness that revealed Teutonic heritage.

Fries looked on impassively. He didn't care whether the tourists went to Potsdam or not. Whichever way it turned out, he'd get to wield his oversized rubber stamp. He did so now, only the movement of his moustache betraying his enthusiasm for the task at hand.

The stamp thumped down on several pieces of paper, some disappeared beneath the counter, others were handed back to the subdued tourists before they crept out of the building.

I put my brochure down and joined Fries at the counter.

"Wait!" he growled without looking up. The rubber stamp was hovering, about to slam down onto the ink-pad again, but he held his hand when I failed to respectfully move away.

He looked up, clocked me. His moustache moved up and down as he swallowed. I wasn't in uniform, but Fries was smart enough to recognise me for what I was, and he carefully replaced the stamp on its stand.

"Comrade," he said in a different tone of voice from the one he'd used with the Americans. Less assertive, but equally bureaucratic.

I unbuttoned my coat and fetched the photograph of Merkur from the inside pocket. Taking my time about it, my eyes never leaving the cop's, I pushed the picture across the counter and Fries lowered his head, dedicating his full attention to the task at hand. When he finally looked up he didn't say anything, but I saw the light of recognition in his eyes.

"Tell me about him, Comrade *Hauptwachtmeister*."

"Yesterday-"

"Wednesday?" I interrupted, just for the sake of it.

"Wednesday the 1st of February," Fries confirmed with a clipped nod. "The person depicted in this photograph, wearing Western clothes, approached the foreigner registration desk of the German People's Police in the *Haus des Reisens* and asked to speak to Frau Gisela Bauer. The subject had a west German accent, from somewhere in the north. I told him that no-one of that name worked here."

"Did you ask for his papers?"

The cop shook his head. "The subject told me he'd call again later and left."

"Why didn't you demand to see his papers?"

"It would have necessitated following the subject outside, leaving the registration desk unstaffed."

"Tell me more about him," I demanded. I didn't give him

much time to answer my questions, hurried him along with more demands. I wasn't here to listen to rambling accounts and evasions.

"That's your lot. He wore Western clothes, had a Western accent, asked for Frau Bauer and left."

"And he waited to hear your answer regarding Colleague Bauer before leaving?"

Fries paused, his fingers found his moustache and twisted one end. "No, he turned away before I could tell him there was no Frau Bauer here—he was half-way through the door before I thought to ascertain his particulars."

Seemed Merkur had had no expectation of meeting Gisela Bauer here. Another point in favour of the message-in-a-bottle theory.

5
BERLIN ALEXANDERPLATZ

I left Sergeant Fries fingering his moustache and pushed my way through the doors and back into the heart of cold, busy Berlin. Traffic grumbled past, whining Trabants and Barkas, moaning W50 and LO trucks, buzzing Schwalbe and MZ motorbikes. Blue fumes hung in the still air, mixing with pungent brown coal dust.

I crossed at the lights and started across Alexanderplatz towards the S-Bahn station. The border crossing point at Friedrichstrasse Station was next on my list—I wanted to take a look at their records, still hoping to establish an exact exit time for Merkur.

Just as I was rounding the corner by Café Polar, I felt a tap on the shoulder. I tensed, bringing my briefcase up to protect my stomach as I turned to see who it was. A young lad stood just behind me, his narrow eyes seeking mine. His hair was cropped close to the skull, ears red with cold. His clothes hung from his frame, his arms drooped at his sides.

He wasn't an immediate threat, so I turned my head from side to side, checking for goons in the background. Berliners, tourists and Poles pushed past us, making their way to the Centrum department store on the other side of the square. The boy jerked his head in the direction the crowds were taking, at the same time pulling down the zip of his winter jacket to reveal a *Telnyashka* undershirt. Green and white horizontal stripes: issued to Soviet border units, but often worn by other branches of the KGB.

He zipped up his jacket again and left me, merging easily

15

with the masses hurrying across the square. I stayed where I was, scanning for potential hostiles, but could see none. A wary glance at the cameras bunched along the Berolina building above the café, then I decided to go and see what the young Russian had for me.

He didn't bother turning to check I was following—his job had been to attract my attention. He'd done that, the rest was up to me.

I could see the lad's bare head as it bobbed through the doors and up the wide staircase of the Centrum department store. I kept about five or six metres behind him, in sight but not too close. On the top floor he slowed down, taking an improbable interest in the racks of men's suits and jackets. As I overtook him, he jerked his head again, towards a door partially hidden by a display of mannequins wearing work shirts and holding leather satchels.

Another look around—just the young Russian at this end of menswear. Further away, a few sales assistants were keeping an eye on the customers in the changing cubicles. I pushed through the door onto a dimly lit staircase. Rough concrete steps led both up and down, and while I was looking over the banisters to check for anyone lurking in the stairwell, I heard the door behind me open again. It was the Russian lad.

"What do you want?" I asked.

But he didn't seem to have any use for language, maybe he didn't speak German. He just pointed upwards.

From where I was standing, leaning over the balustrade, I could see the head of the staircase, it ended at a blank concrete wall. Further passage was provided by metal rungs, leading to a hatch in the ceiling.

I turned to look at the boy for confirmation, but he'd gone. Only one way to find out what this was all about, and that was to see what was waiting at the top of the ladder.

★

I pulled the handle, and shoved against the hatch, the metal was sticky with cold. It swung upwards, pulled by counterweights, and I climbed out, my view of the roof widening with each rung. As I hoisted a foot over the rim of the shaft a figure emerged from the shelter of a heating stack. Civilian clothes—winter boots, dark trousers, dark grey padded anorak and felt hat. Average height and build.

With a glance at the television tower to orientate myself, the bulb at the top of its spindly length vague in the leaden skies, I marched over to the chimney.

I didn't greet the man as I drew closer, even though we knew each other. I didn't salute, and he didn't hold his hand out. So I came to a halt a few paces away and kept my hands tucked in the warmth of my pockets.

This man and I had our history. Short version: he saved my life and in return I did a job for him, a mutually beneficial mission involving illegal border crossings and extra-judicial enforcement action. But far from calling it quits, we were all in agreement that I still owed him. You want my advice? If you ever end up in someone's debt, make sure it's not the KGB.

So whenever Major Pozdniakov turned up—as he had a habit of doing—I counted my toes, fingers and teeth and was always surprised when I still had the full complement at the end of the meeting.

I didn't want to be on this ice-swept roof, but I couldn't leave. A conspirational meeting with the KGB isn't the kind of thing you walk out of.

"I may be of use to you, Burratino," Pozdniakov said, using the codename he had chosen for me. Perhaps I was flattering myself, it may have been the name he used for all his pets.

He lit a short black cigarette then waved the match until he was sure it had gone out and stowed it in his anorak pocket.

It was time for me to say something, and not just because I wanted to know what we were doing up here.

17

"Comrade Major?"

"Good to keep in touch. Sorry, rude of me ..." he held out the soft pack of papirosas. I shook my head. "I thought we worked well together, a few months back, during your Operation Oskar. You helped me, I helped you. And you never know when we might be in a position to help each other again."

I looked up at the television tower again. I couldn't help it, there wasn't much else to see up here. A flat, concrete roof with chimneys and ventilators. The high letters mounted at the edge, lit by neon tubing and spelling out CENTRUM backwards. Beyond the tall letters, the roofs of the other buildings dotted around the Alex. Off to the left, coy behind the chimney, the Interhotel Stadt Berlin. Almost straight ahead of me, the high rise *Haus des Reisens* where I'd just come from, with its socialist bronze frieze and fancy concrete curls.

But I couldn't see the crowds filling Alexanderplatz below, the only human in sight was the disconcertingly cordial KGB officer next to me.

I felt a need to be rude, to demand he tell me straight out what he wanted. But that would have been stupid, even for me. So a deep breath and a polite tone of voice: "Comrade Major, it is a pleasure to meet you again. Is there anything I can do for you?"

"That's better!" Pozdniakov smiled at me, revealing his crooked teeth. But the smile didn't reach his eyes: the one functioning eye with which he was staring at me was as hard as the glass ball in the neighbouring socket. "I think we will be working together again, very soon. There will be things you can help me with, and I believe I can return the favour in advance."

I still had some coffin nails of my own, I pulled them out of my pocket and stuck one between my lips, leaning forward to catch the lit match that Pozdniakov was already cupping in his hands for me. When I had my cigarette going, he turned his hand so the tiny flame was exposed to the wind that had followed him all the way from the steppes. The match guttered and went out, not bothering to put up a fight, but the officer waved it anyway before slipping it in his pocket with the other.

We stood like that, Russian and German, KGB and MfS, a pace or three between us, smoking and inspecting the dull bronze bulb of the Television Tower. I wasn't going to break the silence, I had another few cigarettes and was happy to stand here and let the wind smoke them for me.

"No need to be coy," said Pozdniakov eventually. "You're looking for a man, from the West. Tell me about him."

Should I have been surprised? I'd been on this case for less than twenty-four hours and he already knew about it. No, I felt no surprise. But I did realise that it was too cold for games after all.

"He came over from West Berlin on a day visa," I replied. "Been given the codename Merkur."

"*Merkur*," the major repeated to himself. "Relating to his career in the postal services—yes, most suitable."

I sucked on my cigarette, waiting for the KGB major to stop showing off and start talking.

"And this Merkur has been asking after the colleague you've been trying to find out about? The suicide?"

"Sanderling didn't commit suicide—she was killed," I snapped, I couldn't stop myself.

"What have you got on Merkur?" said the major, ignoring my outburst.

"Merkur is the father of a defector—a walk-up last December, Source Bruno—it didn't end well for him. Yesterday, the father rode into town, asking to speak to Sanderling. Right now, I'm in the process of establishing his movements while he was here in the capital." I doubted any of this was new to Pozdniakov, but hoped I was being co-operative enough to at least keep the conversation civil.

"Your Merkur has booked himself into the Hotel Neptun next week." The Russian lifted a foot and ground his spent cigarette with the sole of his boot before putting the butt in his pocket with the matches.

"Neptun? In Rostock?" It was a stupid question, there's only one Hotel Neptun a Westler would want to visit—the luxurious complex on the sea-front in Warnemünde, a suburb of Rostock.

While I welcomed the information, I couldn't shake the feeling that any intelligence coming from the Russian would have a price tag attached.

"Let's not talk about cost," said Pozdniakov, recognising the direction my thoughts were taking me. "*Drushba*, friendship, is a good that cannot be bought. Instead," he paused, "*usluga za uslugu*—how do you say it in German? Good turn for good turn?"

"One hand washes the other," I muttered the German idiom, still trying to work out the price of his information. Then, aloud, to the major: "Fine. You help me, I'll help you and if you want, we'll call it *Drushba*."

6
BERLIN FRIEDRICHSTRASSE

I paid little attention to the justifications dished up by Passport Control at Friedrichstrasse Station, I was more interested in the relevant records, which I reviewed without comment.

My silence made them squirm, although for a change I hadn't actually intended to intimidate them—I was just preoccupied by the earlier conversation with Pozdniakov. Nevertheless, a reputation as a bastard isn't a bad thing in this line of business, and if PKE thought I was cold and heartless then that counted as a bonus.

Even though the head of PKE outranked me by several chips on the shoulder, I had the upper hand here. We were both MfS officers, but I was from Berlin Centre while he was serving in a deployed unit. He didn't even have the standard MfS uniform—Passport Control are dressed as regular border guards so Westerners don't cotton on to the fact that crossing points are under the direct control of the Firm. But more important than all of that, this unit had failed, and I was the man from ZAIG/II—the department responsible for investigating fuck-ups.

Such was the measure of respect afforded me that I had the only seat in the room. The captain stood behind me, attentively advising on how to wind forward to the footage of Merkur leaving the Capital of the GDR.

The jittery, grainy video of the subject was almost indistinguishable from that I'd seen the day before in the conference room back at Centre. Only someone familiar with this border crossing would know that the cabin shown on the screen was based not in entry control in the body of the station, but in the light and airy exit hall built on the banks of the Spree and connected to the station by a long, dimly-lit and windowless passage.

I watched Merkur collect his passport and follow the stream of passengers through the labyrinthine corridors that we've built to control movement between the two Berlins. I followed his image from one monitor to the next, the captain stacking the tapes in order so I could observe Merkur moving into range of each camera. The final tape I watched showed Merkur boarding the S-Bahn on the upper platform that would take him to West Berlin.

I sat back and closed my eyes, mentally reviewing what I'd seen. The only useful pieces of information were that Merkur appeared to have been alone when he entered and left East Berlin, and that he'd taken only a quarter of an hour to get from the police desk at the travel agency on Alexanderplatz to Friedrichstrasse station—just enough time to walk the distance: no sightseeing, no diversions, no clandestine meetings on the way.

I stood up, informed the captain he could expect further questions regarding the PKE's tardiness in reporting the subject's exit time and left him in the control room with his tapes and machines.

I navigated my way out of the labyrinth, back to the outside world, showing my clapperboard to a sentry at the door to the public area of the station. As I pushed through the crowds of Berlin, I allowed my mind to return to the conversation with Pozdniakov.

If Merkur was booked into the Hotel Neptun next week, his visa should already be on file, and that would show the dates of entry and exit.

Pausing by the River Spree and watching the queues of pensioners and Westerners waiting to be allowed into the exit hall that Merkur had passed through the day before, I decided to take a trip to my old department in Treptow.

Until I'd confirmed Pozdniakov's information, a discreet chat with old colleagues who had the information I needed would be preferable to an official request that would be logged and necessarily mentioned in my next report. It's a policy of mine to only report success.

7
BERLIN TREPTOW

The sentry saw me pull up at the gatehouse of the HA VI compound on Schnellerstrasse, but there was no smile for an old comrade.

I'd seen this man every day for more than five years, and every day, as I passed him on my way to work, he had acted as if he'd never seen me before.

I hadn't been here for a couple of months, not since I'd been transferred to Berlin Centre, but the guard's behaviour hadn't changed. He examined my clapperboard, noting that the stamps were up to date, then transferred his attention to my mugshot. His eyes switched between the photograph and my face, and I dutifully removed my hat so he could see my ears and hairline more clearly.

He returned my clapperboard and, with a salute, silently raised the boom.

I left my Trabant in the car park, mentally going through my short list of victims—which of my old colleagues I could sweet-talk or otherwise induce to check the visa applications for a West German called Seiffert?

I breathed in the familiar atmosphere as I stepped through the doors. *Wofasept* disinfectant, floor polish and hard soap were the standard components of that institutional smell, along with the partially burnt hydrocarbons from the exhausts of two-stroke motors on the main road outside. But the clubhouse, as I used to call the HA VI offices, also had a distinctive, coppery tang from the river just beyond the windows.

I stood for a moment at the bottom of the stairwell, and my nostalgia was my undoing.

"Comrade Second Lieutenant."

The voice came from behind me, through the double doors held open by a sergeant. As I stiffened to attention, a tall, narrow captain with slicked back hair entered the stairwell.

"Comrade Captain Funke," I addressed my ex-boss. This was the bastard who'd sent me to a landfill site on punishment assignment. I'd started the mission with poking through stinking slime and waste on his behalf, and it went downhill form there.

"An official visit?" the captain enquired as he pulled off his pigskin gloves and started up the stairs. "If you have a moment ..." the sentence tailed away as he disappeared round the half-landing and out of sight.

I glanced at the sergeant, who was still at the front door, letting the winter air in, and decided I had no choice but to follow the captain up to his office.

"Settling in at the Centre?" Funke enquired as the secretary brought a tray. "I hear you're doing well."

There it was, I could relax. Word of my supposed success in the Bruno operation had got around, and Captain Funke had obviously decided I was worth a measure of tactical courtesy. We were sitting in the comfortable seating on the far side of the room, well away from his desk, typewriter table and safe.

I didn't bother responding to Funke's polite enquiries. I've already told you what I thought of the way the Bruno situation ended, but I wasn't about to give him the benefit of my opinion.

"Your transfer to Berlin Centre came rather suddenly, we didn't get a chance to say our goodbyes, tie up the loose ends," Funke said as he poured the coffee. The smell of real coffee wasn't the only thing in the air. My nose was picking up on something else: Funke's attitude. "I didn't get a chance to explain the reasons for your deployment to Schöneiche."

This should be good, I accepted the cup and sat back. Was I about to receive the closest thing to an apology I'd ever had from a senior officer?

"You should know, sending you to Schöneiche landfill wasn't my idea. I'd just taken over the position here; the paperwork was waiting on my desk and ... well, orders."

Since the captain was being so polite, I felt I could afford to give him a little push: "So if sending me to investigate workers on the waste dump wasn't your idea ..."

There was a moment's silence as Funke stared into his coffee. He was doing what we all do: adding, subtracting and solving multiple power equations. In a moment, I'd find out whether Funke thought I was worth a straight answer.

"The orders came from HV A," he finally said, quickly putting the cup to his lips as if to hide the words he'd just spoken.

HV A—the foreign intelligence department. They keep themselves apart from the rest of the Firm, thinking they're better than the rest of us. But they'd obstructed the Bruno case, using the most extreme means available, and now I'd found out they'd been interfering in my career.

If I were the paranoid type, I'd say it was personal.

By the time we finished our coffee, Funke and I had started to get used to each other's company. We were never going to be pals, but we'd begun the long process of sussing out whether we could be allies. The thought of asking Funke for Seiffert's visa forms crossed my mind, but trusting the captain that much would have felt a little keen this early in the relationship.

Instead, I dropped a couple of floors and knocked on the second door on the left.

The occupant of the room was a second lieutenant who looked like he shouldn't have passed the fitness requirements for entry into the Ministry. But here he was, sitting in his uniform behind a desk, so he must have managed to scrape through.

When he saw who had arrived, his brow smoothed, and with a smile on his coupon he stood up to unlock the steel cupboard. Clear alcohol and two glasses made an appearance.

"Coffee?" he asked, the pitch of his voice not quite masking the sarcasm.

"No thanks, just had a pot with the captain," I replied in the same tone.

Second Lieutenant Matthias Stoyan hesitated for a moment, uncertain whether I was joking. A shrug, then he poured the schnapps and handed over my glass.

"Your health, Reim—good to see you again."

"You too, Matse."

We knocked back the spirits.

"What do you want?" he asked as he topped us up again.

"Now why would you think I want something?" I took my glass and sipped it, no rush.

"I've not seen you since old Fröhlich was reassigned all of a sudden—you two were close, you know what happened to him?" I shrugged, and Matse carried on. "Then I heard you'd gone to work for the opposition."

"We're all on the same side, Matse," I chided. "Even those of us at Berlin Centre."

"You're not in the clubhouse any more, that's what I'm trying to say."

I liked the way he called this place the clubhouse, as if a little part of me had been left behind when I moved on.

"What have they got you doing over there?" he asked.

"The usual. Paperwork. But I'm fairly sure I'm the only one in the section with any field experience, so with a bit of luck, I'll be taking a trip to the seaside soon."

Matse raised an eyebrow at that, and after another sip of the vodka, I told him what I needed.

"Let me guess—you'd prefer your name not to be attached

27

to this particular request?" Stoyan poured himself another measure, but left my glass out that round. "Nothing changes."

"Where's the problem?" I coaxed. "It's still your job, isn't it? Collating and checking the visa applications—the local offices send copies, you double check they're not letting in anyone they shouldn't."

"That's still my job. But look—if he's coming next week, then the visa application will have long been processed and approved. If I go down to the archives now, they'll want to know why I'm interested in something I should have dealt with weeks ago." Stoyan sipped his schnapps again, working out how much damage to his reputation my request could cause.

It was time to apply some pressure. Blackmail is good, but sometimes you get better results with a lighter touch. Life doesn't always have to be brutal, sometimes generosity works just as well: "I've got Russian vodka—the good stuff. Export quality." I held out the bottle, label showing.

Stoyan took the bottle of fusel, admired the label for a moment, then: "Alright. If I can't do a friend a good turn ..."

"*Usluga za uslugu,*" I replied in my best Russian accent.

8
BERLIN TREPTOW

It didn't take long for Matse to come back with the news:
Merkur had been granted a visa for a seven-day stay in
District Rostock—a room was reserved at the Hotel Neptun,
starting Tuesday.

I finished off my glass of export-quality Russian vodka and
took my feet off his desk.

"Thanks Matse." I shook his hand and let myself out.

On the way back to Berlin Centre, I considered my next
moves. Now I knew that Major Pozdniakov's tip-off was
sound, I could put in an official request to search the visa
records for details of his visit. If anyone was paying attention,
I'd get points for prescience.

But I needed to get the timing right—I couldn't afford to
move too quickly, if I delivered the news first thing tomorrow
morning, the brass would have enough time to dream up a
stupid scheme or two. Much better to request the paperwork
in the afternoon—it wouldn't be processed until after the
weekend, which would give me the chance to get my own
plans in order before letting the upper levels interfere.

9
BERLIN LICHTENBERG

As it turned out, I'd misjudged the timing. I sent the request for Merkur's visa application before I left on Friday evening, but one of the archivists over at HA VI must have been doing overtime. The files were waiting for me when I stumbled in on Monday morning, several hours sooner than expected.

I sat at my desk, head clouded after the weekend's waking vigil, and read the visa application forms, wondering whether anyone would notice if I sat on them until the afternoon. Trouble is, if they did notice—and eventually they would—then I'd be facing more than a few difficult questions.

So I put the forms in a folder and went upstairs to see if Major Kühn had bothered to come in yet.

"Is it urgent?" the secretary demanded.

It was urgent, today being Monday and Merkur due in Warnemünde by Tuesday afternoon.

"He moves fast, your Merkur," noted Kühn when I was finally allowed to see him. He approved of the initiative I'd shown by checking the visa applications, but the good mood soon turned earnest when he pulled a file from his safe and called for his secretary.

"Contact everyone on this list, arrange a meeting for midday," he told her. "Make sure they'll all be here."

The secretary took the list and went back to her office. The major peered at me through horn-rimmed glasses.

"Heym, make yourself available for the meeting—we may need you."

★

I waited in the corridor outside the conference room and counted in the brass—the same caterpillar carriers as last time, all wearing serious faces, all staggering under the power and responsibility represented by the heavy braid on their shoulders. There was Major General Koschack of HV A, accompanied by Lieutenant Colonel Schur from HA II and Major Kühn standing by the door, nodding them in. He went in, and several braces of adjutants followed, the last one closing the door.

It didn't take them long—I was on my second nail when the door opened again. Hastily pinching the cigarette out and stuffing it in my pocket, I straightened my back and waited for the debouchment, but instead of a stream of smug senior officers, only Koschack and his lackeys exited the room.

They left the door open, I could hear murmurs from within. Hoping to overhear, I shuffled along the wall until I was opposite the doorway. I still couldn't understand the whispered conversation, so I edged a little further, just enough to peek around the door jamb.

Schur and Kühn were sitting opposite one another, each leaning over the table. The paperwork had already been packed away, the meeting about to end.

I began my silent shuffle in the other direction, back out of range of the occupants of the room, but too late.

"Comrade Heym—if you please," called Major Kühn.

Ignoring his mistake—I doubted Kühn would ever bother to learn my name, I entered the room and stood to attention in front of the officers. The adjutants hovered on the edge of my vision, down at the far end.

"The committee notes your efforts," Kühn said as he reached for his stack of files and signalled to one of the adjutants. "We have arranged for a secure line for you to brief First Lieutenant Sachse."

Lieutenant Colonel Schur, whose department, HA II, had attempted to recruit Source Bruno, turned in his seat to see me better. His small eyes were magnified behind wide, plastic-rimmed glasses, a flabby chin camouflaged by a greying goatee beard.

"Permission to speak, Comrade Major?" I rapped out, still at attention.

"Thank you, Comrade *Unterleutnant*. Contact Captain Dupski about the call with First Lieutenant Sachse."

Back in my office, I shut the door and went to stand by the window. My hands were drawn into fists so tight I didn't feel I'd be able to unclench them for long enough to light a cigarette.

If I was to brief Sachse, that could mean only thing: he was being sent to Warnemünde to make contact with Merkur.

Of all the people to send after Merkur, they'd chosen Sachse!

Major Kühn himself had told me that Sachse was responsible for Bruno's death, that Lieutenant Colonel Schur had been near apoplectic when he'd found out what had happened to his new source. Nevertheless, the three officers had just agreed Sachse should be the one to talk to Bruno's grieving father.

I didn't care if Sachse spoke to Merkur, but I did want to know who had killed Sanderling, and why. So far, Merkur's arrival had been the first break in my unofficial investigation into my colleague's untimely death.

I marched over to my desk, unclenching my fists for long enough to get the bottle out of the drawer, swearing as I poured myself some schnapps.

Sitting down, I got a cigarette going at the third try and took a puff, then another, hands steadier with each mouthful of nicotine and alcohol.

If I could make some progress in finding out why Sanderling had died, maybe she'd stop visiting me. I wouldn't miss her cold presence in my bed every night.

10
BERLIN LICHTENBERG

I fired another cigarette, took this one slow, drank the second glass of schnapps slowly, too. Feeling more in control, I popped a *Pfeffi* and left my office in search of Captain Dupski.

I found him behind his desk. He gestured me in and lifted the telephone.

"Captain Dupski, ZAIG/II. Has the secure connection to Rostock been booked?" A pause for the answer, then he hung up.

"There's too much traffic on the line," he told me, picking up his pen. "Come back in an hour."

What was Sachse doing up in Rostock? I'd assumed he was working from HV A, either here at Berlin Centre or at their operations centre just outside the city. But he was up on the coast—had he been posted there, or was he in the north for another operation?

As I was rising out of my chair, the door behind me opened, and Lieutenant Colonel Schur's belly appeared.

Dupski and I stood to attention as the rest of Schur entered. He marched around the place a little, then, with both hands, gestured to us to sit. We remained standing, there was no spare chair for Schur, and if he couldn't sit, neither could we.

Seeing our difficulty, the officer headed in my direction, and I stepped aside to allow him to take my place.

He and Dupski sank into their respective seats, and Schur crossed his legs. He looked at Dupski for a while, drumming his fingers on his knee, then turned slightly so that I was in view.

"Comrade Reim, isn't it?"

"*Jawohl, Genosse Oberstleutnant.*" The lieutenant colonel had made the effort to find out my name, and that made me nervous.

"You reviewed the paperwork for the Bruno case?"

"As part of the operational analysis, I also interviewed all field operatives who had contact with the subject, Comrade Lieutenant Colonel."

"But not Comrade Sachse?"

"Access to the team that interviewed the subject was denied. The *Oberleutnant* was part of that team, I believe he was on secondment to HA IX at the time."

Schur drummed his fingers a bit more. "Why weren't you given access?"

"No reason was given, Comrade Lieutenant Colonel."

"But you're familiar with the Bruno material?"

"I have extensive awareness of Operational Procedure Source Bruno."

"And do you think Comrade Sachse is the best man to observe Codename Merkur?"

"Comrade, the interdepartmental committee made its-"

"Comrade Reim, save the verbiage! I want someone from Berlin Centre handling the task—can you suggest grounds for revisiting the decision to send Comrade Sachse?"

I glanced at Dupski, he was sitting behind his desk, wringing his hands. Probably wishing he wasn't within hearing distance of this conversation.

"Well? Any reason not to send Sachse?" Schur demanded. He really did want an answer; perhaps I should think about it.

I didn't want Sachse to do the job either. If he wasn't given the task of liaising with Merkur then it may fall to me, and I was sure Bruno's father must know something—why else had he been dancing the polka with us the previous week?

But what objective reasons could I give to prevent Sachse's involvement? No point telling the lieutenant colonel that

Sachse was responsible for Source Bruno's death—he already knew that. And the only other thing I had on the HV A operative was that Bruno, before he died, had told my friend Holger that Sachse was a double agent.

It was pure hearsay, no proof of it, not even the circumstantial kind. So, unable to come up with the reason Schur was demanding, I kept shtum.

"Never mind," he sighed as he levered himself out of the chair. "I'll kick it upstairs, see what they say. Postpone any contact with *Oberleutnant* Sachse until you hear from me." He fixed me with gibbous eyes, pointing a finger at me for good measure.

As he left, Dupski caught my eye. I shrugged. I could understand why Schur would be unhappy about Sachse's involvement in Secondary Operation Merkur, but was the lieutenant colonel really going to go up against Major General Koschack?

But Schur was a caterpillar carrier, he could do what he wanted. I just hoped he wouldn't drag me into his fight with the HV A.

11
BERLIN LICHTENBERG

The next morning I called Captain Dupski.

"*Hier Unterleutnant Reim*, I have a written order from Lieutenant Colonel Schur—I'm to begin work on Secondary Operational Procedure Merkur with immediate effect."

"I'll get back to you." Dupski hung up.

I smoked a cigarette, blew a speck of lint off my uniform sleeve, straightened the seams of my trousers then stared at the phone. It was another five minutes before it rang.

"Major Kühn confirms your orders, but adds there's to be no provoking the local units, particularly around Hotel Neptun. Have a good trip."

I caught the mid-morning express to Rostock, keen not to give the brass any time to change their minds. As we beat our way through the frosted forests and along the shores of icy lakes, I congratulated myself on my decision to come by train. The heating in my compartment was on the blink, rasping out only the barest of warmth, but four hours in the Trabant would have been a lot colder and a lot more uncomfortable.

Gratified by the thought, I pulled my winter coat tighter, adjusted my hat and put my head down.

I woke as we pulled out of Waren, propped my eyes open long enough to clock the deep snow spilling over roads and onto the frozen lakes and, aiming a hopeful kick at the heating, I pulled my hat over my eyes and settled back for another half-hour.

★

We arrived at Rostock main station at just after half past one. Not having phoned ahead for a car, I had to pick my way along ice-shrouded pavements to August-Bebel-Strasse.

I hadn't been to Rostock Centre before, but like most other MfS District Administrations, the Rostockers had bagsied themselves one of the best blocks in the city. Four storeys of heavy stone and brickwork, with windows that could outstare any local imprudent enough to glance up as they went past.

But I wasn't quite at my destination yet. I didn't take the steps to the main entrance, I walked past the tall red flags, rattling in sleet driven by a hard Baltic wind, finally taking cover in the pre-fabricated offices beside the main administrative block.

I showed my clapperboard to the guard just inside the doors and asked for the transport pool. He pointed the way, and I followed my nose until I was back outside, this time in a sheltered courtyard behind the building. A kiosk at the end of a row of garages seemed my best hope, and I rapped on the glass, rousing an *Uffzi* from his illustrated magazine.

I slipped my paperwork through the opening in the window and gave him a moment to digest what he was looking at. It took him longer than a moment—they're pretty slow up here—but when he finally got to the end, he stood up straight, shouted some orders in the direction of the garages and stamped the forms.

"*Kraftwagen für den Genossen Unterleutnant,*" he snapped as a mechanic slouched over, kneading a rag that had more oil on it than his fingers.

The sergeant handed me a carbon copy and stood up straight again, waiting for me to turn my back so he could return to his dirty mag.

"Anything particular?" asked the mechanic as he led the way to a row of unmarked vehicles.

I looked over the cars: several Wartburgs of various

37

vintages, a recent red Polo, a Volkswagen Beetle with rusty hubs and a dozen Trabants, both saloons and hatchbacks. Most of the vehicles were under several centimetres of soft snow that was crusted with a layer of hard ice.

I pointed to a beige Wartburg 353 saloon in the middle of the row and waited while the mechanic went to find the keys. The courtyard may have been sheltered, but the wind still found a way in, and the sleet fell steeply. My shoes and the cuffs of my trousers were soaked, the shoulders of my coat were powdered white. I wanted nothing more than to stamp my feet and clap my hands together—anything to get the circulation going—but behind me, I could feel the eyes of the *Uffzi* on me, and above and around me, uncounted windows glared down. Right now, as an officer of Berlin Centre, pride was more important than comfort.

Once the keys arrived, I got into the Wartburg and while the mechanic scraped the windscreen clear. I played with the choke and the pedal until the engine finally agreed to fire. As soon as it settled down to a sweet clatter, I put the heating on full and drove out of the compound, stopping only at the boom to show my clapperboard.

I didn't bother with a courtesy call to the Rostock brass, they'd find out soon enough that I was in town.

12
ROSTOCK

As soon as I was out of sight of the District Administration, I pulled over at the side of the road and rooted around in my bag for the map of Rostock.

I opened it up and spread it out on the passenger seat to check my route. Easy enough: stay with the tram tracks for a bit then follow the other cars.

Traffic was light, and despite the ice-slick roads, I was on the four lane arterial to Warnemünde within ten minutes, the shiny new housing blocks of Evershagen, Lütten Klein and Lichtenhagen on the left, the bridge crane of the old harbour and the tensile cable crane of the Warnow Shipyard on the right.

The road narrowed at the edge of Warnemünde, and I parked the car there, leaving my bag but taking the map, and picked my way through back streets until I was on the sea front.

I wanted to get a feel for the place. On paper, Warnemünde didn't look particularly large, but what the map didn't tell me was just how many tourists there were, even in the middle of winter.

I wedged myself against a lamp post and looked out to sea. The rail-ferry was coming in from Denmark, churning the brash ice at the mouth of the terminal. Beyond the wide beach, the Baltic was frozen solid for a hundred metres or more, the grey water beyond hacked at the outer edges of the ice, trying to chisel chunks off, but only succeeding in freezing itself and adding to the mass. Isolated wedges of ice, taller than me, lay aground on the beach, blue in the pallid winter light.

But more than the ice and the sea, it was the wind that got my attention. It slashed at the flags along the Promenade, whipped heavy sleet into my face and continuously grabbed at my hat and the edges of my coat, trying to find a way through to bare flesh. I twisted out of the weather, watching as the ferry turned, the frothing props agitating the sea ice even further.

At the terminal, just visible over metal fences and high, concrete slab walls, a diesel shunter tethered to two lonely carriages sat and steamed, waiting for the boat to dock. I thought I could hear guard dogs barking, but perhaps it was just the scraping of wind over ice.

I wasn't achieving anything out here in the weather, I needed to make plans, and I couldn't do that with the wind whistling through my ears. So I leaned into the storm again and staggered across the prom to the *Teepott*. A ridiculous building that looked like something a child had knocked up one slow summer's afternoon: giant mussel shells resting on an oversized sandcastle. But, true to its name, it was warm inside, and it served tea.

The window seats were all taken, even though their only view was of condensation running down the glass, so I sat at an empty table near the middle. Once my order had been taken, I pulled out my notebook and pen.

I'd spent the last few days manoeuvring, trying to make sure I would be sent up here to Warnemünde. Now I was here, I had no clue how best to find out whether Merkur was a serious proposition, or had just been flirting with us.

I'd have liked a small team for this—a couple of men watching the subject in the hotel, another brace on foot hanging around the entrance, and several more in cars parked in the vicinity. But this wasn't Berlin—this was the Hotel Neptun we were talking about. There were so many operatives in that place, it was a wonder they had enough room for the guests.

But none of those goons were at my disposal. Far from being able to use the assembled forces to keep an eye on Merkur, I'd have to do my best to stay out of their way. None of them were from my department—none of them were even from Berlin Centre. They were all from the District Administration or the county offices, and if they smelt a Prussian in their midst ... let's just say they wouldn't be falling over themselves to help him out.

The tea arrived—I'd ordered tea rather than coffee or beer so I could see for myself how the cultured citizens in this Republic live—and I took a careful sip. I wasn't convinced, but they say black tea is good for the brain. Whatever the truth of that claim, by the time I'd finished my glass, the page in front of me was still empty.

I lit a cigarette.

It boiled down to a straight choice: I could spend my days watching the front door of the hotel, waiting for Merkur to go for a stroll along the front, or I could get in there and see what the natives had to say about him.

Berlin wouldn't be pleased when they heard about it, but they weren't here. By the time my report landed in front of Major Kühn, he might have forgotten the very clear orders he'd given regarding the Neptun.

13
WARNEMÜNDE

From the door of the *Teepott*, I could see the Hotel Neptun further along the prom—it was hard to miss, the tallest building around, with letters a storey high shouting its name from the rooftop.

I edged back into the café to check my map again—my first destination was the *Kurhaus*, and according to the map it was just this side of the hotel, not five hundred metres away. But those five hundred metres were exposed to heavy sleet slanting in from the sea.

The *Kurhaus*, an Art Deco building with a wide flight of steps directly opposite the Neptun, was supposedly the cultural centre of the town—the place old ladies go on summer afternoons to hear the local brass band play.

I ran up the steps and pushed through the doors and into the wide entrance hall. A grey door on my left was marked *Administration*—sounded right to me, so after I'd taken my dripping coat off, I gave it a knock.

A key scratched in the lock, and the door opened a few centimetres. I stood close in, body screening my opened clapperboard from any casual passersby.

A man with grey skin that sagged beneath his glasses and an unkempt moustache below his nose was peering through the crack between door and jamb. He clocked my ID and grunted, but before letting me in, his eyes swivelled over my shoulder to check I was alone.

The room wasn't large, the only light came from dull

sunlight that had struggled through brisk clouds and net curtains. A couple of desks and chairs were in front of me. To my left, beneath the windows, a second operative sat on a platform, peering through binoculars mounted on a fixed tripod. A range of cameras fitted with various lenses were permanently mounted in a row along the windows.

The first operative was still standing in my way, preventing further ingress. He wanted to know who he was dealing with, but wasn't sure how polite to play it—the page of the MfS clapperboard that you flash around shows only photograph and signature of the bearer, along with information about location of your posting and a series of stamps to prove everything is up to date. They didn't know what rank I held, nor which department I represented.

I decided to put them out of their misery: "*Unterleutnant* Reim, from Berlin Centre. I want to take a look out of your windows."

Far from relaxing, the operative began to chew his moustache. He looked to his colleague who was now observing us from the platform—unannounced visits from Berlin were never good news, and these two didn't know what to expect.

"Relax," I told them. "I'm interested in a subject booked into the Neptun."

And the two of them did relax, they told me their names and ranks, I forgot the names immediately, but they were both NCOs, so nothing for me to worry about. Sure, they'd remember my name, and they'd report it back to District Administration, but that was fine—at some point Berlin would get around to informing the locals of my visit anyway.

I took the steps to the platform and picked up a pair of binoculars from the shelf. There was no need for them—less than a hundred metres away, a uniformed doorman greeted guests while a car hop found a spot for the Audis and BMWs in the car park in front of the Hotel.

I watched as a Mercedes R 107 pulled up at the red carpet. The doorman hastened to open the door for a woman in a fur coat and sunglasses while a bellhop opened the boot and took out a set of fawn suitcases.

The driver, wearing a camel-hair coat and pressed trousers, walked to the back of his car to supervise the handling of the luggage. He held on to his hat to keep it firm against the wind that came in hard under the canopy, and with the other hand he took out some money. A green banknote, could have been twenty of our Marks, more likely to be five Westmarks—cheaper for the Westerner, more valuable to the Easterner. The bellhop pocketed the note with an unctuous nod.

Only when the couple had gone into the hotel and the car was parked did I turn back to the colleagues in the room. They were both still gawking at me, waiting for what? Blessings from the capital?

"Do all the guests come this way?" I asked the man next to me. His hair was a little long for the Firm, half-way to his collar, and like his comrade, he had poor skin and an untidy moustache.

"Pedestrians come up from the Prom and use this entrance," said Long Hair, in a wide, slow Mecklenburg accent. "Entrance to disco and bowling alley round the back, but that's in the evening," he added. Long pauses seemed to be part of the speech pattern round here.

I turned to the window again, angling my head low to see the full height of the building opposite. Fifteen floors for accommodation, plus a few storeys at the bottom for entertainment, dining, shopping and administration. Each room had a balcony, tinted windows angled to catch a view of the sea. Large suites at the top for special guests. I'd never been here before, but I'd spent a lot of time in Main Department VI, which kept an eye on tourists, among other things. I'd heard the stories about the Hotel Neptun: everyone from Fidel Castro to several West German Chancellors—Willi

Brandt and Helmut Schmidt among them—had stayed here. It was that kind of place.

I wanted to get inside, have a look around. See where Merkur was staying. But this was a sensitive place—it was obvious why I'd been told to tread carefully: Neptun was a favourite destination of Westerners and a major source of hard-currency, and that was before you considered the columns of workers from our Republic who enjoyed their annual holidays at the hotel, courtesy of the trade unions. Nowhere else in the Republic did East and West mingle so readily, not even in Berlin.

That's why the Hotel Neptun had more informants and operatives fizzing around than the May Day parade on Karl-Marx-Allee in Berlin. With that many colleagues on the scene, it wasn't going to be easy to avoid tap-dancing on a few toes.

14
WARNEMÜNDE

It was warm and dry in the observation room at the *Kurhaus*, so I decided to stay with the comrades, keeping half an eye on the window in case Merkur decided to turn up early.

I knew he'd be travelling by train, and I'd checked the timetable: the daily Cologne to Rostock express stopped at Osnabrück, where Merkur lived, and that seemed the most likely service for him to take—the other connections required several changes, which lengthened the journey considerably. From Rostock main station, a taxi or the S-Bahn would bring him to Warnemünde, where I'd be waiting.

But waiting makes for hungry work. It was a long time since I'd had breakfast, and a civilised cuppa in an architecturally over-reached tea-room hadn't helped to fill the hole in my belly.

"What do the comrades eat when they're on observation duty?" I asked the room at large.

The colleagues shared a look, then the eyes of Glasses-moustache flicked towards a briefcase lined up against the wall next to the door.

"Just outside the back-entrance, there's a *Kaufhalle-*" began the other one.

"But surely assiduous comrades don't abandon their posts?" I tut-tutted, watching as the one with long hair glanced towards a leather satchel, neatly positioned next to the briefcase.

I climbed down from the platform and stood by the bags. "Do you mind?"

They didn't mind. They couldn't see an officer starve, could they? So I helped myself. An apple and a piece of sausage from a battered aluminium lunch box, and a piece of bread and butter from a bright plastic box.

"Thanks comrades," I said between mouthfuls, but they didn't seem to appreciate my attempt at being polite.

It was completely dark by the time Merkur arrived. Buoys and ships winked out at sea, but the Hotel Neptun was lit up like the Palace of the Republic. Even the doorman stood under a bright light in front of the car park.

A blue Volga taxi pulled up, and the staff hurried out to extract the visitor. Merkur was bustled inside before the wind could sweep the old man away.

I angled my watch towards the window, trying to catch enough reflected light to read the time. While I did that, I checked whether either of the colleagues had noticed my interest in the new guest at the hotel.

Glasses-moustache was dozing in a chair, a greasy patch on the wall showing this wasn't the first time he'd rested his head there. Number two was checking his cameras. He'd taken a couple of snapshots of Merkur as he'd exited the taxi, just as he'd done for all the arriving Westerners.

Still staring at the watch face, I considered how long I should stay. Another half-hour would be enough, no need to let this pair know which particular hotel guest I was interested in.

I left the Kurhaus by the delivery entrance, skidding along the concrete service road until I reached the small supermarket on a parallel street, where I merged with shoppers cradling their purchases as they picked their way through damp snow-drifts.

As I came out of the side-street, the wind caught me, and I had to twist away in order to keep my balance. The sleet had eased into wet snow, dampening the exposed side of my face. I bent into the wind, one hand on my hat, the other across my chest, holding my coat tight against the gusts off the sea.

Turning the corner and needing to find my balance again, I shunted myself along the front until I was in front of the Hotel Neptun, then let the wind push me up the path leading to the main door.

The doorman opened up for me, but he didn't smile the way he did for the Westerners. I ignored him, and once inside made straight for the lifts.

Above the main door, directed at the lifts, I murmured to myself as I pressed the button and waited. The cameras were discreetly let into the ceiling panels, not obvious unless you were looking. *Entrance to library, view of reception desk.* Those were the only ones I'd seen so far, but there had to be others— I just hadn't spotted them yet.

The lift pinged, and I climbed aboard. I was alone in the car, and that suited me. No small talk about the storm outside or the comforts inside.

The lift flowed upwards to the sixteenth floor. As I exited, I pressed the button for eleven. I stood long enough to watch the doors slide shut and the indicator tick downwards.

The corridor was dimly lit, the carpet deep and new. A glance up and down to check all room doors were shut, and that no-one was about, then I went to find the stairs.

Up another storey, down the corridor, looking for room 1719, here it was: a door just like all the others, dark wood, polished brass numbers. The next door had no number, it was the one I wanted.

I knocked and pulled out my clapperboard, ready to show it to whomever opened up. A well-built middle-aged man with little hair left on his head looked me up and down, poked his head around the jamb to see up and down the corridor, then opened the door wider to let me in.

"Who's co-ordinating operations here?" I asked as he shut the door behind me.

He turned around and went over to a comfy chair in front of a stack of hardware: several TV monitors connected to VHS video recorders and a few dozen reel-to-reel and cassette tape recorders. The open wrap of sandwiches on the bottom shelf wasn't part of the standard equipment.

"Who's asking?" he said, as I eyed his supper.

"Second Lieutenant Reim from Berlin."

"Well, Comrade Second Lieutenant Reim from Berlin, there's no-one co-ordinating. We all do our own thing here. Maybe there's someone particular you want to see?"

"What do you mean, no-one's co-ordinating? Who's leading the *Operative Einsatzstab*?" I sat down next to him.

Baldy looked at me properly for the first time—he looked me in the eyes, the corner of his mouth playing with the idea of sneering. "There is no unified operational taskforce for these premises."

"Every department for itself?"

"Every department for itself," he confirmed, reaching for his bread.

I shook my head, this wasn't how I'd be running the show if I were in charge—because we all know how dinner turns out when too many cooks get involved.

"Who's here?" I asked, and started the list, just to help him get going: "Department II, Department VI? And 26, along with VIII?"

"Everyone's here," he said, the words coming out of his mouth along with some crumbs. "It's a regular party."

I sat back to think about it a bit. This place was a mess, but that could work to my advantage. If there were no *Einsatzstab* to report to, and the departments weren't co-ordinating their activities, then there would be much less chance that anyone would challenge my presence.

15
WARNEMÜNDE

"Let's see the footage from the reception desk," I told the operative. "Start with three-quarters of an hour ago." I knew what the machinery could do, I'd spent too much time in front of similar monitors and recorders to forget how it all worked. The image on the screen, a capture from the front desk, was recorded onto two VHS tapes, one to keep, one for near-time replay for the times when someone from Berlin Centre turned up, asking to watch a movie.

The operative pressed *stop* then *eject* on one of the machines and took out the cassette. He pushed the new tape home, and when it had settled, pressed the record button.

He pushed the tape he'd just removed into another machine, and turned on the monitor. As it warmed up, the operative rewound the tape. The picture—static and rain—became clearer, and by juggling with the play and rewind buttons, he found the time stamp I'd asked for.

I leaned over and pressed the FF button, watching as the recording sped up. A bellhop arrived, twitched his way across the screen, pushing a trolley with two suitcases. The TV was black and white, but I could guess the colour of the luggage.

I took my finger off fast-forward and the picture stabilised, pausing before running on at normal speed. Merkur came into view, stopping at the front desk, his back to the camera. He stood there, unbuttoning his coat, taking his black felt hat off and running a hand over his grey hair. The receptionist spoke to him while looking down to check something beneath the counter.

"Any sound?" I asked.

"Only for special occasions," replied the comrade. "Did you put a request in for sound?" He knew I hadn't. If I had, there'd have been a chit on the desk.

I watched Merkur's elbow move back and forth as he filled in the registration form and passed it to the receptionist. A short delay as she made a few notes and stood up to reach the room key from the hooks behind her. Merkur looked around the lobby, finally focussing on the short corridor that led off to the side.

"I want to see the registration details for that man," I said, watching as Merkur walked out of shot, heading for the lifts.

16
WARNEMÜNDE

The leader of the reception brigade wasn't surprised by my sudden appearance—no doubt members of the Firm trotted in and out of his office all day. It may have helped that I remained respectful and polite—someone in as public a position as his, in a high-profile, Western-facing hotel like this, would have plenty of vitamin C—*Connections*—to cadre levels in the Party. Perhaps in my Firm, too.

"Who are you looking for, Comrade?" he asked, adjusting his glasses with one hand while picking up a pencil with the other.

"Seiffert, Werner. He checked in," I looked at my watch, "fifty-two minutes ago."

The brigadier checked his own watch, scribbled a note then pushed his glasses to the top of his head. Without a word, he left the office.

It didn't take him long, not long enough to allow me even a brief glance around his office—thirty seconds at the outside. But when he returned, I was standing where he'd left me, hands behind my back, waiting patiently.

"Fourteenth floor," said the brigadier, moving a small *Deutsch-Sowjetische Freundschaft* desk flag aside and slapping a thin bundle of registration cards on the desk.

I sat in the visitor's seat and shuffled through the documents. Everything tallied with the details provided on Merkur's visa application, nothing out of place. No slip-ups, no changes. The only new piece of information was his room number at the hotel.

"Thank you, comrade." I told him. "I shall be sure to report your co-operation."

There was no reply, he was too busy repositioning the flag.

The fourteenth floor corridor was just the same as the ones I'd already seen, except the doors here were closer together—singles and doubles rather than suites.

The deep carpet muffled my footsteps as I paced along, which is possibly why the maid further along the corridor didn't notice me as she let herself into one of the rooms, folded sheets and towels draped over her left arm. By the time I reached her, she was inside the room, the door slightly ajar. I idly checked the number as I went past, then stopped and backed up.

This was Merkur's room. And if Merkur had arrived less than an hour ago then he wouldn't be needing his room tidied, his towels changed or his bed making.

I pushed the door slowly, peering around to see whether Merkur was in residence, or whether the maid was alone.

The room was long, angled at the far end so that the window and the balcony had a view of the beach. The place was tidy, the bed was made, and Merkur wasn't present. But the maid was zipping open one of his suitcases.

"Is this part of the Neptun's famous room service?" I enquired, using a quiet but hard voice.

The maid spun round, one hand over her heart, her eyebrows pulled high in shock, so high that I was concerned for the safety of her eyeballs.

I'd walked into the room unprepared, and now I had to decide who I was. A random guest walking along the corridor? No good—no authority to act. I had a couple of IDs with me, the genuine one from the Ministry in my inside pocket and, in the left coat pocket, my favourite legend, the disc that showed me to be a detective with the *Kripo*.

But I wasn't dealing with a simple case of attempted

pilfering—the maid would have chosen a better time to go through Merkur's belongings, right at the end of the guest's stay, when he'd have less time to notice and report any missing items.

Which meant she had other reasons to take a look at Merkur's luggage, and those reasons were probably very similar to my own. I decided it was the inside pocket I needed —I pulled out the Ministry clapperboard and gave her the briefest flash of my mugshot.

"Where's the occupant of this room?" I demanded.

The maid let go of her heart, and her brilliant blue eyes bounced back to their normal shape. She looked around nervously, as if seeking an exit. Not convinced by her reaction, I took a step forward and leaned over her.

"He's gone to the restaurant complex over the road." Her voice was steadier than I'd expected, but she swapped around some of her vowels, stretching others longer than you'd think a word could take, and her consonants were worn down by the harsh wind that blows off the Baltic. I was dealing with another *Fischkopp*—I had to concentrate a little to understand what she was saying.

I reached behind me and pushed the door to. Merkur would be away for a while if he'd gone for a meal in one of the speciality restaurants attached to the hotel. If the service was anything like in the rest of the Republic, he'd be there for at least half an hour before anyone got round to asking if he was waiting to be seated.

I turned my attention back to the maid. She'd composed herself, was standing and facing me, one hand on the still-closed suitcase, the fingers of the other hand fiddling with the clips that held her blonde hair in the neat braid gathered around her head.

"What's the purpose of your presence in this room?" I asked, still keeping my voice low, not letting up on the hard edge.

She looked sideways and down, her eyes resting for a moment on the suitcase.

"You know who I am," I said, tapping my closed clapperboard against my knuckles. "So tell me what you're doing here."

"I'm ..." another glance down to the suitcase, "I'm required to catalogue his possessions."

It was only then that I noticed the bulge in the pocket of her pinny. I stepped forward and reached in, ignoring her yelp of protest. It was a miniature camera, a Minox 35. Nice piece of kit, made in the West, but well-liked and widely used by the organs of various socialist states, not least because of its discreet size. This wasn't a maid I was dealing with, at least she wasn't just a maid.

"You're an IM?" I asked, losing some of the hardness.

"I'm an informant," she agreed, relieved at finally coming clean. Her shoulders dropped a centimetre or two and she gave me a nervous smile.

I'm a sucker for a nice smile, particularly when it's in the middle of a pretty face. But this was business, and at that time I still had it in me to remain professional.

Officially, I shouldn't be talking to an IM who was being run by another officer—if you want to use an established informant, you go through their handling officer. But here we were, in this hotel room, and both of us wanted to know whether Merkur had anything interesting in his suitcases.

"Who's your handler?"

She hesitated, her right hand rising again to the clips that held her fancy hairstyle in place. Her eyes dropped to the suitcase, then came up again to meet mine. "*Oberleutnant* Mewitz."

"OK, check the luggage, take your photos." I handed back the camera, and she gave me another of her smiles in return. "But I'm staying here. We can finish this conversation once you're done."

The maid got to work, and I stood behind her, careful to make sure there were no additions or subtractions to Merkur's belongings.

"When does your shift end?" I asked once she'd finished her art homework. There had been nothing of interest in the cases, just what you'd expect a Western tourist to take on holiday.

She took her time answering, busying herself with replacing the items in the suitcases. It was a neat job—quick, efficient and exact. Couldn't have done it better myself.

She zipped up the suitcase, placed it on the floor next to the others and only then did she turn around. Behind her, through the window, I could see the twinkling lanterns along the harbour, and off in the distance, the glare of the arc-lamps at the International Port. But, closer to hand, her eyes also shone bright. She'd lost her nervousness, was almost enjoying the situation.

"Eleven o'clock," she said as she pushed past me. "I'll meet you down at the harbour—there's a bar near the end, by the lighthouse—*Fischerklause.*"

I turned, wondering whether to grab her arm before she got the door open, but decided to let her go. She'd identified herself as an informant and had proposed the meet—sometimes, even in this line of work, you have to trust a little.

She left the room, and I followed, pulling the door shut as I went. By the time it snicked home, she had disappeared around the end of the corridor.

17
WARNEMÜNDE

I left the hotel and went in search of my accommodation. The office had booked a room for me somewhere in the west end of Warnemünde, and after wandering around in the sleet and ice for about twenty minutes, I was glad to reach the half-derelict house of my host.

"Come in out of the storm, come in now, leave the storm outside," said the old dear as she levered open the warped door.

She ushered me into the narrow porch and supervised the removal of my dripping coat and sodden boots. A stout tiled stove pumped heat into a parlour crowded with heavy pre-war furniture, every available surface dripping with lace: table cloths, doilies, net curtains, framed samplers. Even the lampshades boasted frothy fringes. Taking the award for most unsurprising prop, a lace-making pillow rested on the filet lace antimacassar of an overstuffed chair arm.

"The comrades from the capital said you'd be coming," she chirped. And with those words, the reverence with which she'd said *comrades*, I knew I was dealing with a veteran of the party, possibly even an officially recognised Victim Of Fascism, a status given to the survivors of the fight against the Nazis—most of whom had seen the insides of the camps during the Hitler time.

"I'll be going out again later," I warned the old biddy, but she chose not to hear.

"A bite to eat, young man?" She was already bustling off, heading for a narrow doorway, presumably the kitchen.

I let her go, fine by me if she wanted to make me dinner. Even if I'd stayed in the centre of Warnemünde, I wouldn't have had much chance of finding anything better than a broiler chicken or a Bockwurst with a dry bread roll, so why not get fed in the warmth of the lace museum?

Appropriately enough, dinner turned out to be *Tote Oma*: mashed spicy blood-sausage which the grandma served up with warm sauerkraut and boiled potatoes. It slid down nicely with a bottle of Rostocker *Hafenbräu*, and with a full stomach and a second bottle in the hand, I was mellow enough to tolerate the old lady's fussing a little longer. But when I saw her reach for the photo album, I scrambled for my boots, still drying on top of the tiled stove. I'd had enough nostalgia for one evening.

"You can't go out again, it's foul weather-" she wailed, but I was already in the porch, pulling on my damp winter coat.

18
WARNEMÜNDE

A whole evening stretched before me—far too much time until the meeting with the maid at the *Fischerklause*—so I headed to the Neptun.

I stuck to the sheltered back streets, but whenever I crossed a road that led down to the sea, hard snow swept into my face, making me splutter.

I found the entrance to the *Diskothek* at the back of the hotel—it didn't require much in the way of detective work, a line of citizens were braving the weather, waiting patiently to be allowed entry.

I headed for the front of the queue, discreetly flashed my tin, the brass disc that showed me to be a detective of the *Volkspolizei*, and the doorman waved me into the warmth.

Ignoring the queue for the cloakroom, I kept my coat on and went through the double doors into the disco. A battery of coloured lights swept over the large room, swiftly followed by a second sweep. It was the biggest lighting rig I'd seen outside an air-defence battalion. The noise was impressive, too. A New German Wave song was playing, some tripe from the West, but the citizens were singing along—they knew every word.

"*Hit des Jahres 1983 ...*" breathed the DJ into his microphone as the song faded out. "*Codo ... düse im Sauseschritt.*" He paused again, sliding up the volume of the track for a moment as if he fancied a job with Radio DT64. "And now-" but his announcement was drowned by the whoops and cheers that greeted a fast, simple beat: New Order, *Blue Monday*.

As the synthesisers kicked in, struggling against the inane hammering of the drum machine, I shoved my way through the dancers. Some rowdy had the nerve to shove back, but I was here on other business so made do with a sharp chop to his kidneys. It was enough, I got the space I needed to reach the bar.

I turned around, leaned against the bar and surveyed the dance floor. It wasn't just young people here, plenty of workers in their best years were trying to keep up. Not too many Westerners though: a pocket further down the bar, a few more in the corner. As I watched the second group, I became aware of a tall fellow with a head of white hair. It wasn't just his age that made him stick out like a painted dog, it was the fact that he wasn't dancing, just standing in the middle while others bopped around him.

I slid along the front of the bar, aiming to get a better view, and as I edged around a gaggle of Saxons, the Westerner looked up. He was about ten metres away, for a moment the lights shone directly on him, and as they switched to strobe, his eyes glinted, staring through me.

The strobe stopped, there was a second or two of complete darkness before the coloured lights returned, and at that moment, Merkur turned away. I was certain it was him, and I also had a strong feeling that he'd seen and recognised me for what I am.

I pushed my way back through the dancers, heading for the entrance. The teenager who had jostled me on my way to the bar saw me coming and got out of the way, his friends giving me ineffectual evils as I shoved past.

New Order died, and the heavy beat of our home-grown *Mont Klamott* took over the dance floor.

Out the door, past the cloakroom and into the storm.

19
WARNEMÜNDE

Merkur had looked directly at me in the disco. These things happen. But the look on his face, that wasn't random—he had been waiting for me, for someone from the Firm to find him.

I angled my head into the wind to let it blow the stupid thought away.

"You're getting old, Reim," I told myself, letting the storm take the stupid words away, too.

But I wasn't getting old, I was on the way up. I'd made a good start in my new department, I had a KGB officer offering help—I'd have a few more pips on my epaulettes before they were finished with me.

I shook my head, letting more wind in through my ears. Winter was making me meschugge. The endless grey more than the cold, it makes everyone go weird.

Or the *Tote Oma*—could be indigestion.

I turned away from the sea, allowing the wind to push me along the Promenade, past the tea pot café and the lighthouse, down to the harbour.

The wind followed me around the corner, both of us heading along the Alter Strom quay. I kept a hand clamped on my hat as I passed piled wooden crates and red-painted trawlers breasted up, their stays clattering and singing. Lines groaned and wooden hulls grumbled on the swell.

On land, snow lay around, hard packets of whiteness shining in the dim streetlamps, warning me to tread carefully. One slip and I'd be over the edge, freezing to death in the oily water, unless I was crushed between the quay and the hull of a cutter stinking of dead fish. I shook my head. Definitely the black pudding talking.

Slippery steps led up to the *Fischerklause* bar. I hung onto the railings and hauled myself past terraced flower beds heaped with snow. The door opened, a couple of men in pea coats and felt caps staggered out, followed by the smell of fresh cigarette smoke and stale beer. The door hung for a moment before it was caught by the wind and banged to. I stood aside, and the two fishermen pushed past, arm in arm, bellowing at each other in *Platt*.

I pulled the door open again and stepped inside, holding tight so that it wouldn't slam.

The bar was narrow and not too long, booths lined one wall, a ship's lantern hung above each table, and marker buoys, nets and large model ships cluttered up what little vertical space remained. Unlike most bars I knew, this one was only dimly lit, which made looking at the clientele bearable.

I found an empty booth—in the summer there wouldn't be space for the likes of me, but on a Tuesday evening in the middle of winter, even I was welcome. I'd hardly sat down before a waitress bought a bottle of Rostocker and a glass. She marked the beer mat and left again, uninterested in whether I had a thirst for anything other than beer.

But beer was what I wanted, the bar was warm, no-one had paid particular attention to my arrival and I had a table to myself. I was beginning to like Warnemünde.

Only when I'd finished the first beer and my fingers had thawed out did I begin to ask myself what I was doing here. The idea of meeting the maid in a pub was wrong, breaking every paragraph and clause in the book. Not only was I meeting someone else's IM, but doing so in a crowded public space.

And what had I been thinking of, turning up an hour early?

But it's not hard to spend an hour in a bar, drinking and being annoyed with oneself. I know, I've had practice.

20
WARNEMÜNDE

At ten to eleven, I started to pay more attention to the door. The place was so small, it wasn't hard to keep an eye on comings and goings—so far we'd lost two fishermen and gained what must have been half a brigade of fishwives. I could tell they'd just finished a shift processing fish at the Fisheries Production Co-op because they were still in their work-clothes, reddened hands reeking of herring.

At seventeen minutes past eleven—just when I was beginning to believe I'd been stood up—the door whirled open, sucking out the warm fug and admitting a young woman in a well-cut woollen coat, a scarf wrapped over her head. I kept only half an eye on her, wondering how someone from the West had stumbled upon this bar. But when she unwrapped the scarf and took her coat off, shaking wet snow onto the floor as she did so, it became clear that this was no *Westler*—under the coat she was wearing a domestically produced sheath dress in a chestnut, mustard and umber Argyle pattern.

Having hung up her Western coat and shaken out her loose hair, she turned to survey the booths. Her eyes met mine, and only then did I recognise her. The maid.

I stood up as she came over, trying to signal to the waitress, who was steadfastly looking in any direction but ours.

"You thought I wasn't coming?" she asked as she settled herself across the table. Behind her, one of the fish workers was telling a story, the others snorting into their drinks.

I looked my guest up and down, admiring the

transfiguration. As if sensing my distraction, the waitress chose that moment to make her way towards us. She edged around the fish processors, adroitly avoiding the stained and scarred fingers of the fishermen.

"*Selters*," ordered my guest. I tapped my beer glass, but the waitress was already on her way back to the bar.

"You look ..."

"Different?" she completed my sentence. "*Feierabend.* End of shift, it's when I let the real me come out."

Music was playing over tinny loudspeakers, *Schlagermusik*, sentimental ballads in German, a far cry from the synth-pop and rock I'd just left behind in the basement of the Neptun.

At the back of the pub, up a few steps in front of the bar, a handful of couples were dancing. I watched them for a second or two, then switched my attention to the fishworkers populating the seats either side of us. More had arrived, several were standing in the aisle next to our booth, too close for olfactory comfort.

"Care to dance?" I asked, watching surprise take up residence on her face. It was quickly evicted and replaced with a vague smile.

"You're forward."

It wasn't a yes, but I took it as such. I stood up and walked around the table to take her arm. As she rose, I closed in and whispered: "Less chance of being overheard."

She didn't say anything to that, but she did come up the steps with me. The music had changed to slow, coastal folk sung in thick *Platt.* Probably about the loss of a mermaid-wife or a worm-ridden barge. Possibly both.

She came into my arms, and I steered her around the narrow dance floor. I'm not much of a dancer—it's not part of my job description—but I did alright at avoiding her feet and those of the other couples.

"What do I call you?" I asked.

"You want my real name?"

I shouldn't know her real name. If I'd gone by the book, I'd be meeting her in the company of her handler, codenames only. But this wasn't by the book.

"I'm Borchert, Wolfgang," I told her, using my current cover name.

"Pleased to meet you, Herr Borchert. I'm Anna Weber." She leaned back far enough to offer me her hand.

I stepped away and shook her hand, then we danced in silence for a few minutes. Anna may even have been enjoying it. The song ended, the next one was just as wheezy, another schnultzy number.

"How long have you been at the hotel?"

"The Nepp? It's my first season there." She leaned back again, this time so I could see her wink. "You're not local?"

"From Berlin. Up here enjoying the fresh air."

"Are we fresh enough for you?"

"So far, all I know is that it's damned cold!" I pulled her closer as I said it and she didn't seem to mind.

We shuffled around the dance floor for a while longer, and I tried to think of something witty or impressive to say, but in the end I just decided she'd had enough of a warm up.

"Have you got the film?" I asked. I had other questions, but they could wait.

She gave me a look I didn't know how to interpret, then: "It's in a safe place, just as it should be, comrade."

I should have taken the camera off her at the hotel. If she'd already passed the film to her handler there'd be a tug of war between the local office and Berlin over who got to see the negatives first.

"Do you still have it?"

She waited before answering, long enough for us to step from one side of the room to the other. "I still have it."

"Bring it to me. Here, tomorrow. If your handler has any complaints, tell him to talk to ZAIG in Berlin."

That impressed her, she went a little stiff in my arms.

Maybe she'd heard that ZAIG has the ear of the Minister?

I let Anna Weber, chambermaid at the Hotel Neptun and part-time informant for the Stasi, leave first, watching her pull on her fancy coat, wrap the scarf around her blonde hair and set sail into the wild weather. I finished my beer and ordered a schnapps. When that was gone, I settled the bill and followed her into the night.

The streets were empty. Other than the bar, there were no lights in any of the windows. Just me and the roar of the storm.

But opposite, on the other side of the Alter Strom canal that sheltered the fishing boats, the ferry port was brightly lit. I stood for a while, observing with professional interest. There wasn't much to see: buildings and walls hid most of the terminal from casual viewers, only the top of the linkspan ramp and an observation tower peeped over the wall.

How many locals and visitors to Warnemünde dreamed of getting the ship to Denmark? Right here in the middle of town, just a few paces from the railway station, the Gedser ferry came in twice a day. A reminder that we were at the edge of the world here, right on the border with the Non-Socialist Economies.

I looked at my watch, shivering as the wind found its way up my sleeve. The next boat wouldn't arrive for another three hours, I wasn't going to wait around just to gongoozle a train-ferry, no matter where it was bound for.

I turned my back on the wind and headed for my lodgings, hoping my decrepit landlady had left the door on the latch.

21
WARNEMÜNDE

I woke the next morning with a headache. A hangover? Not likely, I have to drink far more than that before my liver rebels. Which left *Heimweh*—maybe this was just how I felt when I left Berlin for too long?

I rolled out of bed, ignored the breakfast that the old biddy had laid on for me—*matjes* herring with onion in yoghurt sauce, but I did nearly stop when I passed the coffee pot, steam curling from the spout. I managed to keep my course and left the house.

The wind had died during the night, leaving still, crinklingly cold air. I stamped my feet as I went along and avoided the odd Trabant and Wartburg that were slithering along the iced roadway.

Once at the Neptun, I took a quick look at the breakfast room. It was barely seven o'clock, but the citizens of our Republic were obediently queuing for the first time that day while the Westerners were still tucked up in bed, safe in the belief that there'd be enough food for late-comers.

Returning to the reception area, I took a seat at the Round Bar in the lobby, making sure I had a good view of the lifts and the entrance to the breakfast room.

A coffee arrived, better quality than that my landlady would be serving up—this was the real thing, unadulterated and from real beans, the smell of it was enough to vaporise my headache.

I was on my third cup when Merkur appeared. The lift doors opened, and he stepped out, wearing dark suit pants, a golfing pullover and brown deck shoes. Close up and in the flesh, he didn't look as time-worn as his photographs and video footage—he steamed along, no aches and pains slowing him. As he exited the lift, he took a brief look around the lobby, his eyes resting on me for a measured half-second before he disappeared into the breakfast room.

I checked my watch: nearly eight o'clock. I reckoned Merkur would take about half an hour over his breakfast before returning to his room. After that, we'd find out what his plans for the day might be. I looked at my expensive coffee, still half a cup left. I could make it last.

But Merkur left the breakfast room a minute or two later. He trotted over to the reception desk, looking neither to the left or right, and waited patiently while the staff dealt with another guest.

I left my coffee on the table and headed to the main doors, standing just inside and pointedly hitching up my sleeve to see my wristwatch, as if waiting for someone. I was only a few metres away from Merkur, close enough to hear his conversation with the receptionist.

"I'm afraid not," she told him. "As you may have seen, the sea is frozen—only the main fairways into the Alter Strom and the International Port are kept clear—boat trips will start again around Eastertime. But perhaps I could interest you in a visit to the old city of Rostock? Here's a map showing ..."

Although Merkur wasn't interested in the helpful advice, he was polite enough to wait for the receptionist to finish her recommendations. Then he asked:

"And the coast? How far can I walk along the coast? As far as Heiligendamm?"

It was the first time I'd heard his voice, and I was no expert on the dialects and accents of West Germany, but I'd place him from somewhere in the north-west of the country, possibly a hint of Rhenish in his speech patterns.

The receptionist stopped for a moment, long enough to

wonder whether the information Merkur had requested was the kind she should be giving out—the coast was sensitive: Easterners wondering whether it was worthwhile trying to swim to Denmark would want to scout out sites to launch their venture; Westerners might show too much interest in the various military and border defence stations that lined the coast. "Of course," she replied, "there's a footpath this side of the dunes, but it's too cold at the moment to go far—the next village, Diedrichshagen, is about three kilometres away. From there you can catch a bus ..."

Merkur's attention was wandering again, I could tell by the way he lifted his head to look at the hideous ormolu clock hanging above the key hooks.

"Thank you, I shall walk along the beach after breakfast—you've been most helpful." He left the receptionist to fold her map of Rostock, and me to go back to my coffee.

22
WARNEMÜNDE

By the time Merkur finished his breakfast and went up in the lift, I'd killed my coffee and buried it with a few cigarettes.

I sat patiently, observing staff and guests as they crossed the reception area: the citizens on tip-toe, awed by the splendour of the luxury hotel; the Westerners, self-importantly pacing around, indifferent to the best our Republic had to offer.

Merkur appeared forty-seven minutes later, kitted out in sturdy winter boots, loden winter coat and a warm fleece shapka hat that he must have picked up over here. He exited the lift and nipped across the lobby, reaching the glass doors before the doorman had a chance to open them for him.

I watched through the tall windows as he took the steps down to the promenade, only then leaving my seat at the bar and hurrying after him.

Once on the promenade, it wasn't difficult to see Merkur, thirty metres ahead of me, his long figure easy to identify between the sparse traffic.

I waited at the corner as he hiked further along the edge of the dunes. He didn't stop to admire the sparkling hunks of ice stranded on the wide beach, nor look up to appreciate the flawlessly endless cloud. He tucked his head into his collar, and loped along at a pace a younger man would be proud of.

I lost him to corners of buildings that cut into my line of sight, and decided that was the right moment to fetch my car. But when I reached it, the Wartburg wasn't in the mood to start. Several minutes of jiggling the clutch and repeated pumping of the gas pedal persuaded it to give the idea of firing a go, but even when it caught, it faded again unless I continuously nudged the pedal. I sat in the cold car, watching the heater attempt to defrost the windscreen while the engine finally settled down into a more regular grumble.

After scraping the frost from the side windows, I poured a slug of vodka on a rag and wiped the frozen condensation from the insides of the glass. Once I could see the clouds of blue exhaust through the thawing back window, I put the car in gear and headed towards Diedrichshagen, which as the receptionist had helpfully pointed out, was the next village along the coast.

According to the map, at the end of the Promenade, where Warnemünde called it a day, a footpath threaded between a thin strip of woodland and the edge of the dunes. Further along, I found a garden colony that might offer cover for a parked car, and with a bit of luck would do the same for a stationary observer, too.

Before going into the allotments, I walked along the fence, checking for winter gardeners. The colony was empty, no footprints showed in the snow that blanketed the pathways and vegetable beds. After checking the road was clear, I swiftly climbed the locked gates.

As is the way with tourist maps, the details were vague—a clubhouse was represented by a beer glass randomly placed in the centre of the allotments—but I found the building on the far side, just a few metres short of the coastal path that threaded through winter bare trees.

The clubhouse was a long, flat building of the kind that members often spend years scrabbling and begging for materials with which to build, and, like the gardens, was shut up for the winter. A low wall made of concrete blocks enclosed a beer garden, and a trio of flagpoles stood to vacant attention.

There was no wind at all today, I could feel and smell gelid

71

sea air creeping through the trees from the coast. I could see the trampled path among the trees, but the snow immediately in front of my vantage point lay as smooth as it had fallen, disturbed only by bird and animal prints.

Beyond the trees lay the beach, dusted with snow and frost, then the sea ice, restlessly cracking and rafting up on itself. It was a good place to wait and observe, if a little cold.

Merkur came marching along less than twenty minutes later, as energetic as when he had set off. His head was bare and his coat unbuttoned. He stared straight ahead as he walked, no interest in the trees around him, nor the frost-dusted dunes beyond. I stayed out of sight—the subject had already seen me twice. Even if I was prepared to assume that he hadn't actually noticed me so far, he would if I began to cross his eyeline too often.

As he came alongside, I edged along the wall of the clubhouse, waiting at the back of the building for him to come into view again. Once he'd passed, I lit a cigarette and watched the retreating figure as it flickered between the tree trunks. Should I return to the car, drive a bit further to Diedrichshagen and see if I could pick up his trail there? I was curious to know whether he would get the bus back to Warnemünde, as recommended by the receptionist, or press onwards to Heiligendamm.

I took another pull on my coffin nail and decided I'd seen enough to chalk up Merkur's current outing as an innocent walk. It was time to return to Warnemünde and wait for him in the warmth.

As I was about to turn away, another figure came into sight. He was going at the same rate as Merkur, but with his shorter legs was struggling to keep pace. I recognised the type: a colleague—it's not just the citizens of this Republic that can recognise one of the Firm at twenty paces.

The observer hurried after Merkur, he had no sense of panache or style, was interested only in fulfilling his duty. But to be fair to my unknown colleague, there was only the one path, he couldn't lose his mark—the only skill he needed was the ability to drop out of sight if Merkur unexpectedly started to take more of an interest in his surroundings.

We're like weeds and bad luck, where there's one of us, there's more—although, not for the first time, I was the exception that proved the rule. I lit another cigarette, and remaining under cover behind the building, looking down the side, towards the path and waiting patiently for eye number two. Here he was, nearly a hundred metres behind his comrade and just as out of shape.

When both colleagues had disappeared from sight, I returned to the car, following my own footsteps back through the snow. And as I walked, I thought.

Merkur was attracting a lot of interest—not only had I been sent up here to get a handle on his intentions, but the local office had sent a chambermaid to look through his belongings. And on top of all that, he now had a tail.

What had Merkur done to make the locals start snooping around?

Let's assume for a moment that the receptionist found his query about rambling along the dunes suspicious enough to report—that could, just possibly, explain these two overweight goons on the path. But it didn't explain the chambermaid and her instructions to catalogue Merkur's belongings.

Berlin had ordered me to stay out of the locals' way as much as possible, but I didn't see how I could oblige, considering the level of scrutiny Merkur was being subjected to.

23
WARNEMÜNDE

I wasn't sure of my next move. With a team, I would have been able to cover all the routes Merkur could have taken on his way back to Warnemünde: the bus stop in Diedrichshagen, the Promenade in case he returned on foot, and the hotel entrance just to be sure. Instead, I drove back to Warnemünde and went to see my friends at the *Kurhaus* observation post opposite the main doors of the Neptun.

A knock on the door, clapperboard held up, same procedure as last time. Only Glasses-moustache was alone that day. Enquiring as to the absence of the long-haired operative may have been the polite thing to do, but I didn't bother. My only job was to sit here and wait for Merkur to return—at which point I would latch onto him again and see what he did next.

It was a long wait—Merkur didn't return until after dark. From the *Kurhaus*, I watched him approach the doors of the Neptun, I could see him through the tall windows of the lobby as he pressed the button for the lift. Only then did I slowly cross the car park, adjusting my pace to avoid entering the hotel before he was safely on the way up to his floor.

Once he was out of the way, I sat down in the lobby bar, finding a seat near a few Western businessmen talking about a shipbuilding order. They were a loud group, not only the conversation—their suits demanded attention. I felt well camouflaged sitting behind them.

I passed the time sipping an overpriced Radeberger beer and filling in my expenses notebook. When that was done, I ordered another beer and waited some more.

Folk up here are a bit slow—they take their time when they're speaking and have a good think before they answer any questions. I was never quite sure whether they were being canny, continuously weighing up their options, or were generally just a little backwards. If it's the latter then it was rubbing off on me—I'd sat there for an hour before realising that Merkur might have gone to the nightclub again—he wouldn't need to come through the lobby to get there.

I took the stairs, flashing the *Kripo* disc at the staff member on the door to the Daddeldu and pushed through the already packed club. I headed for the bar first, then worked my way along to the corner where I'd seen Merkur the evening before.

It wasn't the easiest search. Disco-lights flashed and swept across my eyes, Western suits and Eastern teenagers danced to Michael Jackson and drinkers holding the best beers and spirits from East and West obstructed my progress. For a moment I thought I'd found him—a tall man, full head of light grey hair, dark blue check jacket. But when I worked my way round the room far enough to see his face, it was obscured by heavy, horn-rimmed glasses.

I was concentrating so much on figures above average height that I didn't notice the squat man until I felt his eyes on me. I lowered my gaze, searching the mass of dancers. There he was, the one watching me: red face and greasy, thinning hair, grey jacket over patterned shirt, no tie. Not dancing; standing and staring at me. This was one of the goons who'd chased after Merkur this morning.

I crossed the short distance between us, stopping just a few centimetres short. That was enough to make him jumpy— members of the Firm aren't used to being bearded. I tapped him on the chest and jerked my head towards the bar. When I set off, he followed.

Behind the bar, a door led to a stock room, the bar tender took one look at the pair of us and decided it wasn't worth asking what we were up to. I shut the door behind us, pulled my clapperboard and gave the short man a flash.

"This morning you were following a subject named Seiffert. Where is he now?" I said.

His Adam's apple bobbed up and down, and his eyes slid around the room. I didn't need to wait for his answer to know he'd lost Merkur.

"When did you last see him?"

"We followed him back to Warnemünde, comrade. The subject was heading for the hotel, but then ..."

"What time?"

"Twelve-o-four, comrade."

Without wasting another moment, I opened the storeroom door and dived back into the din—Phil Collins was intent on perforating my eardrums with assurances that I couldn't hurry love—but I didn't want relationship advice, I wanted Merkur.

I ran up the stairs, followed by the colleague, crossed the lobby at a fast pace and demanded reception tell me whether Seiffert was in.

The receptionist checked the hook, the key was hanging there.

Merkur wasn't in the hotel.

24
WARNEMÜNDE

It was a little short of the agreed hour when Anna walked through the door of the *Fischerklause*. I watched her slip her woollen coat off, revealing a wrap-over dress with black and red zebra stripes. Her fair skin and light eyes glinted in the glow of the kitschy lanterns, and the red in her dress nicely set off her loose blonde hair. She had a large red *Lederol* handbag looped over her shoulder, and she swung it off as she sat down, letting it fall to the floor under the table.

"For a hotel worker, you seem to spend a lot of money in the *Exquisit* shop," I said in way of greeting.

Anna pouted a little, but didn't deny that she frequented the expensive boutiques that sold limited edition, locally produced clothes and fashion items.

The waitress came over without prompting and examined Anna's outfit, obviously having similar thoughts as I had, although I might have detected a hint of envy in her features.

I ordered another beer for myself, Anna wanted a *Selters* sparkling water, and we sat and smiled shyly at each other until the drinks came.

"No dancing tonight," Anna observed. The music system had been packed away and tables had appeared where the previous night couples had danced. She sipped her drink, looking up from under her eyelashes. "That's a shame."

"We could go somewhere else, if you wanted to dance ..." I suggested.

Another sip of her water, another glance up at me. But in lieu of an answer, she reached into her bag and passed a film cannister over the table.

She watched anxiously as I took possession of the little tin, hiding it in the palm of my hand as I shunted it towards me. She gave a little sigh as I dropped it into my pocket, as if she'd worried I may examine it right there in the restaurant, although I couldn't think why that would have been so bad.

Once the film cannister had disappeared, Anna reached down again, this time lifting her bag onto her lap. She laid a pad of drawing paper on the table, then took out a leather pencil case.

"Do you mind?" she asked, already taking a pencil out.

I didn't object, so, holding the paper at an angle so I couldn't see, she began sketching. She looked up often, her tongue caught between her front teeth as she examined my face.

I drank my beer, ordered another, while Anna, absorbed in her task, left her glass on the table. She had a habit of pushing her hair behind her right ear, I noticed, and her tongue would disappear when she drew, but come out again when she looked at me. I watched that tongue and thought about things I shouldn't have.

Finally, she put the pencil on the table and took a sip of *Selters*.

"May I see?"

She shook her head. "That was just to get a feel for ..."

"For me?"

"Yes." But she was already burrowing in her pencil case again, pulling out a few sticks of charcoal wrapped in tissue paper. She turned the page, starting on a fresh sheet.

Time passed easily without the need for conversation. She drew, I drank. I imagined it was just the two of us in the bar, no need for romantic music, or dancing. I could have sat there all night, watching that tongue dart between those lips.

She let me see the picture this time. She laid the charcoals back on the tissue paper, wrapping them up in a neat bundle, then tore the page out of the pad and laid it on the table.

I turned it around and leaned forward to see it better. It was clearly me she'd drawn, no doubt about it, but it wasn't a portrait of anyone I knew.

"Am I that ... do I really look that brutal?" I asked.

The tongue again, as her eyes scanned my face. "Look at the eyes," she commanded.

I looked at the eyes. Deep, dark rings beneath. She was a good artist, I gave her that, but I wasn't sure she'd captured me.

"Your eyes," she said, packing away her tools. "I see hurt in them."

I didn't know what to say to that, the conversation was far outside my range of experience—that's not the kind of thing men say to each other. That's not the kind of thing my wife would have said to me, even before she left me the first time. And it certainly isn't the kind of thing women usually say to me when I'm trying to seduce them.

I looked up from my portrait, Anna was standing, already wearing her fancy coat, her bag slung over the crook of her arm, ready to leave.

"I thought we could go somewhere else?" I was already reaching for my coat, but she held her hand out, waving me back.

"Work calls. I'm on the night shift."

I relaxed into my seat, picked up the sheet of paper again and began to roll it up.

"Don't roll it, you'll smear the charcoal," she said, already leaving.

After she'd gone, I sat for a while at the table. I finished my beer then rolled the portrait—how else could I get it home?

25
WARNEMÜNDE

I spent the rest of the evening in one pub after another. None of them were quite to my taste, all had been dolled up for the tourists: clean, well decorated, pricey—although I didn't find any as flashy or as overpriced as the Neptun lobby bar.

After the *Fischerklause*, I tried the *Atlantik* on the quay, moved on to the fish restaurant, but left after the first beer— the smell of frying cod was too much to take on an empty stomach. Wondering for no more than a moment whether to go back to the *Fischerklause*, I moved on to the night-bar at the *Teepott*, marvelling at the change of clientele from when I'd been there in the afternoon.

I was devoting myself to drinking—it had taken long enough for the waiter to bring my order, and I had a thirst on me—the schnapps was long gone and the beer wasn't going to hang around much longer either. But my concentration was broken when some fellow, a local by his voice, demanded another guest at my table make space. I looked up, it was the overfed goon from the Daddeldu disco, the one who'd lost Merkur that day. He was squeezing a chair into the narrow gap opposite me.

"Mind if I join you?" he asked, sitting down and trying to catch the attention of an uninterested waiter.

I supped my beer and pretended to ignore him while watching out of the corner of my eye. In my professional and experienced judgement, he didn't look too steady on his pins— I wasn't the only one who'd been drinking that night.

When the waiter finally came over, my colleague ordered

two beers and a couple of chasers. I looked directly at him now, his eyes were blurred and unfocussed, the finger he pointed in my direction was unsteady.

"You're after him as well," he slurred.

"Give me your clapperboard," I demanded.

He pulled it out and slid it across the table—the action reminded me of Anna and her film cannister. I quickly placed my hand over the bound cardboard booklet to conceal it from any observers, not that anyone was interested, opening it below the table and flicking through until I reached the interesting pages: Unterleutnant Lütten Horst, Rostock District Administration of the Ministry for State Security.

"So Horst Lütten," I said in a quiet voice, leaning forward. "Which department?"

"Department II."

"OK, what's counter-intelligence's interest in the subject?"

"We get our orders, we do our job. How about you, what's your interest?" Lütten leaned forward, placing one hand on the beer-damp table to steady himself, the other hand stretched out, wanting his clapperboard back.

"I get my orders—what else?" I said, keeping hold of his ID for the moment.

"So you won't tell me?"

There wasn't anything else to say, this conversation obviously wasn't going anywhere, so I handed over his clapperboard and stood up. But as I did so, Lütten rose with me. He pressed his beer belly against the edge of the table, his slack face leered at me.

"You, comrade," he said in a voice suddenly sober. "I know your kind, I've seen enough of them—you don't get to sleep at night, do you?"

26
WARNEMÜNDE

Saturday morning found me in my seat at the Round Bar in the lobby of the Neptun. It was called the Round Bar for a reason: everything was circular, from the wooden counter itself to the bucket seats and the tables. I felt a little out of place, holding the rectangular guide book that was my excuse for sitting here.

I was waiting for Merkur, but I had enough to occupy my mind without having to read the guide book. This morning, I'd spent a few minutes in the old biddy's bathroom, looking at myself in the lace-edged mirror. I couldn't see anything different in my eyes, they were as they always were. Perhaps not such a deep brown as they used to be, certainly more bloodshot, but still mine. There was nothing that told of the broken nights, the visits by a dead operative—the dark bags that Anna had drawn so precisely weren't eloquent. And Lütten had seen nothing, it was just the drink speaking.

But don't they say that drunks and children speak the truth?

At just before eight o'clock, Merkur exited the lift, took a brief look around the lobby and headed into the breakfast room.

Glad of the distraction from my own thoughts, I opened my notebook to note down the time, but looked up when he appeared again. He spoke to the receptionist—the same woman as the day before—who seemed confused by whatever he was asking.

Slipping notebook and pencil back into my pocket, I left my

coffee and walked over to stand by the main doors. Repeating my performance from the previous day, I checked my watch and tapped my foot: impatient man waiting—a hackneyed but effective role, not least because I could hear the conversation going on at the reception desk.

"... can I walk along the coast as far as Heiligendamm?"

"If you walk as far as Diedrichshagen then you can catch the number 36 bus back." After an initial slip, the receptionist had done well in covering her irritation at fielding the same questions she'd answered just twenty-four hours previously.

"Thank you, you've been most helpful," replied Merkur, and went for his breakfast.

When Merkur came out of the breakfast room and entered the lift, I remained in my seat, hiding behind my tourist guide. And I stayed right there when he came back down, fully togged up in his boots, shapka and loden coat, and strode purposefully to the doors.

I watched him through the window as he descended the steps and disappeared from sight. A moment later, he was back in view, stalking along the Promenade in the direction of the lighthouse and harbour.

I waited a little longer, and was rewarded when *Unterleutnant* Lütten entered the frame, hastening after Merkur. Only then did I pick up my book, drain my coffee and follow them into the cold.

It was another dry day, but clouds were massing overhead, giving the impression they might lower themselves onto the town at any point, suffocating us with snow and freezing fog.

I pulled on my gloves as I went, taking care to keep Lütten in sight, but also aware that Lütten's colleague should be nearby. He'd be staying warm in a car if he had any sense.

At the *Teepott*, our little convoy turned right, heading down a back lane parallel to the Alter Strom quay. Past narrow houses, tight shops with empty shelves and long queues, grannies with red hands, shiny with arthritis, clutching shopping bags.

Merkur had reached the end of the lane where it widened out to meet Kirchenstrasse and the bridge to the railway station. A grey Wartburg was waiting at the side of the road, the driver had opened the door and was climbing out, ignoring the Barkas impatient to get past. As Lütten drew near, Merkur was already half-way over the bridge, and the two goons switched places, Lütten quickly putting the Wartburg into gear and making space for the greengrocer's van to squeeze past. Lütten's colleague hurried after Merkur, the Wartburg shuffling over the warped planks of the bridge.

I waited by the Alter Strom and watched the procession— Merkur had already disappeared into the train station, the road layout forced Lütten in his car to turn right onto the main road to Rostock, while the goon on foot had reached the booking hall, was cautiously opening the heavy doors to peer inside.

Lütten parked his Wartburg behind a row of Danish and Swedish lorries and hurried back to the station to see what was happening.

A rake of double-decker carriages was waiting at the platform next to the station building, a heavy diesel V180 droning away at the head, working itself up to pull the train to Rostock. After a moment's hesitation, I boarded the first carriage, quickly working through the connections between the cars to the end and finding myself a window seat upstairs. The lower part of the window could be wound down, leaving a gap of about thirty centimetres, just enough to angle my head out to see along the length of the train.

I'd guessed right: just as the dispatcher appeared, carrying her whistle and her green and red lollipop, Merkur hurried out of the ticket office and marched across the icy cobbles to the nearest carriage. The platform manager, about to raise the signal, shouted in irritation as Lütten hurried after, jumping aboard as the whistle blew. The doors shuffled and clunked home and, with a jerk and a scream of exhaust, we set off. As the platforms of Warnemünde station slid backwards, I made myself comfortable in a seat from which I could see Merkur or Lütten, should either decide to alight at any of the stations between here and Rostock.

27
ROSTOCK

Lütten's colleague was waiting for us at Rostock, pretending to make a phone call from the box outside the station, his Wartburg idling at the curb. Lütten himself paused to study the timetables on the noticeboard, and I dawdled at the ticket counters.

Merkur, the only one of us with no reason to hang around, headed directly for the tram stop.

Lütten decided he also had to make a call, so left the ticket hall and waited outside the phone booth, studiously avoiding eye contact with his colleague, who was still managing to hold a one-sided conversation down the line. I switched to the queue at the Mitropa kiosk, deliberating over the display of newspapers and magazines on the counter. I had a good view of Merkur at the tram stop, staring at the parade of flagpoles and their charges of national and red flags. They didn't stir or flap, but drooped in the dead air.

When the Gothawagen rumbled around the turning circle, activity returned to our little tableau. Merkur boarded the first carriage of the tram, Lütten's colleague finished his call and went back to his car, searching one pocket after another for his keys. Lütten was having problems with his pockets too, fishing around for coins for the telephone. Meanwhile, I decided that the nearest magazine would suit my needs and paid hurriedly.

Along with several other passengers, I boarded the trailer car and pretended to flick through my purchase, a little unsettled to discover I'd picked up the women's magazine,

Sybille. Through the windows I could see Merkur in the other carriage, fumbling with change, trying to pick out a twenty Pfennig coin for the ticket box. He found one just as the doors concertinaed shut and the tram hummed into life. The money dropped into the box, he pulled out a ticket and found himself a seat at the front, not paying any attention to Lütten and his friend, who were both climbing into the Wartburg behind us.

We weren't on the move for long—Merkur got up as we screeched around the curve into Lange Strasse in the centre of Rostock. The doors scraped open and Merkur climbed down the steps, looking around, as if to orientate himself. He took a street map out of his pocket and unfolded it, giving me a chance to alight while he was distracted.

We were on a traffic island in the middle of the road. Beside us, Lütten's Wartburg puttered, giving way to the passengers who wanted to cross from the tram stop to the side of the road. He glared at me as I walked in front of his car, I could still feel his eyes on my back as I reached the pavement in front of Hotel Varna.

Once safely out of the traffic, I dropped to one knee and retied my lace, taking a discreet look to each side as I did so. The tram had moved off and was gaining speed, Merkur was waiting for a gap in the traffic, wanting to cross to the far side.

A further glance over my shoulder, I could see the Wartburg doing a U-turn at the next junction then pulling up to let Lütten out.

I stood up and moved towards the hotel, using the reflections on the bronzed windows to keep track of Merkur— he was heading for the Centrum department store.

Once he'd disappeared through the doors I turned around, better to observe Lütten, puffing along the pavement and into the store.

As every watcher knows, department stores are a nightmare. Multiple floors, multiple exits and plenty of customers to provide cover. Poor Lütten, having to follow the subject through the Centrum on a Saturday morning!

Rather than head into the store, I decided to wait where I was, keeping an eye on the Wartburg and Lütten's colleague, now standing beside it. The two Rostockers would be in radio contact so the second goon could intercept Merkur if he left by another exit.

It was ten minutes before anything happened, ten minutes in which to reflect that no matter how cold it was, it was at least a calm day—no wind, no snow and no sleet. That was when Lütten's colleague reached in through the open window of his car and picked up the radio. He looked up and down the pavement, then spoke into the microphone.

It was the way he scanned his surroundings—not a good sign. A moment later, Lütten came out of the store, he spoke to the driver, they both scanned the street again before exchanging a few more words. Not friendly ones, by the look of it.

The colleague got into the Wartburg and drove off, leaving Lütten staring at the doors to the Centrum, doing his best to ignore me, even though he must have been aware of me, watching on the opposite side of the street.

Seeing a break in the traffic, I sprinted across the road.

"Hope you haven't lost him!"

Lütten didn't answer, he was too busy staring at the doors of the department store.

"You have, havn't you?" I demanded, but there was no need to wait for an answer. These two clowns had managed to lose Merkur. Again.

It didn't take me long to find what I was looking for. My kind of place: open early in the day, dingy, no tourists.

"*Einen Klaren*," I said to the barman. He didn't reply, just got the bottle out. My kind of barman.

I downed the schnapps and let gravity put the glass back on the counter, ready for a refill. My barman obliged.

This time I took it to a table, ordering a beer as I went.

Either Merkur was cannier than I'd given him credit for, or the two colleagues from Rostock Department II were more useless than I'd feared. Which was it?

The beer arrived and I sank the schnapps in it. Lifting the glass to my lips I re-ran the film of Merkur, the one I kept in my head: Merkur getting on the train at the last minute. No, rewind a bit further: Merkur in the hotel lobby this morning.

Why had Merkur talked to the receptionist—on two mornings running—about walking along the beach to Heiligendamm?

"How far is it from Warnemünde to Heiligendamm?" I called out to the barman.

He stopped rinsing glasses and looked up, not in my direction, just vaguely upwards. There was silence, long enough for me to decide he hadn't heard me, or hadn't understood the question. Then came his answer.

"Depends how you get there." Another Mecklenburger, slow to answer, vowels so steady you could fall asleep between the syllables.

"On foot, from Warnemünde."

He nodded and turned back to washing his glasses. I watched him put them on the side to drain: one, two, three— then an answer: "Be about three and a half hours, three at a trot."

Three hours. A pleasant stroll in the summer, not so much fun when it was minus twenty in the shade. So why the insistence that he wanted to go to Heiligendamm?

I stood up and went to the bar, coins in my hand, ready to pay.

"And what's the best way to Heiligendamm from here?" I asked.

28
HEILIGENDAMM

The next day, back in Berlin, I would sit at my desk and write the investigation report on Secondary Operational Procedure Merkur:

I determined the direction of travel of the subject through deployment of political-operational search methods. Consequently, I was in position to regain operational contact with MERKUR on the platform of Bad Doberan railway station.

It would have been more honest to state that Merkur was expecting me, but that's not the kind of thing the brass like to read in reports. Nevertheless, there he was when I got off the train at Bad Doberan.

The train to Heiligendamm was standing at the other side of the platform, one of those toy trains that we seem to have a lot of in our Republic: narrow gauge steam engine pulling mismatched dinky carriages, each with an open platform at either end.

The locomotive gave a long, plaintive whistle, and Merkur stamped out a cigarette and climbed aboard. I chose a different coach and stood on the outside platform until the couplings stiffened and the train jerked into motion.

First we picked up some speed, but almost immediately slowed to a crawl as we crossed the main road and ratcheted down a shopping street, a warning bell clanging away as if the Young Pioneers had taken over the footplate. Trundling along, I admired the decorations in each of the empty shop windows as we passed: the banners proclaiming the *Day Of The Soviet Army* and the upcoming *Day Of The Postal And Telephone*

Workers. But of more concern was the fact the train was moving slowly enough for Merkur to jump off anytime he liked.

But why would he? He'd practically invited me along for the ride.

The steam engine dragged us through Bad Doberan, stopping a couple of times to allow housewives with shopping baskets and workers travelling to late shifts to board. We finally left the town and picked up some real speed, boiling smoke and soot obscuring the view. The bell had stopped, but the steam whistle whooped every so often, perhaps worried we might fall asleep and miss the excitement.

Heiligendamm was the next stop, and as the train whined and screeched through a sharp curve and clacked over a set of points, I went to wait on the platform above the couplings.

Sure enough, as soon as we pulled to a halt, Merkur jumped down and headed through the woods at his usual brisk pace.

As I hurried down the woodland path after him, a short whoop of the whistle and the regular chug of steam told me the train was leaving.

The subject led me across a road and into another loose woodland, some kind of park. He left the path, cutting across the virgin snow under the trees with the certainty of a man who'd been here before.

It took less than five minutes from station to beach, but Merkur didn't stop there. He turned right along the edge of the dunes, leaving the buildings of Heiligendamm behind him.

The wind blew in over the sea-ice, a gentle breeze, yet colder even than the driving storm of the other day. I shivered and walked on, half an eye on my surroundings, the rest of my concentration on Merkur. To my right, a marsh frozen hard, to the left, on the beach side, large boulders protected the roadway from erosion.

Up ahead, Merkur was waiting for me.

29
HEILIGENDAMM

"I came here as a boy." Merkur stared out to sea, his eyes focussed on the waves scraping the edge of the ice, a hundred metres or more from the shore. "It was summer, first time I ever saw the sea."

"Weren't you here yesterday?" I asked. I had no idea whether he'd come this far after giving Lütten and his goon the slip, but it was as good an opening as any.

"I wanted to get rid of the other two, didn't want them spoiling our chat."

I thought about this. It made sense, not wanting those two clowns hanging around. "The others, they're ... you're aware that we're all in the same club."

"I doubt that. You're in a different league."

It was meant as a compliment, but try as I might, I couldn't strangle the thought that I hadn't been doing so well in this championship either—after all, I'd been sussed by a postman. I didn't argue the point.

"How did you know you were being followed?"

"Dogs."

"Dogs?" I asked, gathering my patience—I hate it when a subject comes over all arcane.

"When you're a postman, you learn to keep an eye out for them. Dogs are territorial—you stop in front of their house, come into the hallway of their flats—so they see you as a threat. Postmen always have to be on their guard.

"Little dogs are the worst, terriers, I don't like those—you have to watch out for terriers, vicious breed. Under bushes, behind bins—never know where they might be hiding."

I had my arms across my chest, trying to keep the cold out, but Merkur stood easily, hands by his sides, still staring over the frozen sea.

"What do you want?" I asked.

"What makes you think I want anything?"

"Let's talk *Tacheles*, Seiffert. You didn't come over here to throw names around on a whim, you knew it would get our attention. So now you have our attention, what do you want to do with it?" I'd been preparing for this conversation for days, yet now I couldn't wait for it to be over. It was too cold for flirting.

"I want to find out about my son. I want to know why he had to die."

That was a good reason, but I wasn't sure I believed it was the only reason. Naturally, he wanted to know how and why his son died, but was the ice-bound northern fringe of the GDR really the place to start?

It felt like a lifetime ago when I'd first heard of Source Bruno, Arnold Seiffert. A lifetime, and somehow only two months. And now I had his father standing in front me, asking why he no longer had a son.

"I understand your son's death occurred in West Germany. You ought to direct your enquiry to the authorities over there," I suggested helpfully.

"Your lot were involved, don't pretend otherwise."

"There is no reason for the German Democratic Republic to have any interest in your son's activities."

"Don't take me for a fool—Arnold was over here, in the East. He visited his aunt and uncle and soon afterwards he was dead. Something happened while he was here, and I want to know what—you must know something, why else would they have sent you?"

"I looked at his file before I came here. I can assure you, there was nothing in it. He had a visa to visit his relatives in

District Frankfurt-Oder. He arrived in the German Democratic Republic, registered with the local police and deregistered when he left. Your son wasn't of any interest to the organs of our country. He left our jurisdiction on the third of December and that is all the information we have."

Merkur sliced his hand through the air, cutting me off. It was a practised gesture, authoritative.

"I asked for Gisela Bauer because my son mentioned her. He said she was one of yours. If you don't know anything, I'm sure she will."

"I'm afraid I don't know of any Frau Bauer, I checked the records, but no-one of that name works for the Ministry of State Security."

Merkur finally turned away from the view, it was the first time I saw his face close-up. It was a fine face, the moustache and hair well groomed—a Western face, one that had known a good life, nutritious food and a warm house.

"Listen, if you won't tell me what I want to know, then you should go back to Berlin or wherever you've come from. Go back and tell your ministry this: Arnold Seiffert's father is here, and he knows that Arnold offered to work for you. Wait!" his hand shot out and grabbed my forearm even before I'd started to turn away from him. "There's more ... tell them this: just like my son, I am prepared to offer my services for Socialism."

30
BERLIN LICHTENBERG

"I had the distinct impression, comrades, that Merkur was well-prepared for this mission. He was able to identify and monitor operational observation by myself and members of Department II of the District Administration in Rostock." I paused in my presentation, took a peek at the caterpillar carriers seated around the table. They looked bored, preoccupied with greater concerns.

"Furthermore, there are no operationally relevant indications that source Bruno, when still alive, had operational contact with the operative working in the operational area under the name Gisela Bauer," I continued, internally wincing every time I said the O-word, not for the first time wishing our Ministry wasn't so obsessed with labelling every possible activity as being operational. "Consequently we can exclude the possibility that Source Bruno had awareness of any operationally significant information regarding the identity of Comrade Bauer."

"Comrade *Unterleutnant*, the committee would be thankful if you would confine your report to operationally relevant information and evidence gained during your operational activities in District Rostock."

They wanted facts: *what did I do, who did I see, what did they do and say?* There was zero interest in my appraisal of Merkur, my assessment of his training and objectives, whether or not he was an unreliable witness and what irregularities there may be in his legend.

So I gave them what they wanted, and remained at

attention while they didn't ask their follow-up questions.

When it was clear that my verbal report had provoked neither interest nor reaction, Major Kühn dismissed me. "Keep yourself available, Comrade Second Lieutenant."

It was a polite way of saying I wasn't going home that night—but good manners are no substitute for a bed. Not that I'd have slept much under my own blankets, but at least they'd have been my blankets.

I took myself to Operational Technical Sector. As soon as I'd arrived back in Berlin last night, I'd handed them the film canister that Anna had given me. I wasn't expecting anything much from the photographs, but they'd be ready by now, and going to fetch them was just one way to delay writing my report.

The photographs weren't waiting at the secretariat, but a message was.

"The technician wishes to speak to you," the secretary informed me, already lifting the phone and pressing buttons.

"This film, domestic manufacture, brand: ORWO," said the techie once I'd found his lair, a narrow store-room equipped with red lights, white lights, washing lines, bottles of chemicals, trays and mechanical bits and bobs I couldn't begin to identify. "But this film has been exposed."

He stood in front of me, wringing his skeletal hands, bushy moustache and sideburns moving as he chewed something, possibly his tongue.

I didn't follow for a moment—of course the film had been exposed, that's why I'd wanted it processed. Then the *Groschen* dropped. "You mean daylight?"

"Deliberately, I'd say. Normally you can salvage an image or two from the beginning of the roll, particularly where later frames have wrapped around and protected them from accidental exposure. But this has been completely pulled out under sunlight or other bright light then wound back into the canister."

"Fingerprints?"

The techie shook his head, gestured at the baths of chemicals behind him. "The film has been through a dilute acid solution, then washed. Good luck getting prints off that."

31
Berlin Lichtenberg

I took the envelope of empty negatives back to my office and sat down at the typewriter. I fed a sheet of paper in, typed my personal code in the top right-hand corner and pushed the carriage back a few times. Then:

Zentraler Operativer Vorgang BRUNO
Operativer Teilvorgang MERKUR
Ermittlungsbericht

That's as far as I got. I picked up the envelope with the negatives, held one up to the light. As blank as you'd expect, nothing in the frame.

Deliberate, the technician had said.

I lifted the phone and dialled the operator.

"Hotel Neptun in Warnemünde, Cadre Department," I told her, and waited while she looked up the number and connected me.

Two hundred kilometres to the north, an extension rang.

"*Kaderabteilung, Wiersinski am Apparat.*"

"*Obermeister* Teichert, K in Berlin," I told him. If Wiersinski felt the need to check, the Berlin *Kriminalpolizei* would be happy to confirm the existence of a senior sergeant named Teichert, unfortunately not at his desk at that precise moment. "Do you have a Weber Anna on your housekeeping staff?"

Wiersinski grunted. There was a thud as he laid the phone on the desk, then the rustle of papers. Another clunk as he picked the receiver up.

"When did you say she worked here?" he asked.

"Right now. She worked the late shift last Tuesday."

Another rustle of papers. "No, sorry, Comrade *Obermeister*, no-one of that name."

I put the phone back on its cradle and leaned back in my chair. No Anna Weber, room maid at the Hotel Neptun.

In my safe was a phone directory for all official Ministry offices, I checked then dialled the central number for the MfS District Administration in Rostock.

"Second Lieutenant Reim, ZAIG in Berlin. Put me through to First Lieutenant Mewitz."

"Which department?"

"You tell me."

A sigh transmitted down the line, followed by the creaking of a wooden chair, drawers sliding open and being pushed shut. Words exchanged in the background, then the phone was lifted again.

"No-one of that name here."

"What about the county office?"

"As I said, no Mewitz here."

So that was the news: *Oberleutnant* Mewitz didn't exist—which made him the perfect handler for the equally non-existent informer Anna Weber. But how to make that fit the Merkur case?

Until now, I may, just about, have been prepared to accept that Merkur was a harmless old man, too clever for his own good, but merely looking for meaning in his son's death. The kind of asset best sent home and forgotten about.

But now I'd established the non-existence of both Weber and Mewitz, I had more questions—too many questions to allow Merkur to slip over the border back to the West.

32
BERLIN LICHTENBERG

"What did Merkur suggest he could offer in the service of Socialism?" asked Major Kühn later that evening.

"Comrade Major, the subject emphasised that his co-operation is conditional on access to information regarding Source Bruno's death. Providing he is given such access, Merkur is willing to exploit his position as mid-level official in Osnabrück postal sorting office. He indicated awareness of the presence of IMs in the *Bundespost* who currently work to ensure packages carried within West Germany are redirected to the territory of the GDR. He further indicated willingness to facilitate the activities of any such IMs who may be within his area of organisational responsibility."

Kühn steepled his fingers and thought about the offer. The parcel operation run by Department M was something nobody knew about, and at the same time, something everyone knew about—the parcels sent from the West to addresses in the GDR and searched before they reached their destination, the tapes, money, medicines that were removed—we'd all seen the plunder. I'd even heard rumours that the brass had access to a warehouse to the east of Berlin where they could take their pick of the goods.

But until Merkur mentioned it, I hadn't heard anything about parcels posted and addressed within West Germany being deliberately diverted over the border by agents in the West German Post Office. Presumably they ended up in the same warehouse in the Freienbrink complex.

"Another thing, Comrade Heym, we have received several

communications from the District Administration in Rostock, not to mention the Cadre Manager at Hotel Neptun."

I stiffened. It was clear what was coming next—complaints of flattened toes from the very people whose toes I'd been told to avoid. "*Jawohl, Genosse Major.*"

"The interdepartmental committee has reached a decision, Comrade Second Lieutenant." Instead of bollocking me, Kühn changed the subject—was he sparing me the embarrassment, or was he just realistic enough to realize there'll always be a little sawdust when you plane a plank? "Secondary Operational Procedure Merkur has ended." Kühn slid a couple of forms from the file in front of him and passed them over. "Merkur's visa has been revoked, and you are to travel overnight to Rostock and escort the subject to the border."

"Permission to speak, Comrade Major?"

"The committee has made its decision, take the lieutenant from Rostock with you," he shuffled his papers again, looking for the name. "Second Lieutenant Lütten, take him. I want a written investigation report on Merkur before you leave this evening, and the final report on the secondary operation on the day of your return."

When a superior won't let you speak, you hold your clapper and bite the sour apple, no matter how much he needs to hear new information about exposed rolls of film, non-existent chambermaids and fictitious handlers.

"*Jawohl, Genosse Major.*"

33
ROSTOCK

The train arrived at Rostock half an hour late, but still in the wee hours of the morning. It was the darkest and quietest time of the day, night workers only half-way though their shift and everyone else abed. All except for Lütten, his glowing cigarette visible in the shadow of the shuttered ticket office.

We stood facing each other while the other passengers filtered into the night. I had my bag in one hand, the other was in my pocket. Lütten sipped placidly on his cigarette and stared past me, as if he were still waiting for me to arrive.

"Are you here to give me a lift?" I asked. I was as proud as the next man, but it was too late and too cold for this kind of game.

Lütten dropped his cigarette, putting his foot on it as he pivoted around to the main entrance. I followed him.

More snow had fallen since I'd left the night before. It was yet to be cleared and troughs stamped through the drifts showed the most popular routes. We took the path to the right where a familiar Wartburg stood, its engine ticking over, puffing smoke like an addict.

Lütten held the back door open and I climbed in, dragging my bag after me. I was surprised when he walked around the car and got in next to me.

"We've got a few hours, Merkur's train leaves just after nine. I've sorted out a bed for you," he said, looking the other way.

"I want to hear about the plan before I turn in."

"We knock on his door at six o'clock, watch him pack,

accompany him downstairs and put him in the car."

"And what are you going to do until his train leaves?" I demanded. "You plan to sit in the car with him for two and a half hours?"

We'd left the station now, were driving towards Warnemünde. The driver showed no signs of listening, his eyes staying on the road and the wing mirrors.

"That's not what we're going to do," I told Lütten. "The subject arrives for breakfast between a quarter to and five to eight—so we fetch him at twenty to eight. I want a man at either end of the corridor and two knocking at his door. In addition, there's to be two men on each entrance of the hotel, starting immediately. Got that?"

Lütten finally turned around to face me. Maybe he was bored with the view outside.

"And I want good men knocking on that door," I continued. "There's to be no fuss. Any complaints from the Neptun, I'll point them in your direction. Now get on the radio—sort out the personnel, then take me to my bed."

34
WARNEMÜNDE

I waited in the back of the Wartburg while they hauled Merkur out. They were as discreet as they could be under the circumstances: Lütten directing operations, a local heavyweight bringing up the rear, carrying both of Merkur's leather suitcases in one hand. Lütten stopped at the door, his arm extended as graciously as a gentleman considering how best to drape his cape over a puddle.

They took the downstairs entrance, the one used for the Daddeldu disco: crowded in the evening, it should have been empty at breakfast time. Yet a member of staff was wiping down the cloakroom counter—he knew exactly what was going on and suddenly found his task fascinating, bending over the desk so far his eyeballs almost touched the wood he was polishing. A couple of Westerners who had no business being there weren't so reserved. They stood around at the foot of the stairs, watching as the procession passed through, at least until the hotel management turned up and toadied them upstairs to the breakfast room.

Lütten ushered Merkur into the back seat of the car, and the Wartburg sank on its suspension as the big goon clambered into the front passenger seat. Lütten got behind the wheel and we pulled out of the hotel car park, a Rocar minibus with the rest of Lütten's men tucked in tight behind us.

"Can you tell me where you're taking me?" asked Merkur. His voice was as steady as the day he and I had chatted by the sea at Heiligendamm.

"I'm afraid there's been an administrative error regarding

your visa, Herr Seiffert. Unfortunately you'll have to cut short your visit to the German Democratic Republic. As an indication of our regret at this unfortunate situation, we're giving you a lift to the station where you'll be able to catch the train back to Osnabrück."

"How kind," murmured Merkur, watching the lights of Warnemünde through the car windows.

The Inter-zonal train came in from Stralsund, a rake of West German *Bundesbahn* carriages hauled by a thrumming Ludmilla diesel. We stood at the far end of the platform at Rostock main station, Merkur and I together, Lütten and his goons a few paces away, giving us some privacy. Not that I needed privacy—I had questions for Merkur, but not out here in the open.

There were passengers throughout the first carriage, so I sent Lütten along to clear out a compartment in the middle. Once that was done, I heaved Merkur's suitcases into the luggage racks and invited him to sit next to the window.

"You and one man stay at the end of the carriage, dismiss the others" I ordered Lütten as I slid the compartment door shut and locked it with a square railway key. I drew the curtains on the corridor side and sat down in the seat next to the door.

Merkur was looking out of the window, watching the snow-capped platforms jerk away as the train gathered speed. We rattled over points, past the sparse lights of a marshalling yard and were soon free of the town. The snow was thicker here, covering sheds and skeletal vegetable plots of endless allotment gardens. After that: open fields, bare trees and lifeless villages. Merkur turned away from the grey dawn unrolling outside the window.

"I suppose I was naive to think this might end any other way," he said. I didn't know whether he was talking to himself or to me.

I pulled my bag off the luggage rack and fetched a book out: a red bound hardback that looked and felt impressive: Chromow's biography of Felix Edmundovich Dzerzhinski, hero of the Russian Revolution and forefather of all Chekists. It wasn't something I wanted to read, it was the kind of tome you keep on your bookshelves for those occasions colleagues drop by to examine your collection. I'd just brought it along to send a message.

After I'd looked at the first line of a randomly chosen page for a few minutes without taking anything in, Merkur broke the silence again.

"How did this ..." he waggled his fingers and looked upwards for inspiration, "these administrative errors arise? Last time I looked, my visa was perfectly in order."

I closed the book, but kept a finger in the page, just in case he was paying attention.

"You're here on a tourist visa, yet I'm sure you'll admit you've hardly been a model tourist."

"Ah yes. But I did enjoy my walks along the coast. Does that not count for something?"

I opened my book again, but paused. My orders were to escort Merkur out of the country, file the obligatory report and then forget any of this had ever happened. But I had questions, and it didn't take a trained interrogator from Main Department IX to notice that Merkur was feeling talkative.

"About those walks you took. You always seemed to come back alone—not a bad trick."

Merkur allowed a smile to flit across his features.

"How did you evade your tail?" I persisted.

"Dogs."

Again with the dogs. I let his answer echo around the compartment for a moment or two, the interval timed by wheels drumming over frozen track joints.

"Dogs? We talked about dogs last time we met."

"Yes. You see, dogs are wonderful things. When a postman

comes to deliver a letter, to the dog's mind he is invading their territory. The dog reacts. The dog has to react, has to see off what he sees as a threat to his pack."

More clacking of wheels while Merkur chose how and when to get to the point. He was enjoying all this talk about dogs, making me wait.

"I was a postman for more years than I can remember. Every day, whatever the weather, carrying letters and parcels. Some dogs aren't sophisticated—for them, it's all about strength. Sharp teeth, big muscles. Other dogs you can do a deal with. Biscuits and treats, a scratch behind the ears. I told you I don't like terriers, didn't I? They're the worst ones, not just terriers—all the little ones. They haven't got the strength, but they still have their pride, which is why they're not interested in a deal. They ambush you, really, they do. Spend all day working out where best to hide, what the best angle of attack is and then they wait for the postman to come down the garden path so they can ambush him from behind."

He pulled a silver case of cigarettes from his jacket pocket, opened it up and slid one out before pointing the case in my direction. I helped myself, Merkur lit me up with an American Zippo lighter.

"Over the years, you get used to keeping an eye out for them. Under bushes, around corners, in doorways, behind cars. You learn to spot the hiding places first, and only then do you look for the dog." Merkur drew on his cigarette, perhaps marshalling his thoughts, straightening up his words, arranging the punch line. "When a postman is on a dog's territory, it doesn't just see him the way a human does, the dog hears the postman, it smells him. Seeing the hiding place can be easy, but shaking off a dog without losing the cuffs of your trousers is always the hard part. Compared to dogs, humans like your colleagues are easy to shake."

I turned back to my book, wondering what type of dog Merkur thought I might be.

35
INTER-ZONAL TRAIN

Over an hour had passed since Merkur gave me his spiel about the dogs; we'd left Bad Kleinen behind, were nearly at the border. There I'd take my leave of Merkur and make my way back to Berlin. Write that report, forget about Merkur and his dog stories, let Anna disappear into the gaps between the files. Return to a life behind a desk.

But even if my book had interested me, I doubt I could have concentrated—I still had questions. I put the book down.

"You said you went to Heiligendamm as a child?"

Merkur didn't answer, the window had his attention again. Outside it was as light as it was likely to get. Another dull day, heavy clouds moving inland on an arctic wind.

"Did I? You must have misheard, I said when Arnold was a child."

"That makes a bit more sense. You see, I've spoken to a few people, found out a little of the history of Heiligendamm. Until 1939 it was an exclusive resort for rich people, not the kind of place a worker's family would go for a holiday."

Merkur was no longer gazing out of the window, he was looking at me. Not staring—his face was politely pointed in my direction, as if we were having an everyday conversation in his local bar.

"So you were what, seven years old in 1939? A child," I continued, keeping my tone conversational, even nodding a little, as if a little puzzled by what I was saying. "The last time anyone went to Heiligendamm for a holiday was in 1939. After that came the war, then liberation and rebuilding the country. The next time anyone had a holiday at Heiligendamm was spring 1950. By then you were eighteen and married. No longer a child."

I fished out a nail, offered the pack to Merkur, but he waved them away. Cigarettes are a boon to an interrogator—you can regulate the flow of conversation with a cigarette. It was time for a short break, give Merkur a chance to think about what I'd just said, and playing around with a pack of cigarettes is the best excuse I've come across.

"I'm glad we cleared that misunderstanding up, that it was your son you took on holiday, it was his holiday you spent on the coast. I wonder whether you had a nice time? You and the wife and little Arnold? Going by the look on your face the other day, I'd say you have fond memories of the place. Miles away, you were. Remembering summer days at the beach."

Merkur was no longer playing along. He leaned his head against the headrest, eyes half closed.

"But of course, you left the GDR before Arnold was born— he was born and grew up in the West." Another puff or two on the nail, blow smoke in Merkur's direction. "For the sake of argument—just out of interest—let's say the authorities allowed you and Mrs Seiffert and little Master Arnold into the country. A nice wee holiday by the sea. Let's pretend, just for a moment, that it happened."

I stubbed the cigarette out in the ashtray fastened to the wall of the compartment, all the while staring at Merkur. He had shifted position slightly, head back, eyes half shut. But there was no nervous tic, no tapping of foot or finger.

"You see, Herr *Seiffert*," I made a meal of pronouncing his name, stretching the double-F and rolling the R. "After 1950, there were three classes of families invited to spend their holidays at Heiligendamm. Number 1: workers at the Ministry for Culture of the German Democratic Republic." I held my index finger up, not that Merkur was looking. "Number 2: workers at the Culture Ministry of that fraternal socialist state, the Czechoslovakian Socialist Republic." Another finger held up. "And finally, little kids from our very own, home-grown minority group: the Sorbs. Are you a Sorb? Grew up in the Spreewald did you? Or maybe in the Lusatian hills? Because you don't have the right accent for either of those places. Quite impressive—not a trace of an accent left."

I knocked the lid of the ashtray. It gave a satisfying crack as it snapped shut.

"What do I call you, then? Because I know you're not Werner Seiffert."

It was obvious I wasn't going to get an answer out of Merkur, I was just letting off steam before some valve in my head blew.

Even if I was right and Merkur wasn't the father of Source Bruno, he wouldn't admit to it now. Another ten minutes and we'd be at Border Crossing Point Herrnburg. I'd leave the train, he'd show the Passport Control Unit his West German passport and his cancelled visa and forty minutes after it rolled into the station, the train would start up again, pick up speed as it passed floodlamps, fences and watchtowers and just a few kilometres later, enter Lübeck station, over in the West. All he had to do was keep his mouth shut for less than an hour and he'd be safely home.

Convinced that Merkur wasn't going to say another word, I turned back to my book. But my ward had other ideas.

"You're right—I'm not Werner Seiffert. Arnold wasn't my son, he worked for me. I was his superior."

I stared at that same sentence in the book while my brain caught up with my ears. It was one thing to work out that I wasn't dealing with a working class postman from Osnabrück, but I hadn't conceived of the possibility that I was sharing a compartment with a senior officer in a West German police agency.

Book still open on my lap, I checked my watch. Ten minutes before we reached Herrnburg. Ten minutes to decide what to do with the class enemy sitting opposite. Do I give him a pat on the back and send him on his way to the West, pretend this conversation never happened? Or keep hold of him until I received further orders from Major Kühn?

Problem was, it was Saturday morning. Kühn and all the other brass would be at their weekend *Datschen*, playing happy families with their wives and kids—it could take me until Monday morning to get hold of anyone willing to retroactively authorise the detention of Merkur.

The Westler seemed to understand my difficulty, after all, it wasn't that hard to work out. But this man knew which buttons to press, and he pressed them now:

"Do you want to know why I've been asking about Gisela Bauer? Because the night Arnold died, her whole group was arrested—she was the only one to get away."

36
GÜST HERRNBURG

I swallowed Merkur's bait, how could I not? How else would I find out what he knew about Sanderling?

Unlocking the compartment door, I looked along the train corridor until I spotted Lütten and gestured for him to come closer.

"Change of plan, we're taking the subject off the train. You look after him while I deal with PKE."

When the train squealed to a halt at Herrnburg station, and the Pass and Control Unit took up position, I opened the carriage door.

Ignoring the shouts to get back on the train, I waved my clapperboard at the small knot of armed operatives that had appeared around me. They calmed down when they saw what I had in my hand, but still hung about, practising how to look menacing while fingering the straps of their machine pistols.

"Detain this person, these other men are with me." I waited for the nearest NCO to salute, then: "And I wish to speak to your CO."

The NCO turned to run along the platform to the office where the Head of PKE must have been hanging out. He came back at the double, saluted again and requested I follow.

"Stay with the subject, make sure he's comfortable," I instructed Lütten, then followed the *Uffzi* along the platform as the train doors slammed open and the Passport Control Unit and customs climbed aboard.

Herrnburg is a nowhere town with a station to match, the kind of place no self-respecting train would bother stopping at if it weren't for the border just beyond the end of the platform. Points, signals and extra tracks had been added over the years, along with all the observation bridges, watchtowers, walls, fences and lights that are usual on our Western frontier.

The NCO ushered me into the presence of a major. I saluted, informed him I was from Berlin and that I had detained a passenger and would be taking him back to the capital. The officer nodded absently and continued shuffling the paperwork for the train around his desk.

"Request the use of your phone, Comrade Major?"

Another vague nod from the officer, I lifted the receiver and dialled the number for ZAIG at Berlin Centre.

"*Unterleutnant* Reim, phoning from the office of the Head of PKE, Border Crossing Point Herrnburg," I told the duty NCO at the other end of the line. "Message for head of Section II begins: subject detained pursuant new operational information. Request further orders. Contact via District Rostock, Department II. Ends."

I stood to attention and thanked the major, but he wasn't looking.

"Make sure to take down the comrade's details, those of the detainee, too," he told the *Unteroffizier*, who was still by the door.

We left the office, boots crumping through compacted snow. On the train I could see PKE and customs move from compartment to compartment, a brief salute to the passengers inside, then the brusque demand for papers.

The NCO took me to a door in the station building. A corporal behind a desk, in the corner, a pot-bellied stove that belched out smoke and heat in equal measure, and a private standing in front of a closed door. Lütten and his man filled the remaining space in the small office.

"Is the detainee in there?" I asked the corporal, who had stood up to acknowledge my presence.

"Comrade Second Lieutenant," said the sergeant behind me,

"if you'll permit?"

I handed him my clapperboard, and he took it to the table, copied out my name, rank and ID card number before asking the corporal if he had the detainee's paperwork. He made a note of Merkur's details, and I didn't bother telling them that they were false, that we weren't dealing with Werner Seiffert but an unidentified officer of the West German security organs.

Formalities over, I had a question for my colleagues: "When's the next train out of here?"

"The train for Wismar is due to depart from the other platform, Comrade *Unterleutnant.*"

37
GÜST HERRNBURG

Felix Edmundovich Dzerzhinski, the first Chekist, was clearly in whatever place Bolsheviks go after they've ended their material revolution—and he was looking down on our efforts that day. Either that, or the planners at the *Deutsche Reichsbahn* had broken the habit of a lifetime and timetabled a connection that worked for the passengers.

I didn't have anything against Herrnburg, nor against the languid Head of the Passport Control Unit there, but I was pleased that we didn't have to wait long for our train. Right now I had enough logistical problems to solve without spending half a day on a freezing platform that wasn't only within sight of the border, but also within reach of a telephone that connected to Berlin Centre.

But first things first—get the subject and the rest of our party on that train out of Herrnburg. It was a stopping train, with an open-plan saloon layout, so I remained with Merkur at the back of the last carriage until Lütten and the heavyweight had scared off the other passengers. The final pair, an old married couple, put on a big show of having to move, in the end the goon carried their bags into the next carriage while they leaned on their walking sticks and grumbled.

Once we had the carriage to ourselves, I told Merkur to sit in one of the middle seats and locked the connecting door. But before I could take my own seat and relax, I had to deal with Lütten—I didn't owe him an explanation for my actions, but he seemed to expect one. And I wasn't going to tell him what my plans were because I didn't have any, leastways, not yet.

So I took him to the end of the carriage, out of sight of the others and did my best to pacify him: "It's the weekend, it'll take them a while to get hold of my superior officer," I explained. "Until I receive further orders, our primary task is to remove the subject from the security zone along the border. After that, we'll need to find a suitable place for his detention." Lütten nodded along, as if he had any say in the matter.

The best way to calm a nervous subject or operative is to give them a task: "Comrade Lütten, we need a *konspirative Wohnung*. Do you have access to such a safe house?"

Lütten turned his mind to dealing with his new duty and I lit a cigarette while his brain shifted into gear. The train was already slowing for the next stop, and I watched with satisfaction as Lütten's goon positioned himself by the doors at the centre of the carriage to prevent any passengers boarding.

"Bad Doberan," Lütten announced once we'd got moving again. "There's a number of KWs in that town, they don't get much use. I can call ahead and check when we change at Bad Kleinen."

Bad Doberan sounded good to me—close to Rostock, but not in the city itself, far enough from both Merkur's stomping grounds around Warnemünde and the Ministry's District Administration.

Nevertheless, I wanted to limit the number of people who knew we still had hold of Merkur. Even the discreet booking of a safe house without mention of the subject might spark interest at the county office—if our breed is good at anything, it's officiousness and inquisitiveness.

"Don't phone ahead, we'll take our chances. Do you know where they keep the keys?"

Lütten nodded, but he was already thinking again. "What about transport? The four of us can't traipse around Doberan, looking for an available KW."

The Rostocker had a point. "OK, phone when we change trains at Bad Kleinen, ask for a vehicle to be left at the station. But don't mention that we need a KW or that we're detaining a subject."

A Moskvitch stood outside Bad Doberan station, the keys waiting for us on the front tire. We got Merkur into the back seat without arousing too much interest from the locals—a couple of babushkas on the platform had themselves a good stare at the strangers, but they soon went back to comparing the contents of their shopping bags.

With everyone arranged—Merkur in the back, sandwiched between the goon and myself, Lütten driving—we set off, reaching our first destination within a couple of minutes: Schillerstrasse.

Lütten slowly drove past the large villa: no vehicle on the drive, garage doors closed. The curtains were open, the rooms beyond unlit—if anyone had been home on a dreich day like today, there would have been a light burning in at least one of the windows.

"Prager, take a closer look while we drive around the block. If the place is empty, get the key and open up the garage."

The goon let himself out and walked up the path to the front door as we drove off, wheels slipping in pockets of ice on the cobbled road. By the time we'd done a few left turns and were passing the villa again, the garage stood open. Lütten steered us in and Prager closed the doors behind us.

Another door led from the garage to the main house. I went first, taking in the shadowy corridors and rooms, the chipped and gouged marquetry on the stained wood panelling. Art Nouveau chandeliers hung from the ceilings, branches twisted and dusty, bulbs missing.

We put Merkur in an upstairs room with barred windows and a heavy door. He had been entirely passive during the journey from Herrnburg, smoking cigarettes from his silver case and remaining silent unless directly addressed. Now he spoke up:

"I should like to eat something, I had to go without breakfast this morning."

He wasn't the only one who could do with some food, but it was Saturday afternoon and the shops had already shut. We'd all have to make do with whatever we could find in the kitchen.

Lütten sent the goon Prager back to Rostock but agreed to stay with us at the house in Schillerstrasse. He spent half an hour coaxing the coal powered central heating into life while I raided the kitchen cupboards. Dusty boxes of *Tempo* dried peas, *Kuko* parboiled rice and a few packets of instant soup were the most edible findings, and I started work on something I hoped could pass for a meal, or at least put some bulk in our bellies.

"What's this?" Merkur lifted a spoonful of reddish gloop, allowing lumps of rehydrated pea to dribble back into his bowl.

By way of seasoning, we had the choice between a jar of tomato ketchup from which I'd scraped a skin of mould, and a bottle of Bino sauce. Merkur read the labels carefully, his face betraying not only his scepticism, but his hunger. He put both the ketchup and the Bino back on the table and lifted the spoon again. This time it made it as far as his mouth.

The pair of us sat in the dining room, accompanied by the ticking and the gurgle of the ancient heating as it creaked into life. For a while, Lütten had observed my attempts at cooking then decided to leave, putting his faith in his ability to forage some edibles in this small county town.

"Anything to drink?" my charge asked hopefully once he'd swallowed his first mouthful.

"There's some instant rosehip tea in the cupboard." But our situation wasn't quite as bad as all that—an investigation of the cellars revealed a couple of wooden crates of Rostocker beer. I brought one of the dusty crates up to the kitchen and Merkur rinsed out a couple of glasses.

"*Prosit!*" we clinked glasses and turned back to the soup.

"I've had worse," Merkur said after he'd finished. He patted his belly and poured more beer into his glass. I waited for some qualification, some remark about rations during military service or the hunger winter of 1947, but nothing came. As insults go, it was mild.

"What say you and I have that conversation?" he asked after another sip of beer.

I lit a cigarette and leaned back in my chair. Protocol was clear, I should make further efforts to contact my superior, and failing that, hand Merkur over to IX, either the Main Department in Berlin, or the local boys in Rostock. They were responsible for the remand and interrogation of detainees, they were the ones Merkur should be having a conversation with.

But Merkur knew more about Sanderling's last operation than I did—he'd given out just enough to tempt me. Don't think I was too slow to realise I was being played, but I was still trying to work out the West German's plan, not least because he'd made me part of it.

Of course, I should step away from him, follow protocol and take him back to Berlin, but then I'd never find out what he knew about Sanderling.

38
BAD DOBERAN

"My name is Doctor Andreas Portz, I hold the rank of *Polizeirat* in the Federal Crime Agency." *Polizeirat*, equivalent to Major in our organs. Which meant Merkur was fairly senior, perhaps even head of a section in the BKA.

We were back in his room on the top floor. He was on the bed, leaning against the wall and smoking the last of his West German cigarettes. It was the usual set up—thin single mattress on a divan base, a hard foam wedge instead of a pillow. We'd found fresh bedding in a cupboard and had hung it over the bannisters to air.

I sat on the deep windowsill, sometimes watching Merkur, sometimes gazing out of the window at the fieldstone wall that surrounded the grounds of the Minster. A light blanket of frost-proven snow lay about and a heavy wind blew more in from the Baltic.

"I was Arnold Seiffert's superior officer, but we knew each other socially—Arnold was often at my house, my wife liked to feed him up. She said he needed to find a woman, and if he didn't then she'd have to start match-making." He paused, either to reminisce, or to allow me some time to consider the close relationship he'd had with Source Bruno.

I let him blether on, I was impatient to hear about Sanderling, but I already knew Merkur well enough to realise he wouldn't be hurried. He had his plan and he'd stick to it. He knew that I'd have to hand him over before too long, and had no doubt factored this into his timetable.

I was considering lighting another cigarette when I heard

the creak of a floorboard. The click of shoes on bare wood came closer.

Merkur appeared not to have heard, he was giving me some story from the time when Bruno first joined his section and didn't even pause when the footsteps started up again, softer this time, fading into the background creaks and knocks of the old house—Lütten had returned, he'd listened at the door for a moment but had been sensible enough not to disturb us while the subject was talking.

While Merkur blethered on, I took out a nail and absently tapped it against the packet. I became aware of how the Western policeman was following the movement of the cigarette. I offered him one.

Out came the Zippo, and as he lit up, I took the opportunity to speak. I decided it was time to interrupt Merkur's deliberate rambling, to take control of the interview.

I wouldn't achieve that if I stayed with any of the expected topics. The first questions any interrogator could be expected to ask would be why Merkur had come to the GDR, why he wanted to stay—what about his wife, the property he owned over there in the West? And why he kept name-dropping Sanderling? But Merkur would have prepared answers for those topics. I needed to ask something unexpected.

"Tell me why I shouldn't just take you back to the border and throw you out of the country?"

He exhaled, half a smile forming. The hand holding his cigarette dropped to his lap and he watched the blue smoke curl up to join the smog collecting beneath the ceiling.

"You mean other than the fact I'm expected in Berlin?"

"At my discretion—you only go to Berlin if I like what I hear. Otherwise, back to the border with you. So tell me something useful while you still have the chance."

Another draw on his cigarette, wasting more time, watching the rising smoke.

"OK, I understand. You wish to establish my bona fides?

How about this: I'll give you a network in Rostock to prove my value," he said eventually, looking out of the window to gauge the remaining daylight. "But you'd better be quick."

"Why quick?"

"If I'm not behind my desk on Wednesday morning, my colleagues will wonder where I am. And when they find out, they'll start rolling up the network themselves. So, as I said, you'd better be quick."

39
WARNOWWERFT

It took quite a while for someone from the works Party Secretary's office to come and sign us in, and while we waited in the Moskvitch, the works security in their police-like uniforms watched us from their cosy gatehouse.

My own eyes were drawn to the cable crane that rose higher even than the Herculean shipbuilding halls. A skein of cables hung between two gantries, each pair supporting a trolley and hoist mechanism. The trolleys travelled back and forth along the wires, stopping and letting down or lifting loads. Massive slabs of steel dropped into a half-finished hull, further over, several trolleys working together carried engines the size of buses.

"Our ladies do a grand job."

My eyes returned to earth, focussing on the suit wearing a yellow safety helmet. He gazed upwards, just as I had done, admiring the trolleys spidering between the gantries. Lütten watched us both, his eyes glinting in amusement.

"Ladies?"

"Oh yes, that's our women's brigade up on the crane. They've got the knack. A nudge here, another centimetre or two there. Requires concentration and co-operation that job, proud of our crane drivers, we are."

Lütten shrugged, and the suit turned around to face us. I held out my clapperboard long enough for him to work out what he was looking at, short enough to keep him wondering.

"I see," he said, waving away one of the works security who was brandishing a pen through the window, his free hand placed on the visitors log. "Let's go somewhere warmer."

We passed through the turnstile gate and towards the administration block directly behind the gatehouse. Once in the building, the suit stamped the snow from his boots and gave himself a shake.

"Know who you're here to see?"

"Cadre department," Lütten answered brusquely.

We went up to the second floor and through a secretarial office, the suit pausing to knock softly on the next door.

"Visitors, Willi," he called and pushed open the door. He ushered us in and left us to talk to Willi.

"Comrades," he said, rising from behind his desk. He had us pegged even before we opened our mouths. "A coffee? The poppy seed cake from the kiosk is good—Elsa, three coffees, and some of that poppy seed."

"Thank you comrade, won't be necessary," Lütten interrupted, closing the door on the secretary who was already hurrying to the coffee maker.

"I want to know when the people on this list will next be at work." I laid a piece of paper Willi's desk and remained standing, close enough that he had to lean back in his chair if he wanted to see as far as my face.

Willi adjusted his glasses and ran a finger down the names, then angled his head up to address me. "I'd have to ask Frau Richter."

Lütten already had the door open and was ushering the flustered secretary in.

"Elsa, could you check which shifts these workers are down for?"

Elsa Richter took the page and read, her face growing paler the further down the list she got. She scurried back into her office and Lütten followed her while I sat myself opposite Willi. Leaning forward, I placed my elbows on his desk, hands clasped between his telephone and a nice collection of rubber stamps.

"Your name, Comrade?"

"Noack Wilhelm, *Kaderleiter.*"

"Well, Noack Wilhelm, *Kaderleiter*, tell me: did you recognise any of the names?"

"No, comrade, no." Willi shuffled back in his chair, trying to put some distance between us. I decided he looked nervous, but not duplicitous. "Should I have?"

"Just so we understand each other: other than you and Frau Richter, nobody will ever find out that those names were on any list. Clear?" I waited for him to nod. "Your socialist duty, Comrade, your socialist duty." Another nod.

I left Willi at his desk, closing the door on him and joining Lütten and the secretary. She had several shift plans unfolded on her desk, cross-referencing the names on the list with those of the brigades in the shipyard. Lütten stood next to her, jotting down the information in his notebook and interrogating her about the four subjects.

"Have any of them ever been in trouble? Any accusations or investigations—no matter how small?"

Elsa denied knowledge of any wrongdoings, insignificant or otherwise.

"And this one, Frau Drews—know her?" he tapped the name on the list and we both watched as Elsa rubbed the palms of her hands against her thighs, her eyes scooting towards a corner where the top layer of the battered lino had cracked and curled. "So you know Frau Drews?"

"We chat in the canteen. Sometimes. I don't see her outside work, we're not in the same brigade, you see, so it's only now and again for the midday meal ..." The secretary admitted, her tone apologetic. More importantly, her mouth was running away from her, spilling out ever more details of how she didn't really know Colleague Drews.

"Talk about home, does she? Over dinner in the canteen? Well, does she?"

"She has a son, there's no man around, it's just the two of

them … I picked the son up from Kindergarten once when a meeting ran later than expected. Well, I suppose it might have been a few times."

Lütten chucked me a look, wanting to know whether to continue the interrogation, but I shook my head. I stayed by the door while Lütten indoctrinated Elsa in the importance of confidentiality. He was less aggressive about it than I would have been, but he had the local accent, she knew he would always be close by. No need to be so antagonistic if the subject knows you could waltz back into their office at any time.

40
WARNOWWERFT

"What have we got?" I asked once we were back in the car.

"We've got a secretary in the works party organisation— that's the one our Elsa Richter didn't want to admit being friendly with. A couple of manual workers and the last name on the list belongs to one of them women crane drivers." Lütten peered at the floodlit crane through the windscreen, his hand groping for the key to start the engine so we'd have some warmth from the heater.

"Do you think we'll have to go up there to get her?" I wiped the condensation from the window and joined my colleague in staring at the nearest crane gantry.

"Hope not, that thing's higher than the three tower-blocks in Lütten Klein—and I get nervous just looking at them."

I could see a lamplit staircase threading up the central stanchion of the near gantry, leading to a series of cabs suspended more than sixty metres above the slip. Even when they weren't in use, the heavy cables swung and jerked in the winds that funnelled through the river mouth.

"May be easier to pick her up at home?" Lütten suggested.

I nodded while I lit a nail, passing the packet over.

"Shouldn't we get this investigation on a proper footing?" asked Lütten once his cigarette was going. "File the operational plan? We could do it up here if you want, through my department."

I didn't answer. Lütten was fishing, trying to find out what was going on and what I might be planning. He wanted to know how much trouble he'd be in if he hung around with me for too long.

But he had a point: urgency wasn't a reason not to follow the rules, not when it comes to the Ministry. Merkur had told me that his colleagues in the West wouldn't act before Wednesday morning at the earliest—that was more than enough time to write a report about what we'd found out.

And why not do that? Because, best case, it could take several days for the apparatchiks at Berlin Centre to react. By then it would be too late to wrap up the network in the shipyard—assuming there was one and we hadn't been fed a few random names by Merkur.

But more likely, once I told Major Kühn what was going on, he'd pass the operation back to Counter-Intelligence and Merkur would be lost to me. Whatever information he had about Sanderling would disappear into the system.

I was right to sit on this and keep hold of Merkur for the time being. Let Monday morning take care of itself.

But Lütten was still being over-helpful: "It's urgent, isn't it? The lads up here are good, I can have them knocking on doors within the hour, collecting background information from the neighbours—have the officer of the day issue an emergency warrant and we'll get them picked up on their way home from work."

Perhaps Lütten was right. Let Rostock District Administration do all the work and tell Major Kühn that I tried to get hold of him but, lacking the necessary authority to do otherwise, had been obliged to involve the Rostockers.

If I gave Merkur to the local lads, I could try to persuade Kühn to let me do liaison and co-ordination. That way I'd have eyes on the transcripts, maybe even wangle it so I could sit in on an interrogation.

Far from ideal, but it could be a way through this mess I'd landed myself in. Providing my superior really was still incommunicado—I'd have to try phoning him again, if only to shore up my alibi.

"Let's go," I said. I'd think on the plan while we drove back to Doberan—perhaps put in another call to Berlin from the county unit there, and if Kühn still hadn't been unearthed from his weekend then I'd send Lütten off for reinforcements. That would give me at least an hour to chat with Merkur before the party started.

41
ROSTOCK LICHTENHAGEN

"Maybe you don't want to hear this," said Lütten as he started the Moskvitch and steered us onto the dual carriageway back to Rostock. "But I've been there—you're in the middle of a job and before you know it, the parameters have changed. If you do it by the book, try to change the operational plan, then the brass want to stick their oar in. It slows everything down ..."

Lichtenhagen loomed out of the darkness ahead, the lit windows in the high concrete flats multiplied as we drove towards them.

"I get it, I really do. It's late on Saturday—what are the chances you're going to be able to reach the very person you need to sign off on changes to the operational plan? That's why I'm offering my lads. The chief is good, I know exactly where to get hold of him this weekend, and he understands operational necessity, he's happy to bend a few rules if he thinks it'll get a result."

We'd reached the centre of the new town now, barely a decade old and the concrete already stained and matte in the orange sodium lights. Glazed tiles set into parts of the facades glinted, but the fitful glimmer of reflected light just made the whole place appear even more dingy.

The traffic signals up ahead changed to allow passengers from the S-Bahn station to cross the busy road, and we slid to an untidy halt at the front of the centre lane, our headlights illuminating the pedestrians that were walking out in front of the cars. The usual babushkas returning from a Saturday out in Rostock, some kids wheeling bikes and a young woman.

Everyone had their heads down, hurrying to get out of the flinty wind that swept down the wide road. Lütten was still blethering on about operational certainties, revolutionary diligence and the necessity of flexibility when realising operational goals. Possibly he meant well, was intent on providing support for a fellow Chekist, but he could equally have been out to advance his own career over the corpse of mine.

It was stuffy in the car, the smoke from our cigarettes still hung around, barely shifted by the singed air gusting from the heater. I wound down my window, turning my head to breathe in the cold air that seeped in.

Most of the pedestrians had reached the other side, the kids huddled together on the corner, chatting before they went their separate ways. Only a babushka was still steadily making for the safety of the pavement. Lütten had his eye on the lights, hand already on the gear stick, impatient to get going.

The young woman who had passed in front of us was quite a way along already, crossing the side road in front of a quad of flats. I watched her progress with idle interest—she had a shopping bag which looked heavy, but was nevertheless going at quite a clip. Something about the colour of her coat reminded me of ... what? Tan coat, mustard and chocolate check scarf over her head.

"Turn right! Now! *Rightrightright!*" I shouted.

Lütten was already putting the car into gear as the lights turned. He twisted the wheel, then braked almost to a halt as the car in the right-hand lane refused to give way.

"Down there!"

Lütten eased up on the clutch and the Moskvitch jerked over the painted line into the lane to our right, forcing the other car to a stop.

"Down there, other side of the road!"

Once we were on the intersection, Lütten put his foot down, hard. The engine, still in first gear, howled as we slanted across to the wrong side of the road, Lütten tweaking the headlights at oncoming vehicles as they slalomed past. The woman in the scarf and tan coat heard the honking and the shouts, she turned slightly, clocked the Moskvitch heading straight towards her and broke into a sprint, cutting the corner of a car park and ignoring an oncoming rubbish truck as she ran across a minor road.

"Down there, that road by the car park!" I shouted, but Lütten had already caught on, was still accelerating down the wrong side of the road, the heel of his hand pressed on the horn.

A Barkas swerved to avoid us, the Trabant immediately behind didn't notice our approach in time, and as the driver began to react, Lütten swung the steering wheel to the left. A jolt, the tyres groaning as hubcaps ground against the curb. Lütten hit the brakes and the Trabant scraped past, leaving behind a wing mirror caught in my open window. As soon as the other car had cleared my door, I pushed it open and ran around the front of the Moskvitch, but my foot slid out in the icy gutter, my shin hitting the same curbstone that had already damaged our car. I jumped up and carried on after the woman, ignoring the pain morsing up and down my leg.

She had about seventy metres on me, but I was fresh and didn't have a heavy bag—I'd already reached the minor road she'd cut across, I'd made the wide pavement on the other side, half of it covered in fresh snow. Deep footsteps showed me the way, but I'd seen where she was heading—she'd disappeared into a shadowed nook in the wall of the flats, some kind of entrance.

I reached the point just ten or fifteen seconds after her, sliding again on the ice as I tried to take the corner. This time I went down all the way, my shoulder twisting as my hip punched the concrete. I pressed on the ice with my hands, pulling my legs under me and launching myself into the dimly-lit entryway that led from the street into the yard behind the flats. I shoved my way past a mother, her pram hitting the side of the building, and slowed slightly as I left the passageway, finally stopping to scan the yard.

Five storeys of flats above me on all sides, a free-standing, low building to the left—nursery? day-centre? polyclinic? Bins in drunken rows to the right, behind them a line of cars, all covered with varying amounts of snow. Every twenty metres, entrances with steps up to the doors. Footsteps in the snow everywhere. But no woman in a tan coat and woollen scarf.

I walked along the row of cars, checking nobody was hiding behind or between them, but other than a child's football, nothing.

I'd lost her.

Still breathing heavily, I went back through the ginnel to the road. Lütten had parked in a no-stopping zone, his door was open and he was standing by the side of the car waiting for me.

I limped back to the car and my colleague gave me a sympathetic pat on the shoulder as I went past.

"Want me to call it in?" he asked. He already had the radio receiver in his hand, the spiral cable stretching through the open door.

I shook my head and lowered myself into the passenger seat. Lütten climbed in and fired up the engine, easing back into the traffic. Once my breath had slowed enough, I lit a cigarette. We headed deeper into Lichtenhagen, looking for a way back onto the arterial road to Rostock.

"So who was that?" Lütten asked, shifting down and taking a left.

"Know an *Oberleutnant* Mewitz? Might be in your department?"

Lütten shook his head.

"What about the county office? Any Mewitz there?" But I didn't bother to wait for him to shake his head again, I already knew the answer. "The lady I was pursuing, you saw her?

Brown scarf, brown coat made in West Germany, name of Weber Anna. An *Inoffizielle Mitarbeiterin* for a certain First Lieutenant Mewitz of the District Administration. Since you've just told me there's no Mewitz in your unit, I have to ask myself which is more likely: that you're mistaken, or the lady isn't who she said she is."

"Got one of those for me?" Asked Lütten as he turned left.

I fed him my cigarette, I hadn't made much progress on it anyway.

"It's not just about the grey haired man we left behind in Bad Doberan is it?" he asked. I decided to ignore his question, but he hadn't finished. "It's bigger than just some Westler behaving suspiciously. Want to tell me how this woman fits into the picture?"

"I don't know," I admitted, wondering what would happen to my lungs if I took another coffin nail.

42
BAD DOBERAN

Back at the Schillerstrasse villa in Bad Doberan, Lütten's big goon was sitting on a kitchen chair at the bottom of the stairs, arms crossed over his broad chest. When we came in through the connecting door to the garage, he bobbed up, feet together, fingers pressed to the seams of his beige trousers.

"*Na*, Prager?" said Lütten, looking around the hallway.

"No incidents to report, Comrade Second Lieutenant."

"Very good, at ease. Bit chilly in here, isn't it?" He put a hand on the cast iron radiator.

"Furnace went out an hour ago, thought it better not to leave my post to tend it."

Lütten took his goon off to the cellar to get the central heating going again, and I headed upstairs to see how our charge was doing.

Merkur was still on his bed, overcoat wrapped around him, fleece shapka keeping his head warm.

"Did you get them?" he asked.

I gave him a cigarette and parked myself on the windowsill to admire the moonlit view: the old monastery walls, a couple of barns, one with fire-blackened ribs exposed to the snow; beyond that, the thin copper spire of the minster pointing at the moon's flat face.

Merkur was smoking his cigarette with the intensity found only in those who have had to do without for a while. He watched the glowing tip between puffs, reluctant to let it out of his sight for more than a second or two.

"We confirmed that the people you named actually work at

the shipyard," I told him. "But so far we only have your word for it that they're working for an imperialist agency."

He bowed his head, as if conceding the point and took another toke on the almost spent cigarette. "I'm sorry I couldn't provide proof—the BND run them, not my outfit. Those are just names that recently crossed my desk, I happened to remember them. I have others—if you're interested?"

"You just happened to remember a handful of names?" I eyed him from my place by the window. The bit about the BND, the West German foreign intelligence service, that made sense, but I didn't like the rest of his explanation—too verbose. Wordy answers often point to guilty consciences. I watched him finish the nail and mash it onto the saucer that served for an ashtray. "No need for more names just yet, there'll be time for that later."

I turned my back on him, looking out into the night again, re-running the conversation. If Merkur only had a non-specific and possibly historical awareness of the network he'd just betrayed, then why would Bonn be so anxious to extricate them the moment he returned late from his holiday?

Contradictions. All Merkur had offered since the moment I first saw him on that video screen in Berlin were contradictions. He wasn't who he'd first claimed to be. He didn't want to be tailed, yet was happy to meet and talk with me. He had information he knew I wanted, but whenever we got close to talking about it, he retreated into diversion and dissimulation.

The more time I spent with him, the more I felt my nerves stretching. And now my patience was going the same way. When I'd entered the room just a minute or two ago, I'd had a mental list of questions for Merkur, now that list had blurred and unravelled. There was only one thing I could still remember. I turned away from the window and observed Merkur for a moment, noted with gratification how the fingers of his right hand were drumming on his lap—the first sign of nervousness I'd seen in the man.

"A young lady, late twenties. Blonde, long hair. Fair skin and blue eyes. Above average height, slight build, fine features," I described Anna Weber, the mysterious maid from the Hotel Neptun, the woman who had got away from me not half an hour since.

"Sounds like you like her?" It was an oddly flippant remark, particularly coming from Merkur. I ignored it.

"Recall seeing anyone of her description, perhaps in Warnemünde?"

"She one of your honey traps?" Merkur's gaze was loose, but his fingers had stopped their drumming. "Plenty of those in the basement disco at the hotel—what's it called? Da Drin?"

Daddeldu, but I didn't bother telling him.

"Could you be more precise?" He asked, fingers dancing again. "It could be anyone, the person you describe. Plenty of pretty girls around."

I considered giving him Anna's name, watching for a reaction. Instead, I left the room.

Downstairs, Lütten was poking around the food cupboard in the hope of finding more appetising ingredients than I had earlier. There was no sign of the big goon.

"Told Prager to remain available," he told me. "Good man, but won't get much further than *Feldwebel* or *Oberfeldwebel*. Not too fast on his feet, you see, but reliable." He closed the cupboard doors and turned to face me. "There really isn't anything to eat, is there?"

I opened a bottle of beer and sat at the table, facing the open door to the hall so I could keep an eye on the staircase.

"If you can hold out for an hour or so, I'll go and find something," he suggested.

I nodded agreement, even though Lütten was already pulling on his coat.

"Wait, I need a favour—can you check for any Westerners with the name Weber Anna? And their current registered whereabouts?" I gave him her description for good measure. "Get someone to phone around the police stations in Rostock and the surrounding counties."

Lütten returned within the hour. He hefted a nylon shopping bag onto the table and took out bread, a jar of sauerkraut, potatoes, Leberwurst, a few apples and a pot of mustard. From another bag he pulled three portions of Bockwurst wrapped in newspaper and three bread rolls to go with them.

"I've got someone working on finding your Weber, but it'll take a while. I'll phone later to check on progress."

Fair enough, the right people wouldn't be around on a Saturday evening, everything slows down at weekends. I grunted my thanks as I put one of the sausages on a plate, cut the roll and smeared mustard on the side to take up to Merkur later. I could have invited him down to the kitchen to eat with us, but I wasn't in the mood to listen to him any longer.

More importantly, I didn't want Lütten listening to him, either.

"What about tonight, watching the subject? We could do half and half?" Lütten asked, his eyes on the crate of beer in the corner, wondering whether to take another one.

"I'll take the first shift."

"Fine. I'll turn in then, it's been a long day. See you at 0200 hours."

Compared to sentry duty when I was doing national service, standing for hours in sun, rain and snow, this was an easy watch. I had a chair, I was indoors, I could move around as much as I wanted to. Embrace the boredom and don't fall asleep—that's all you have to do.

The house creaked in the wind, and as the furnace died down, the radiators ticked and clattered and the cold crept through the cracked putty of the window frames and under the door to the cellar. Lütten snored, interrupting himself with nonsense words. Perhaps he dreamt in Russian.

Merkur slept quietly. Too quietly. Once or twice I crept to his door and listened, wondering whether he'd found a way to cut through the bars and escape, but the silence was punctuated every so often by a short snore.

Nobody with a conscience could sleep that easily.

43
BAD DOBERAN

I was woken by Lütten knocking on my bedroom door the next morning. After he'd relieved me in the early hours, I had gone to bed but hardly rested, my frustration with Merkur somehow bringing an ever sharper and clearer Sanderling to my dreams.

"You shout in your sleep," he told me from the doorway.

I rubbed my eyes, tried to think of a comeback, but let my head fall back on the pillow. I wasn't in any state to be witty.

"Breakfast downstairs, coffee's on the boil."

"Coffee?" I lifted my head again, but Lütten had already gone. I could hear his footsteps on the stairs.

In the bathroom, I splashed some water around then pulled on my clothes and went to check on Merkur.

"Morning," I offered, but Merkur was too busy to answer. He was on the floor, doing press-ups. "Coffee's on the way."

Down in the kitchen, Lütten was playing mother. He had slices of bread piled up on a plate and he'd laid the table for two.

I stuck a knife in the Leberwurst and scraped it onto a slice of bread, did the same with the mustard and then held a cup out for Lütten to fill.

He poured the coffee slowly, taking care to ensure most of the grains stayed in the pan. "Subject gets his breakfast first, does he?"

I couldn't think of a witty response to that either.

★

"Breakfast!" Merkur seemed pleased enough with what I had to offer, even if it didn't come close to the standard he'd enjoyed at the Hotel Neptun. "Will we have another chat today? Perhaps about Gisela Bauer?"

I didn't answer. It seemed I was developing new habits.

"So what are you going to talk to the subject about today?" asked Lütten, when I arrived back in the kitchen.

He was still pushing, trying to find out why I was unwilling to give up Merkur. Fair enough, he was helping me, and there was no need for him to do so.

"When will you hear back about that search for Weber?"

"I'll head out and find a call box now." He washed down the last mouthful of bread with strong, black coffee.

Lütten left, and I took a notebook and pencil out of my bag and made some notes. I knew what questions I wanted to ask the subject, I just wasn't sure how best to get the answers I was after.

Today was Sunday, I'd have to pass Merkur on to HA IX first thing tomorrow morning. So if I didn't get the information I wanted today, I possibly wouldn't ever get it. I'd already crossed the line, ach, who am I kidding? I'd crossed several lines, and I'd have to face the consequences. I just hoped whatever Merkur knew about Sanderling and her death would be worth it.

I finished jotting down my questions and walked around the kitchen, calming my nerves before heading upstairs.

"Ready to begin?" chirped Merkur as I walked in. He was back in position on his bed, feet on the floor, back straight. I noticed his forefinger, tapping his thigh again. Good, nicotine withdrawal was still doing its work.

Over at the windowsill, I lit a cigarette I didn't need, pretending not to notice the subject's eyes follow the blue smoke as it swirled gently upwards.

"Tell me about yourself, Herr *Doktor* Portz."

Merkur pulled his eyes away from my cigarette and bent his fingers into a fist to stop them fidgeting. He took a deep breath. "Do we assume I'll soon be handed over to the professionals?"

I didn't react.

"We could just cut to what we both want from this—what do you say to that? You want to find out more about Gisela Bauer, who you call Sanderling. I don't know why you're interested in her, I don't need to know—but I'll tell you what I have. And I'll tell you why I came over here. The deal is, you have to promise to do your best to make sure I get what I want. How does that sound?"

"Depends on what exactly you want."

"It's simple: make sure I don't get sent back to the West. I want to stay here, I'm prepared to work. I'm prepared to talk to your counter intelligence and foreign intelligence. It'll be full disclosure on operations and operational procedures, but I won't name any names. I don't want anyone to suffer because of my decisions."

"Sounds reasonable." It didn't sound reasonable, it wouldn't be as easy as that when it came to the proper interrogations, but why tell him something he already knew?

"I want a decent life here. No prison, no house arrest. Just an ordinary life. I'd like to bring my wife over, we get to have a normal life. Is that a deal?"

Once again, he was trying to take control of the interrogation before I'd even started, but I didn't mind. Promise him whatever he wanted, find out what he knew about Sanderling. Depending on how quickly he was prepared to talk, I could take him back to Berlin and hand him over that same evening.

But his proposal also bothered me—it was too simple. After all the deception of the last eleven days, it sounded too easy.

"OK, let's say I'm interested. But why me? What makes you

think I can give you what you want?"

"You're from Berlin, you're not one of these local fish-heads. You're carved from different wood than that fellow you've got downstairs. You also know about me, more than you're letting on—how else did you know to ask about this Sanderling?"

I turned to look out of the window, just in case my face betrayed any reaction. Hadn't Merkur been the first to mention Sanderling? When was it? On the train to Herrnburg a couple of days earlier? Or had he already mentioned it on the frozen coastline at Heiligendamm?

My cigarette had burnt down to the cardboard filter, so I stubbed it out on the windowsill and left it there, already reaching into my pocket for the next one. Outside, children were playing in the snow—snowballs, snowmen, snow-angels. Adults walked around the monastery grounds, admiring the brickwork or giving praise to god—whatever it is that normal people do on a Sunday.

"So is it a deal?" Merkur asked again.

I turned back to him. Cigarette packet in hand, I crossed the room. He took a nail and I lit him up with a match. It was as good as a handshake.

44
BAD DOBERAN

"Arnold Seiffert and I, we had it all worked out. We spent months putting together material we thought would be useful to the German Democratic Republic. But then you lot sent him back—that's where it all went wrong. Arnold was arrested. They couldn't prove anything, though, we were too clever for that—he'd registered his intent to visit his aunt and uncle over here and I'd signed it off and passed the paperwork to the relevant departments. Everything was above board, no rules broken, so in the end they had to release him.

"But they kept him under house arrest while they sniffed around a bit more, looking for anything to back up their theories. Because I signed off on those visits, suspicion also fell on me. For all I know, my superior was a suspect too—he hadn't objected to Seiffert's trip either. But sooner or later they'll find out about me and Arnold, about our plans to come over and bring the material with us. So now I'm here to ask for help."

I'd taken it slow, feeding in the odd question or prompt to keep him talking. But now it was time to steer the conversation to what I was interested in. IX would get the rest out of him in good time. "Was that when you became aware of Sanderling?"

"No." He shook his head. Then, contradicting himself: "Yes. Arnold told me she'd made contact."

"When? After his visit to Beeskow, when he returned to Bonn?"

"Before that. It was when we were still preparing our own

144

plans. We thought about asking her if she could help, but in the end we decided a direct approach to Berlin would work better."

"Did you at any point have operational contact with Codename Sanderling?"

"Not me, I never met her. But Arnold did, several times." Another shake of the head. "Before he came over to the East."

"You told me yesterday that Sanderling's group went into the net—how do you know that?"

"I was informed, as a matter of courtesy, after the fact ... Some of her group were picked up in Bonn, in an empty shop opposite Arnold's flat, another couple were arrested at a safe house in Cologne."

"But you know that Sanderling escaped, that she returned to the GDR?"

"Yes, she had someone with her—a man. That's all they told me."

He knew more, although perhaps he wasn't even aware of it, or he thought it not worth mentioning. Given time and careful questioning, we'd get to that information. But right now, I wanted to find out what Bruno and Sanderling had talked about.

But before I went into that, there was something else I needed to ask—I just wasn't sure what it was. A nagging voice —that of Major Renn, my old tutor at the Ministry's high school in Golm—he was in my head, eyebrows wiggling as if with a life of their own, telling me I'd missed something.

I mentally reviewed Merkur's last few answers, trying to localise whatever it was that Renn was badgering me about. Then I had it: Merkur had twice stated that Bruno and Sanderling were in contact before he came East to defect—yet she herself had told me she'd had no operational contact with Bruno. She'd claimed her activities had been limited to observation only.

"Herr *Doktor* Portz, you said that Arnold Seiffert and

codename Sanderling were in contact—how did that contact come about?"

"That's not the question you should be asking."

I'd like to see him pull that kind of trick on the interrogators from IX—they know how to deal with wise guys like him. Speaking from personal experience, sleep deprivation and hunger was a decent enough cure for that particular kind of sickness, as well as many others. But I didn't have enough time, so I played along.

"What should I be asking?"

"Don't you find it interesting how they knew exactly where to find Sanderling's team? The observation team with eyes on Seiffert, the safe house in Cologne. It all happened conveniently quickly."

"I'm sure you'll tell me why."

"We had information, from Berlin. Your half of Berlin. Someone in your firm told us about Arnold's defection, and about the team you had in Cologne and Bonn."

I turned to look out of the window, hiding my features again, just in case he was good at reading faces. This was old news, I knew there had been a mole in HA II, counter intelligence, and I'd dealt with the situation. But it sounded like Merkur could be talking about a different mole.

"What can you tell me about this informant?" I asked, turning back to the room.

Merkur shrugged, his eyes on my cigarette again. I gave him the packet and he got his Zippo out. He lit up, inhaled, held the smoke in his lungs, then let it go.

"Someone in foreign intelligence."

"When you say foreign intelligence, you mean HV A? Or do you mean the counter intelligence department, HA II?"

"I know the difference between foreign intelligence and counter intelligence." There was iron in his voice, he didn't like his expertise being questioned.

There was a whole catalogue of questions I wanted to ask:

how did Merkur know which department his alleged mole was in? Was he aware of any characteristics which might help identify the mole: age, length of service, classification levels of the material provided?

But before I could put any of this to him, there was a knock. I left the windowsill and opened the door. It was Lütten. He didn't look very happy.

"Not a good time," I told him, about to shut the door again. But instead, I took another look at his face and decided to join him in the corridor.

"You need to know about this," Lütten said, moving away from the door. "Come downstairs."

I followed him down. Irritated, but hopeful he'd brought news about the elusive chambermaid, Anna Weber.

It was only when we reached the first floor that I spotted the shadows in the doorways. They sidled out, cutting me off from the stairs back up to Merkur.

"Sorry, Reim, new orders." Lütten still looked troubled, genuinely so.

I could do nothing but watch as two operatives went upstairs and into Merkur's bedroom. Another one, Lütten's favourite heavyweight, remained at my elbow.

"You're to return to Berlin immediately, Prager will take you."

45
BAD DOBERAN

"I need my bag," I told Prager. He wasn't about to let me past, but a look from Lütten and he stepped out of the way.

I went into the kitchen, and while I was there, I poured myself a glass of water from the tap. When I turned around, Lütten was behind me, like a dachshund with sad eyes.

"Any news about the Weber woman?" I whispered before he could start apologising again.

"We've got a Westerner fitting her description, registered as visiting Frau Jakopaschk, number 11 on the Lichtenhagen pedestrian zone—near where we saw her yesterday."

I patted his shoulder as I picked up my bag and passed him. I probably wouldn't be able to use the information he'd just given me, she'd be long gone by the time I had a chance to look her up.

"Prager will take you to the county office—you're to contact Berlin before you set off."

I nodded, put my coat on and threw a last look around the hall. Lütten was in the kitchen doorway, Prager was by the passageway that led to the garage. No sight or sound of the goons who had gone up the stairs, they were probably waiting for me to clear the safe house before they brought Merkur downstairs.

"What's going to happen to the subject?" I asked, nodding upwards.

"Back to Herrnburg. This time he's to leave the country."

"Better twice than not at all." A weak smile from Lütten, no reaction from Prager.

I ducked through the doorway into the garage and folded myself into the passenger seat of the Moskvitch, bag on my lap. Prager got behind the wheel and we drove out of the garage, past a blue Shiguli and a sand-coloured Wartburg parked on the drive, then onto the cobbled roadway and up to the junction with the main road.

We slowed down as we came to the level crossing where the narrow gauge railway runs through the town—a double hoot from the Molli steam train warned us to give way.

It came from the left, coal bunker first, pulling the same mixed rake of carriages I'd travelled on when I'd followed Merkur to Heiligendamm a few days before. Another whistle as it came up to the road, steam hissing from valves, brown smoke gusting from the funnel. I watched the locomotive rattle over the road crossing, trailing a dark red luggage van and three passenger carriages.

As the luggage van cleared the junction, I shoved my bag at Prager, pushed open the car door and ran toward the train, hooking the grab rail and pulling myself up the steps onto the platform at the rear end of the first passenger carriage.

I heard Prager shout, but didn't turn to see how far behind he was. He had strength, but I was hoping his bulk would slow him down.

Slamming open the door to the carriage, I ran up the aisle, the shuddering train throwing me against seats and outraged babushkas. Out onto the front platform, finally risking a look back. The Moskvitch was still on the main road, both front doors open, no sign of the goon—he wasn't running alongside the train, he must have jumped aboard. Crossing the platform, I leaned out to see what was coming up: we were almost into the town centre, slowing down as the street tapered. A Dacia pulled up at the curb to give the train enough space to sidle by, and as we pulled past, I jumped down. Instead of the efficient parachutist's roll that I'd intended, my feet hit a frozen puddle and my right leg snapped forwards. As I went down, my left leg scissored backwards—I swung myself about, dragging my left leg around before it had a chance to introduce itself to the train's wheels. I'd hurt myself, but ignoring the pain, I crawled around the parked car until I was lying along the pavement, out of sight.

I lay in the slush, the soot and the brown coal dust, listening to the wheezing, clattering carriages as they straggled along the tracks, just waiting for Prager to find me, pick me up and drag me back to the Moskvitch.

A sharp puff of grey exhaust smoke in my face told me the Dacia was about to drive off, so I propped myself on my knees and limped into the recessed doorway of a shop. The train's bell was clanging, reverberating off the buildings on either side of the narrow street, dimming and deepening as it pulled further away, hopefully taking Prager with it.

I released the air caught up in my lungs, willing adrenaline to drain away, but not too much, I might still need it. I prodded my hip and my knee, still hurting from yesterday's chase and kneaded the back of my ankle, a new injury. All were sore, but the ankle hadn't yet begun to stiffen—I was still mobile.

Another cautious peek around the edge of the doorway to check what was happening down the street. The Moskvitch stood abandoned at the junction—a cop had already turned up, was leaning in, checking the interior. He stood up again, closed both doors and went to talk to the driver of the first car in the queue caught behind the stationary Moskvitch.

The cop was occupied, he wouldn't take any notice of a limping pedestrian a hundred metres down the road, this was a good enough time to leave my cover, but a shout sent me back into the recesses.

I pressed myself into the corner as the heavy crunch of rapid footsteps approached. Prager went past on the opposite pavement, looking neither right nor left, focussed on the cop and the Moskvitch.

Another peek around the corner, the policeman had marshalled a couple of drivers and was directing their efforts to push the car to the side of the road.

"Hey!" shouted Prager again, trying to attract the cop's attention. A good time for me to move.

A narrow lane opened out a few metres further down the other side of the road and I headed for it, hoping Prager would be interested only in recovering his car. I risked a look over my shoulder as I crossed the street, the cop and Prager were arguing, the big man was trying to open the driver's door, but the policeman was standing in the way, being difficult.

I'd reached the curb on the far side when my luck broke.

"Oy!" This time, Prager's shouts were for me.

Wincing, I pushed my legs into speeding up, I had a good head start, if I could ignore the various pains then I might still keep my advantage. I reached the entrance to the lane and swung around the corner, hoping nobody was coming the other way.

"Reim!" It was Prager again, but I wasn't in the mood to stop and see what he wanted, so I scurried along, watching for ice and cracks in the flags. Further on, this lane opened into the next road, slightly uphill, past low cottages, some in good shape, others falling apart, spewing rubble onto ice-slick pavements. Another junction, straight on or off to the left? I took the left—it curved around, I'd be out of sight once I hit the bend. The slope was steeper here, the pains in my leg were joined by keen daggers of cold air slashing my lungs with every breath I took. Over my panting, I couldn't hear Prager, neither his shouts nor his heavy footsteps.

A crossroads—I took the road that led further up the hill, just because Prager might expect me to take the downhill option. Up ahead, on a bend, the slope evened out—if I got that far I'd slow a little, catch my breath—with all these turn-offs, I might just have shaken off the goon.

I kept my eyes on that goal, ignoring the twitching net

curtains in the houses I passed, working up that hill, ears stiff from listening for the drumming of footsteps behind me, or worse, the growl of the Moskvitch engine.

I got to a bend, pressed myself flat against the wall and stopped, half-turning, looking back the way I'd come. Still no sign of any pursuit, so I gave myself a few seconds, leaning over, hands on my thighs, breathing in the frigid air.

My lungs eased a little—they still burned from the cold, but were ready for the next round. A final check backwards, and there he was, at the last junction, looking around, trying to decide which way to go. I straightened up, pushed myself off the wall and started to run.

46
BAD DOBERAN

By moving so suddenly, I'd alerted Prager to my presence—he gave another shout, but I was already around the bend, out of sight.

Finally, a downhill stretch, my stride lengthening. If my feet found an icy patch I'd be down on the ground again, at Prager's mercy. Eyes wide, scanning the cobbles and flags ahead, I counted my paces, not daring to look over my shoulder.

At the bottom of the hill I hit a wide marketplace. To the left, another residential street, leading up an incline—cottages and small houses jostled along either side, steps and gateposts jutted out onto the pavement. Thick snow lay on the roadway, children were playing, sledging down the middle.

I slowed as the slope steepened further, looking around, hoping for somewhere to hide, to give my lungs and my leg a break.

Yards opened between each house, the next set of gates on my right stood open, and I darted in, leaning against the wall and bending over in an effort to get some air into my lungs. When I looked up, a little girl, perhaps eight or nine years old, was standing by the gatepost, staring at me, her mitten clutching a length of string that led to her sled.

"This is my house." She had a soft Mecklenburg accent, her eyes were wide with disapproval.

"Is there a man down there? A big man? By the market?"

The girl held the string tighter, looked down the hill then back at me. She shook her head.

I reached into my pocket, pulled out my wallet and extracted a note, the first one I found—twenty Marks. Too much, but I didn't have time to waste looking for anything smaller. I showed the green note to the girl, folded it up so she could see Goethe's face and offered it to her.

"In a moment, a man is going to come running out of that road on the right, I want you to tell him that you saw me ... You saw me running that way."

"Towards Mollistrasse?" she asked, watching my arm point down the hill.

"Exactly, Mollistrasse. Will you do that for me?" I held the money out.

She looked at me, she looked down the hill towards the market, then she pushed her sledge until it was out of the road, resting against the house and trotted off down the hill, pigtails bouncing.

I pushed the twenty Marks into a joint in the seat of the sledge, then looked down the hill again, keeping out of sight as best I could. Prager had finally turned up, was staring around the marketplace and up the street I was on. The girl was still on her way towards him, jumping over snow that had drifted up in the gutter, but as he came towards her, she stopped and waited, planting her feet wide and putting her hands on her hips.

Prager halted, I watched as she pointed in the other direction, towards the marketplace, but ducked back behind the side of the house as Prager looked around again. I peeked out again, needing to know how he reacted, whether he believed the girl.

The clattering whir or a two-stroke engine broke through the everyday background noises of the small town. The pitch tightening into a whine as it came closer, and a vomit-green Trabant slithered to a halt in the street next to the gateway I was standing in. A woman in the driver's seat sat and looked at me. Her eyes moved to the right, noticing the twenty Mark note on the sledge, then, face clouded with suspicion, she opened the car door and stood in the road, leaving the engine running.

"Who are you? What do you want?"

I peered around the corner of the building, Prager was heading the other way, the girl still stood there, hands on hips.

This was my moment. I ran onto the road, reaching into my pocket for my clapperboard. Thrusting the identity card in the woman's face, I pushed her onto the pavement and got into the Trabant.

It was pointing the wrong way, so I drove into the bank of snow on the far side of the road, wrestled the gear lever into reverse. The woman was shouting, her words unintelligible over the skirling of the engine. The tyres slithered on the thick snow, finally gained traction, slipping, biting, slipping again. Far enough. Back into first gear and off up the hill, away from Prager.

I could see him in the mirror, he had turned, alerted by the yelling woman. Closer to, the woman was still standing in the road, her hands placed on her hips, just like her daughter.

47
KRÖPELIN

I found my way back to the main road and pointed the Trabant west. As the car lumbered its way up to a reasonable speed, I kept one eye on the mirrors, the other on the road ahead.

After ten minutes I had to slow down again as the road dribbled its way through the small town of Kröpelin—past the usual piebald buildings and shops closed for Sunday.

After taking a promising-looking junction, the small houses that lined my route faded away, leaving allotments to one side, new blocks of flats on the other. Feeling this could be the place I'd finally find some luck, I entered the car park in front of the flats, looking for a vehicle that wouldn't be on the Firm's watch list.

At the gable-end of the block of flats where no windows overlooked the car park, I found what I needed—a grey Wartburg with a stencil on the door proclaiming it the property of an agricultural co-operative—the kind of company car used by management. It wouldn't be missed before the boss decided to go to work on Monday morning.

I parked up next to it and got out of the Trabant to check the door of the Wartburg. Locked. Nothing a pocket knife couldn't fix.

I didn't give my surroundings more than a once-over before I broke the lock—best thing to do in situations like this is to act like you belong. Don't peer over your shoulder or bend down to examine the lock. There's nothing so obvious as furtiveness.

With the door cracked, I got into the Wartburg and leaned down to strip the steering column. Touch the ignition wires together, the engine firing immediately. A moment to set the heater to full, and I reversed out of the car park and drove back to the main road.

At the junction I had a decision to make: where next?

There was no point in going after Merkur, even if he was still at the safe house in Bad Doberan, I'd never get close enough to him to find out what else he could tell me about the mole in HV A.

So my destination was Lichtenhagen—I was determined to take some kind of success back to Berlin, no matter how minor, and finding out what the Westerner Anna Weber was up to might make the difference between a mere demotion and cleaning the toilets until I retired.

My route took me back through Bad Doberan, but I was no longer in the car they were looking for. Unless they'd set up a roadblock and were checking each vehicle, I'd be fine.

Perhaps I had found my luck in Kröpelin—I rolled into Bad Doberan ten minutes later and passed through the crossroads where I'd escaped from Prager—the Moskvitch was gone, not even a white mouse traffic cop was still at the scene. Wherever they were looking for me, it wasn't there.

On the outskirts of Rostock, I took the arterial road north to Lichtenhagen, turning off at the same place where I'd chased Anna Weber, the day before. A little further on, I pulled into the car park that served the nearest block of flats and found a nice gap between two other stationary cars—all the better to hide the stencil on the doors. I shut the door of the Wartburg and walked away.

Block number eleven was at the far end of the pedestrian zone. In the summer it would be a pleasant walk between young trees and fountains, but it was less fun in the middle of winter when the Baltic winds thrummed between the high buildings. No wonder I was the only person out there.

I examined the doorbells outside number eleven, Jakopaschk, the woman who was allowing Anna Weber to stay in her flat, was the third name down on the right. Mentally rehearsing my cover, I stood for a moment, finger poised to press the bell. An old man struggled up the steps to the door, his reddened eyes rheumy, his back bent against the wind.

"Come along in, young man," he rasped as he aimed his key at the keyhole. His hand was far from steady, which put his aim off. On the third go, he hit the bullseye and twisted the lock.

I pushed the door open for him, holding it while he shunted himself over the threshold.

"Frau Jakopaschk?" I asked.

"That meddling woman?" He directed his tired eyes upwards and shook his head. "Fourth floor."

I took myself off up the stairs, but waited on the half-landing, leaning over the banisters to see which way the old man went. Still shaking his head at the folly of strangers, he played catch the keyhole on a door on the first floor, and once he was safely inside, I went back down to check the name on the bell: Carlson.

Up on the fourth floor, I had the choice of three doors, Jakopaschk was in the middle. Adjusting my legend slightly—a functionary on door-to-door enquiries—I started with the neighbour to the right. I pressed the bell and knocked loud enough for the neighbours to hear.

No answer. Good, that saved a little time.

Counting to twenty before turning to the middle door, I pressed the bell and held it down.

"All right! All right, coming!" the voice within came almost immediately, as if the owner had been waiting at the spyhole. The click of a lock, and a middle-aged woman in a purple dederon housecoat opened up. Permed hair, bottle blonde, a duster in her left hand, the right still on the door latch.

"Frau ..." I made a show of peering at the bell. "Jakopaschk, is that right? My name is Sandek, from the *Volkssolidarität*. We're concerned about Herr Carlson on the first floor. Would you be able to confirm the reports we've received regarding his continued ability to live independently?"

Jakopaschk crossed her arms beneath her bosom and nodded meaningfully. "That old fool? Doesn't know what's good for him. Of course, he's done a lot for the Party, but that's in the past. Now he's nothing but a danger to himself and the rest of us in the block."

"Would it be possible to come inside to discuss this further?"

She mustered me from top to toe, wondering whether I could be trusted to see the inside of her flat.

"*Volkssolidarität*, you say?"

I nodded, selecting a charitable face to wear, the one I hoped was most fitting for a worker of the welfare organisation.

"I haven't got time for nattering." She waved her duster around a bit.

"Anyone else here I could talk to?"

But Jakopaschk was already closing the door on me. I'd pushed too hard.

Jakopaschk's other neighbour was more accommodating. A widow with an immaculately kept flat stuffed with furniture from a previous era, she invited me in for a coffee, only too delighted to tell me all about Herr Carlson's distinguished service to the Party during his working life at the International Port on the other side of the river, and about his current struggles to do his shopping. I finally managed to turn her naturally enquiring mind to neighbour Jakopaschk.

"Well, I don't like to speak out of turn, but she is an odd one," she confided.

A little more encouragement, and it all came out, her tone brimming with reluctant disappointment. "It's her political standpoint. She harps on about other people, but when it comes to doing her part in the block, not to mention around Lichtenhagen ..."

"Does she live alone? Any visitors?"

"Visitors? So many visitors! Oh, I don't mean like that, not *gentlemen* visitors, leastways, not that I've seen ... But in summer—the holidaymakers, you know? It's not official, of course, the Travel Agency of the GDR hasn't inspected the rooms, not to my knowledge, but it stands to reason, doesn't it? They'd never allow her to rent out that boxroom to holidaymakers, would they? But she takes in paying guests anyway and for all I know she doesn't register them in the housebook. Well, I wouldn't actually know whether she does or not—she keeps the book for the whole block, you see. It's all very well for us to have to go knocking on her door to tell her about *our* visitors so she can enter them in the book, but we're not allowed to know who's staying at her place."

"Anyone there at the moment?"

"Slip of a girl. No idea what her name is, but out all hours, she is." She lowered her voice and leaned forward. "A Westerner, the local beat policeman told me, just imagine that!"

I gave her a shocked look, and she sat back, gratified by my response.

"And is the Westerner there, right now?" I asked, lowering my voice too.

"Oh I wouldn't know a thing like that, would I? What do you think I am—a gossip?"

48
ROSTOCK LICHTENHAGEN

On my way out, I had a look at the back of the building. A door let onto a car park, but since Anna Weber hadn't been in a car when I'd last seen her, I decided she may not have access to a vehicle and I should concentrate on watching the front.

Leaving the building by the main door, I was heartened by the discovery of a pub directly opposite, and, what's more, it was open.

I crossed the gusty walkway, keeping my head down against the snow that whipped between the flats. I pushed at the aluminium and glass door and stepped into the warm, smokey interior of the bar.

The tables by the front window were empty, and I chose the one furthest from the door. Draping my coat over the back of a chair, I took a second look around: the inevitable veteran clutching his nearly empty glass, and a middle-aged man behind the bar, his sideburns long enough to underpin his jowls. Neither had paid any attention to my entrance, both were watching a black and white portable television, some report on Sigmund Jähn's 1978 trip to space on board a Soyuz rocket. We enjoyed celebrating past successes in our Republic.

The barman finally looked over, jerking his loose chin by way of a greeting.

"Beer and a hot grog," I called, then stood up and peered into the darker corners of the room. "Toilet?"

The barman jerked his head again, towards the back, and I set off to explore. The toilets were off a short corridor: the usual cracked and leaking bowl, plastic sink with plastic taps.

Further down the corridor, I found a tiny kitchen with an outside door. I pulled on the door and peered out. Another car park, the mirror of the one I'd just seen over the way.

Pushing the door shut again, I returned to the bar and settled in to observe the block of flats opposite. I didn't know whether Anna Weber was at home, and if not, when she might turn up—or even whether she'd still turn up. But I had a comfortable seat in a warm bar, I could think of worse places to wait.

It was a couple of beers later before anything happened. Comrade Carlson shuffled his way down the outside steps, searched his pockets for a minute or two, then turned around and hauled himself back up to the front door. A young mother jostled a pram down to the street and headed north.

But halfway down the third beer, a Barkas van nosed its way along the pavement. I couldn't read the decals on the side, but I didn't need a sign to tell me what was going on. As two workmen pulled toolboxes from the back of the van, I drained my glass and pulled on my coat. The workmen were setting up camp by the door of the flats opposite, one slowly swinging it open and shut, the other standing by, shaking his head thoughtfully.

Repairs. On a Sunday. The Firm needed to think up some new tricks—those two weren't out in the cold mending a hinge, they were there to intercept Anna Weber when she returned, to politely guide her round to the back door. Along the way she'd be bundled into a strategically placed vehicle.

I stood up, having to hold on to the edge of the table for a moment while I reacquainted my bruised knee and twisted ankle with the idea of movement, then headed for the back door. I laid three one-Mark coins on the counter as I passed, and by the time I was in the corridor to the toilets, the barkeeper had scooped up the money without even looking away from the telly.

Out of the back door, down the steps to the car park, penknife ready to crack another car door—then I spotted the dark blue Shiguli, about fifty metres away. Comrade Lütten leaned against the wing, tweed hat pulled low over his eyes, cigarette at his lips. He flicked the cigarette away and nodded. Not at me, but to someone over to my right.

I turned my head in time to see Prager materialise from the shelter of a doorway. A glance to the left—a second operative of the same species was stepping out of another doorway. They stopped a respectful couple of metres away, but their intentions were clear. I looked over the icy concrete at Lütten, unconsciously rubbing my leg and wondering whether I could even begin to run.

"I've got your bag," called Lütten, opening the back door of the Shiguli for me.

49
NEAR WITTSTOCK JUNCTION

Lütten and I sat in the back of the Shiguli, too far to feel the benefit of the feeble heater on the dashboard. Cold seeped from the leatherette seat and through our winter clothes.

Outside, dusk turned the world ever greyer. Traffic had thinned soon after leaving Rostock, but Prager kept a reasonable speed, he was a careful driver, aware that the Autobahn was icy. Seemed none of us were in a rush to get to Berlin.

For the first hour or so, the only sound above the beating engine was the thrum and ticking of tires as they ran over joints in the concrete surface of the motorway. Lütten's head rested against the side window, he gave a good impression of being asleep.

"Boss," said Prager from the front, eyes aimed forward, hands at a regulation quarter-to-three. We had just passed through Wittstock junction where the big BMWs and Audis from Hamburg joined us on the journey to Berlin, although they were headed for the other half of the city. "Boss? We need to pull in for petrol."

"Then do so," replied Lütten, not moving from his position.

In a few minutes we'd be at the service station, the restaurant would still be open—perhaps we'd stop for a cup of coffee? And if we did, how would I use the opportunity? Commandeer a car and drive off?

But what would be the point? They'd set up a road block at the next junction, perhaps I'd even merit a helicopter. I shifted my legs a little, my knee and ankle reported in, trying to dissuade me from making any sudden movements.

Blue signs rose out of the night, flashing past in the headlights, but not before they'd told us how far to the service station. Prager put the indicator on, a VW Sirocco overtook us, front wheels squirming on the slick surface.

Our driver nudged the brakes, repeatedly tapping them to slow us down in time for the sharp turn-off.

When we drove onto the forecourt, the Sirocco was already there, tanking up on 98 octane. We pulled in next to a pump with lower rated fuel.

As Prager filled the tank, Lütten leaned forward between the two front seats, twisted the dial on the radio until the news report filled the interior of the car:

... the workers of the Soviet Union have called for a four-day period of mourning after the death of our dear comrade Yuri Vladimirovich Andropov, General Secretary of the Central Committee of the Communist Party of the Soviet Union, Chairman of the Praesidium of the Supreme Soviet ...

"Why did you do it?" Lütten asked as he slid back into his seat.

Through the window I watched Prager. He in turn was watching the numbers tick around on the pump. I didn't answer.

"I didn't have any choice, I needed to call it in to protect myself," Lütten continued. His voice was steady, low. A hint of urgency, but none of apology. But he didn't need to apologise, I would have done the same myself.

I looked at him, he was back in his corner, hat pulled low, shading his eyes. To a casual observer, one without ears, he would seem asleep.

"Was it the subject, that old man? He knows something, and it's important to you—or someone? Maybe a colleague?"

"A colleague. Full marks. Now leave me in peace." answering his question seemed easier than listening to his guesses.

"A colleague, then. And this Westerner knows something ... An operation, perhaps, over there, in the West? Something went wrong, and you're looking for someone to blame?"

He was getting close to the truth, and since I'm not one for sharing, I changed the subject: "What's happening with Merkur?"

Lütten looked up, not at me, but through the window, checking Prager's movements. He'd hung up the nozzle and was heading to the cashier's office to sign for the fuel. Another minute and he'd be back—that would be the end of the conversation with Lütten.

"On the train. Should be in the West by now."

The car listed as Prager got in. We nosed back onto the motorway and the noise from the engine was loud enough to silence the newsreader.

50
BERLIN LICHTENBERG

The sentry at the entrance to Berlin Centre was expecting us. He checked Lütten's clapperboard, then saluted and waved us in. All very polite, all very ominous.

As we rolled into our assigned parking place in Yard 5, a figure detached itself from the shadows outside the officers' mess and marched briskly towards us. Prager was out of his seat and saluting the uniformed officer before he was close enough to read the pips on his shoulder, but even from that distance, I recognised the tall, thin man, too narrow for his own uniform, steel glasses: Captain Dupski.

Lütten and I were trapped in the back seat, unable to open the handle-less doors—Prager hadn't worked this out yet, but Dupski saw the problem, and the hand raised to return Prager's salute flicked sharply into a command to let us out.

Prager turned to open Lütten's door, then hastened around to my side. I climbed out, rolled my shoulders and stretched my arms. Then, pretending to notice Dupski for the first time, gave him a laconic "*Jut'n Abend*, Comrade Dupski."

"Comrade *Unterleutnant* Lütten?" Dupski asked, ignoring me for the moment.

Lütten clicked his heels and fumbled when confronted with Dupski's extended hand.

"The canteen is that way, House 18. Take yourself and your man over there for some refreshment," he ordered, and Lütten and Prager snapped out another salute, just for practice.

"In trouble again, Comrade Reim?" Now he'd got rid of the other two, my superior relaxed a little. I would have been flattered, but I knew it wasn't personal. "Word to the wise: the head of section isn't happy, you've put him in a difficult position."

I considered this for a moment. It wasn't much of a revelation, more interesting was the way Dupski had said it— neither gloating nor malicious, his tone tending more towards pity, sympathy even. He'd be no good in a field role.

The captain accompanied me to my office and told me to wait. So wait I did. I put on my uniform, straightened my cuffs, polished the dull alloy buttons with a handkerchief, switched on the radio to hear the latest on the Soviet leader's death and sat at my desk to start my written report, all while trying my best to ignore the bottle rattling away in the drawer.

It was after midnight when the knock came. Not brass—they don't bother knocking—so probably some flunkey with a message.

"*Herein,*" I called, and the door opened. Lütten.

"I guessed you might still be here," he said as I gave him a nod to let him know he could come in. He checked the corridor before entering. "The brass have all gone home, thought you'd want to know."

"Home?"

"I saw them leave, that captain who met us in the car park, and the major, too—he had me in for a while, asked lots of questions. Afterwards, I was outside, having a cigarette and I saw them leave the building, the captain and the major. They got into their cars and drove off."

My shoulders sagged as I expelled the air in my lungs. I pulled my tie loose, undid my top button and reached down to open the bottom drawer, all in one practised sweep.

"Fancy a drink?" I asked my visitor.

★

Lütten didn't stay long, just a couple of glasses to check there were no hard feelings. Sure, he'd shopped me to the brass, but before that, he'd gone along with my freelance mission.

Even if he hadn't grassed me up, I would have run out of time anyway. Still, another ten minutes with Merkur would have been nice, I might have been able to narrow down the information he was peddling about the mole in HV A. Maybe he would have finally told me what he knew about Sanderling.

When Lütten left, I set up camp on the floor behind my desk, just a greatcoat over the lino, my bag for a pillow. Until a few months ago, I'd had the soldier's ability to sleep whenever and wherever needed. Now I'd be glad if I managed a short doze.

My travel alarm-clock went off at four-thirty the next morning—if Major Kühn wanted to catch me out he'd need to get up earlier than that. A catlick wash in the toilets down the corridor and a moment in front of the mirror, pondering my future. I'd been ordered to wait in my office, but I hadn't eaten since breakfast in the Bad Doberan safe house. I needed food.

The schnapps had taken the edge of my hunger last night, but it wouldn't be a such a good idea to start drinking again this morning—I needed solids in my belly, if only to dampen the smell of stale alcohol on my breath.

A glance out of the window to check Kühn's car wasn't in its parking place, and I left the building, hurrying across to the canteen. I was back at my desk within ten minutes, admiring the tray loaded with boiled egg, sliced bread, margarine and mixed-fruit jam. And the top-prize: two litres of strong coffee in a flask. If being confined to Berlin Centre looked like this, then I had no complaints.

I had more than enough time to think about my situation while I ate breakfast, not that there was much to think about, and not that I hadn't had enough time to dwell on it already. I'd borrowed time over the weekend, hoping to find out more about my dead colleague, and now I had to wait while the brass calculated the interest. The initial failure to follow orders may have been tolerated if I'd immediately delivered Merkur into custody, but by hanging on to him I'd gone against virtually every standing order pertaining to the detention and interrogation of subjects. Now it was time to face the consequences.

And one of the more minor consequences would inevitably involve Kühn trotting out the old Chekist chestnut about steady hands and cool heads.

51
BERLIN LICHTENBERG

"Steady hands! Every Chekist needs steady hands—but without a cool head and a firm class standpoint the operative is at the mercy of the hot heart that beats for the class struggle, for the strengthening and the protection of the achievements of Socialism!"

I stood in front of Major Kühn's desk, back as hard and straight as the bed I'd lain on that night, eyes burning holes in the wallpaper exactly forty-five centimetres above Kühn's receding hairline. I wasn't listening to what he was saying, but I wasn't expected to listen—just to be present and at attention.

He had my written report in front of him—perhaps he'd even read it—but first he wanted to share his concerns.

"This is ZAIG, we're the ones who ensure the comrades in other departments have unfailingly clean hands. We have a reputation to uphold, far more so than other staff at the Ministry—how can we do that when you're up north causing this, this ..." and here the major struggled to find a word that could contain what I had done. "We now have a political-operational *Havarie*," was what he finally came up with. Not a bad attempt: a technical catastrophe.

His clockwork slowly ran down, first there were gaps between the sentences, then between the words. I stood there and didn't let my eyes move from the chosen spot on the wall, but I had registered the slackening force and rhythm of Kühn's speech.

When my ears picked up the rasp of rough paper being turned over, I started to pay more attention. I allowed my eyes to dart downwards, far enough to confirm that Kühn was leafing through my report. I'd restructured my reasons for taking Merkur off the train, moving his revelation about the mole forward and remaining silent about the morsels of information about Sanderling with which he'd tempted me.

"A mole?" the major asked, his voice sharp with apprehension. "The interdepartmental committee took the decision to close Secondary Operational Procedure Merkur on the grounds that the subject did not meet the degree of reliability and factual accuracy necessary to authorise a continuing investigation. Yet you, without authority, effectively re-opened the operational procedure!"

My field of vision extended far enough to see his hairline lift as he raised his face to look at me. "And a *mole*? Comrade Second Lieutenant, could you not have found any other reason for disobeying orders?"

Another lift of the head, longer this time, he was staring at me. "At ease, Comrade Reim," he sighed.

I spread my legs a little and allowed my back to relax, but kept my eyes on the wall. I could understand his wariness— any news of a mole is bad news. Always. Regardless of whether the information is true or not, the hunt for a mole turns whole departments upside down, causing trouble throughout the ministry. Questions would be asked of the interdepartmental committee, the first would be why they had not just once, but twice ordered the removal of Merkur from the territory of the GDR. Kühn had good reason to be sore at me, I was the one who'd dumped this *Havarie* on his lap.

I got off lightly—a bollocking from the major and suspension from duty while the interdepartmental committee considered whether and how to act on Merkur's information. In fact, Kühn had been so exercised by the idea of the mole that he hadn't thought to ask about the maid from the hotel, even though Lütten must have told him how I'd been picked up while observing Anna Weber's lodgings.

Captain Dupski levered himself off the wall he'd been propping up while I received my lecture, and accompanied me back to my office. He didn't say anything, not because he wanted to show his disapproval, it was just that he didn't care any more. He was coming up to retirement and his career was at a dead end. Maybe that's why I risked a question.

"Were you at the committee meeting when they decided to expel Merkur?"

Dupski didn't respond. He stood in the doorway while I changed back into civilian clothes. He didn't watch, as far as I could tell, he was just standing there, bored. Eyes glazed.

I picked up my bag and waited for him to give me space to pass through the door, but he didn't move. His eyes shifted, focussed on me, then he gave me a nod. Not a *ready now?* kind of nod, it was an answer to the question I'd asked five minutes earlier, the significance underlined by eye contact that went on longer than comfortable.

"Is that a yes?" I asked. "You were there? Anyone particularly keen on making sure the subject left the country?"

Dupski stepped back from the doorway and we walked out of the building. Halfway across the courtyard, he turned his head and, in a tone of voice usually reserved for commenting on the weather, said: "HV A," and gave me the same long stare.

So foreign intelligence had been the ones pressing for Merkur to be sent home. Perhaps not that much of a surprise.

We arrived at the Magdalenenstrasse exit, I showed the sentry my clapperboard, then surrendered it to Dupski, giving him a sloppy salute as I did so.

Dupski didn't frown or smile or return my salute. He turned to trudge back through the snow-pocked courtyards to his warm office.

52
BERLIN FRIEDRICHSHAIN

I took the U-Bahn home and went to bed. There would be blank days stretching ahead of me, nothing to do but sit and indulge my preoccupation with Sanderling. Maybe she'd let me sleep, maybe she wouldn't. If I drank enough, it wouldn't matter.

Afternoon came and I got out of bed. I took a shower, exercised the stiffness out of my knee and ankle then crossed to the window to admire the monochrome world of Berlin in winter. Steel cloud above, dirty snow and ice below. The car opposite was grey too, but it wasn't as familiar as the weather.

From this angle I couldn't see inside, but the driver-side window was cracked open a couple of centimetres. Only one reason to have a window open in winter, and that's to stop the windscreen fogging up when you're sitting inside.

I pulled on my clothes and went down to the street. The driver of the grey car saw me coming and looked the other way, perhaps hoping I'd be stupid enough to believe he was waiting for someone.

A rap on the window and he turned to face me. A young operative, bum-fluff on his upper lip, warm woollen cap on his head. Probably his first field experience.

"Comrade, I need to go shopping, give me a lift, won't you?"

Poor lad didn't know which way to look or what to say. Didn't make any difference, because I was already pulling open the passenger door and climbing in.

"Centrum department store at Ostbahnhof," I told him. I

watched his eyes widen as he processed the information, probably remembering the course on tracking, the bit where they told you department stores are the most difficult environment to keep hold of your subject's tail.

But that wasn't the reason I wanted to go to the Centrum—I no longer had access to the small but well stocked supermarket at Berlin Centre, and around here the Centrum was my best shot at getting a decent range of goods without having to queue in the cold for a trolley.

But I was kind to the lad. I made no attempt to shake him off in the Centrum. I even gave him my shopping bags to hold as collateral. In fact, with an extra pair of hands and a vehicle, I could pick up a few of crates of beer and a few bottles of *Doppelkorn* along with the rest of my shopping. I made sure to buy some food as well as cigarettes and alcohol—reports would doubtless be written about this trip, and I wouldn't want anyone to get the wrong idea.

I piled a few kilos of potatoes, a loaf of grey bread, a pack of overpriced coffee, a few shrinkled apples, a triangular carton of milk and a few cans of Eberswalder sausages in the trolley before leading the kid back to the car.

A familiar-looking, dark blue Shiguli with Rostock plates was parked on my street—I spotted it as we turned the corner, but was careful not to look inside as we drove past. The kid parked opposite my flat and helped me schlep my purchases up the stairs before I sent him back to his post in the cold. I didn't feel like company, and even if I did, I wouldn't want to share my space with a little *Pinscher* like him.

After putting some potatoes on to boil, I went back to the window and looked down the street to the corner, standing off to one side so the young operative couldn't see me. The Shiguli was still there, and from this angle I thought I could make out a figure behind the wheel, although it may have been the head-rest.

Stepping further away from the window, I broke a fresh deck of cigarettes and wondered what Lütten wanted. Had he been here on official business, he'd have been knocking on my front door by now. If he was here for his own reasons, he'd have to wait for an opportunity to get into my block unobserved. Either way, it wasn't my problem.

I went back to the kitchen and checked how the potatoes were doing.

It gets dark early at this time of year, the windows in the flats opposite were already lit up by four o'clock, but I didn't bother switching my lights on yet. I moved a chair so I had a good view of the street below and drank a beer. Lütten and the kid were within thirty metres of each other, but I was prepared to bet a crate of beer that Lütten was the only one who'd clocked the other.

At exactly 1630 hours, the kid started his car, it snorted blue smoke from the exhaust for a while before he drove off. The only other cars that had arrived and departed since I'd cracked my first beer were neighbours that I either knew personally or at least recognised. The kid hadn't been relieved—Lütten was the only observer left.

He waited another twenty minutes before pulling out and driving down the street. He went slowly, but not too slowly. I couldn't see him in the dark interior of his car, but I knew he'd be checking his wing mirrors, looking into each vehicle as he passed, alert for anybody sitting, watching.

The Shiguli turned the corner at the end and disappeared from view. I checked my watch, having another bet with myself—I reckoned it would be five minutes, ten if he couldn't find a place to park.

It was 1704 before the buzzer went. I pressed the button to let him in and waited by the fish-eye lens in the flat door, only opening up when I saw Lütten was alone.

"Thought you might appreciate one of these," he said,

brandishing a bottle of Neubrandenburger Kümmel. He was beginning to grow on me.

Back in the living room, I drew the curtains before I switched the lights on, then went to find a couple of schnapps glasses and a second beer glass. I poured Lütten his beer, and he measured out the Kümmel.

"*Proost,*" he toasted me in his Mecklenburg accent.

"*Prosit.*"

He downed the spirit and started on his beer, all the while swivelling his head to take in what he could of my flat. There wasn't much to see: telly in one corner, door to the bedroom opposite, couch in between. Tiny kitchen next to the bedroom and a short corridor to the front door, with the bathroom on one side and coat hooks on the other.

"Nice gaff. You here by yourself?" he asked.

I drank my beer and waited for him to tell me why he'd come. It took a while, but he got there in the end:

"Your friend, the tall blonde girl? I've been talking to her."

"You found Anna Weber?"

"She found me—was waiting outside my lodgings."

"She followed us from Rostock?"

"That's the least scary explanation I can think of."

I took a sip of beer. Anna Weber, following us all the way from Rostock, and somehow keeping track of Lütten—not bad going for a hotel chambermaid.

"You reported the contact?"

"Wanted to know what you thought about it first—she gave me a message to pass on." Lütten poured himself more beer. "She said the old man is back in town. He wants to meet you tomorrow midday."

53
Berlin Friedrichshain

Whoever was handling Anna Weber was security aware, I'll give them that much. My first rendez-vous was just before midday at a telephone box on Helsingforser Platz, and you'll get no bee stamps from teacher for guessing what would happen next.

I was in the yellow booth, my elbow draped along the top of the payphone in such a way that I could discreetly keep the cradle depressed while talking into the receiver. I probably needn't have bothered, just moving my mouth like a goldfish would have been enough—there was no way the queue outside the phone booth could hear my pointless ramblings over the grumbling traffic on Warschauer Strasse.

Through the window, I watched steam rise from the cooling tower of the power plant just up the road. It hung for moments at a time before being snatched by the wind and merged into the general smog and low clouds. But still the telephone didn't ring.

Lütten had helped me slip my guard dog. It hadn't been hard, Berlin Centre had sent the lad to freeze his brasses off outside my house more as a message to me than in any real attempt to clip my wings. So when the Rostocker sidled through a neighbouring block of flats and into the common drying green, he'd had no problems reaching the back door unobserved. I'd left him with a few bottles of beer and the television, and he'd promised to tweak the net curtains every so often so the kid in the company car wouldn't start worrying.

A woman with a tight perm escaping from her hat rapped on the glass with a coin, mouthing impolite encouragement. I turned my back on her and checked my watch: already two minutes beyond contact time. If the phone didn't ring within another minute, I'd have to resort to the fall-back location.

The second-hand on my watch ticked down to 6 and started its climb back up the other side. The phone rang.

I waited for three rings, aware of the disquiet spreading through the queue behind me, then lifted the receiver. I waited for the message.

"Oberschöneweide," said a woman's voice. Young, with an accent from the Baltic coast—perhaps Anna Weber? "Phone box opposite TRO. Thirty minutes."

She cut the call and, ignoring the restless line of residents who were demonstratively stamping their feet and burying heads and hands in collars and sleeves, I left the phone box and jogged towards the S-Bahn station as fast as the icy conditions allowed. Half an hour to get to the transformer factory in Oberschöneweide was tight timing, and deliberately so. I understood the reasoning: keep me running so I couldn't make contact with anyone on the way. It reduced the chances of a line trace being set up on the phone box. But the short timescale wasn't without risks—any delays on my journey and I'd miss the next phone call and we'd have to start this game all over again.

Darting between the traffic on Warschauer Strasse, causing a W50 lorry and trailer combo to brake sharply, I reached the far side of the road, skidding, sliding, ignoring my stiff knee and running towards the station. No time to buy a ticket, I pounded down the steps, feet crunching over grit and splashing through puddles of meltwater, I jumped the last few steps onto the platform and dived towards the train standing there. I had to push back against the door as it began to slide shut, the bell ringing shrilly and the angry tannoy yelling—
Zurückbleiben!

The train shuddered into motion, and I found a seat. I had ten minutes or so until we reached Schöneweide. Enough time to catch my breath, give my knee an encouraging rub and worry about ticket inspectors.

I pulled the doors open as soon as the train eased into Schöneweide station. Before we'd even gasped to a halt, I had one foot ready to put down on the platform.

Down the steps, through the ticket hall, past the banners celebrating the electrification of the mainline railway, out into the open. The tram stop was hard by the station, but the crowds of passengers showed that no tram had been past for a while—not a good sign.

I checked my watch, ten minutes left—too late to cover the distance on foot, no choice but hope the tram came soon.

If I'd still been in possession of my clapperboard, I could have commandeered a policeman or hijacked a passing car, but here I was, reduced to watching minutes tick by on the station clock.

The ivory-painted Gothawagen heaved itself around the corner just three minutes later, wheels shrieking on the curved track. I climbed aboard and positioned myself next to the doors, immune to the pointed comments of Berliners forced to squeeze past me.

It was only three stops, but I found myself checking my watch again and again, sighing in exasperation as traffic choked each junction. We ground to a halt on the bridge over the river, then got going again, passing the traffic lights responsible for the hold up. When we screeched around the corner into Wilhelminenhofstrasse, I turned to face the doors, impatient to get down the steps and onto the street.

It was going to be OK, I told myself, checking my watch yet again. I still had two minutes and just another hundred metres to go. Attempting to calm myself, I fell back onto old habits, discreetly checking passengers who were getting up and moving towards the doors.

As we slowed to a halt and the doors wheezed open, I jumped down, but still had to wait for the tram to move off, then for the traffic caught behind to clear. I used those seconds to note which passengers were heading in which direction. An old couple shuffled towards the *Poliklinik* attached to the factory behind, most were waiting with me to cross.

Finally, we had the chance to step out into the road, at the other side, my fellow passengers peeled off, some heading down a side street, others walking to blocks of flats. I stood outside the yellow phone booth for a moment, ostensibly searching my pockets for the right change, but really making sure no-one was moving suspiciously slowly or taking a sudden interest in loose shoelaces, shop windows or the wing mirrors of parked cars.

Satisfied, I pulled open the door of the payphone—no queue here, perhaps it was out of order? I lifted the receiver and, reassured by the buzz in my ear, replaced it and waited for the call.

"Tram to Köpenick," said the voice down the line, same one as before, but now I was certain it belonged to Anna Weber. "Number 25. Get off at Müggelseedamm and walk through the Spreetunnel." A click and she was gone. No instructions on how long it should take, which could have meant I was now under observation.

I was a good boy. I left the telephone box, resisted the urge to scan the dusty windows of the flats on this side of the road, or those of the factory opposite. I waited patiently at the tram stop, neck pulled into my upturned collar, hands buried deep in pockets.

Anna Weber picked us up when we jerked around the corner into the wide road that runs along the side of the Wuhlheide park. I watched from the back of the number 25 as she pulled out of a parking place and tucked in a few cars behind us. A grey Trabant hatchback, Berlin plates—nice choice if you wanted to fade into the scenery.

She was good at what she did, had obviously researched the route, to the extent that she could turn into side roads when she was too close, and appear again before the tram reached the next stop. Whenever we screeched to a halt, Weber was there again, making sure I was still on the tram.

As I observed her driving, I became aware that not only was she keeping me in sight, but her patterns of movement were allowing her to perform counter-surveillance—she was dry cleaning, making sure no other vehicles were tailing herself or the tram.

As for the other people on board, I had them in my sights. From the back, I could not only keep an eye on Weber following in the Trabant, but I could monitor the passengers seated in front of me.

As we neared Köpenick, the passengers thinned out, which would made it harder for a tail—if there was one—to blend in.

Just before my stop, Weber pulled out to overtake us, blue-grey exhaust swirling past the tram windows as she put her foot down. A little further on, she turned right, towards the river. With a rumble and a jolt, the tram halted and I climbed down the steps onto the roadway. In summer, this was a popular destination, but in the grey of winter I was the only one alighting.

I stood at the side of the road until the tram had rumbled away, then I walked to the turn-off that Weber had taken. I searched for a cigarette, stopping to pat each pocket in turn, then fumbled with my matches while I had a quiet look around. The usual rough rendering on the houses, stained with soot and dirt. Windows hung with net curtains, some as dusty as the buildings themselves, others shining like white squares on a chess board. No-one to be seen on the street, the few cars that passed weren't showing any interest in slowing down or stopping.

Nothing was amiss, so I turned the corner and into the side road, glancing into each parked car as I went, all the while heading for the warm smell of malt emanating from the Bürgerbräu brewery just ahead.

It was a couple of hundred metres from that corner to the winter-stripped park set on the mouth of the Müggelsee. Here the shallow lake gives the River Spree a chance to hang back for a last taste of bucolic woodland before braving the pollution from the factories in Oberschöneweide. In warmer months, the Müggelsee is full of day-trippers bathing, drinking beer on *Weisse Flotte* pleasure boats and racing dinghies through the shallows. Now it was just me and a few ducks who were less than happy about how their lake had turned into an ice cube.

On the edge of the park, at the point the Spree reluctantly narrows back into its bed, a low stone building with a hipped roof provides cover for the steep steps that lead to a dank passageway under the river.

Standing at the top of the stairs, I peered over the ice, trying to see what was on the far bank. But both banks of the river were clear of people, no Weber, no Merkur, no anyone in sight. I hesitated a moment longer, then took the first step down into the tiled depths.

54
BERLIN KÖPENICK

I emerged into unpromising daylight on the south bank of the Spree. Bare trees guarded the entrance to the tunnel, frozen lake to my left, a path leading to a bathing area and the road to Köpenick to my right. The locked river creaked and crackled behind me. Before me, the forest closed in, coniferous trees screening whatever lay ahead.

I hesitated, unsure which way to go. There was no welcoming committee, no subtle clues as to which path to take. I listened, hoping for the swish of clothes, the crunching of feet over snow and pine needles, but it was just me and the low building that marked the entrance of this end of the tunnel.

I lit a cigarette and waited. No wind in the trees, ducks grumbling off to the left. Somewhere ahead, a crow announced the end of the world. Then, finally, footsteps. Echoing and repeating, reverbing from the mouth of the tunnel.

I'm not the type to play hide and seek, and anyway, the spindly trees around me couldn't provide much cover. Whoever was coming through the tunnel was likely to be either with Merkur and Weber, or a civilian out walking his dog. As a concession to caution, I moved back a few paces, if only to avoid presenting an easy target from the bottom of the steps.

The footfall drew nearer, the decaying echo segueing into the slapping of boots on concrete. A mustard and chocolate woollen scarf rose from the depths, followed by wisps of escaped blonde hair and the lapis eyes of Anna Weber.

She arrived at the top of the stairs and stopped close enough to reach out and touch my cheek, close enough to knife me. I stood my ground.

"Hundred metres that way, the boat club," she said, smiling a little. But her eyes were as cold as the Müggelsee.

I dropped my cigarette and followed the path along the shore of the lake that she'd pointed out, half-turning to look back a couple of times. Weber had posted herself near the entrance to the tunnel, close enough to hear anyone coming under the river.

I had to admit, this was a good place for a meet—any tails would have to come through the pinch point of the tunnel, or head back to the next bridge, a twenty-minute drive at the least. A meeting could be finished and the parties scattered in that time.

When I saw the fence through the trees, I paused long enough to give the site a quick survey. A yacht club—sailing dinghies under wraps for the winter, icicles hanging from stepped masts that peeked from under tarpaulins. Just the two buildings: clubhouse and what looked like a storage space or workshop. Other than footprints in the snow that showed the way through an open gate in the boundary fence, there was little sign of human occupation.

I followed the tracks into the compound, pushing the gate shut behind me. Things looked much the same on this side of the fence: traces of old bootprints lost in fresh snow, an area of gritted and trampled snow over by the clubhouse, and the fresh marks I was trailing.

The spoor led me around the far side of the workshop. There was little point in playing it careful, every step I took was accompanied by the snarling of snow crushed beneath my boots, if anyone was waiting beyond that corner, they'd hear me from a hundred metres away.

I was at the corner of the building when Merkur appeared.

His grey hair had been clipped into a short back and sides, his eyebrows trimmed, and he'd shaved off his moustache—the overall effect was to show the years he'd lived through. The shorter hair somehow made his neck look scrawny, the lines from mouth to nose and around his eyes showed deeper, harder. But it was the same man I'd seen just a couple of days before.

"Thanks for coming, Second Lieutenant." He offered his hand, but I ignored it. Merkur shrugged and put it away.

"How did you get over here?" I asked. Until this moment, I hadn't actually accepted that Merkur could be in East Berlin.

"Different passport, different border crossing. I'm here on a day visa." The kind that is issued at the border, no need to pre-register and no problems as long as your passport is genuine, you have the same face as the photograph and the name you're using isn't on one of our blacklists. Just make sure you leave before midnight or we'll come and find you.

I leaned against the rough-rendered wall and reached for my coffin nails, but Merkur had his silver case out before I even had the glove off my hand. We each took one of his cigarettes and he lit us up with his petrol lighter.

A deep drag, waiting for the nicotine hit, I looked up at the wall of the building. Glass bricks at head height, a proper window further along, covered with brightly painted rebar welded into star patterns, same as the fence around the yard.

While I examined the metalwork, Merkur was examining me. He was in no hurry to talk, but at least we weren't doing the onerous check-in that happens when runner and agent meet. *How long do you have? Are you safe? Anyone follow you?* This meeting was strictly between professionals, if there were any safety announcements, we'd make them without the fuss and feigned concern that are the mark of a good handler.

"I need your help," he finally said.

"You don't say. One of these days, someone will drag me halfway across Berlin just to say they're going to do something for me—it would make a nice change. And while I'm bellyaching, tell me this: what's *she* doing here?" I stabbed my cigarette in the direction of the tunnel, where Weber was presumably still waiting. "You want my help? First thing you have to do is send her back!"

"You want to find out what happened to Sanderling, I want to find out who murdered Arno Seiffert." Merkur did a good job of ignoring my kvetching.

"What happens when you find whoever's responsible?" The man he was looking for was called *Oberleutnant* Sachse, but I wasn't about to tell Merkur that—not without good reason.

"I'm going to destroy him." Merkur nipped at his cigarette then checked to see how much he still had left.

"And how will you do that?" As always, he expected me to drag each piece of information out of him. No wonder I was crabby—if he wanted help, he should just come straight out with it.

"I know how to destroy his career, I know enough to put him behind bars." Merkur finished his Gauloise and flicked it into the snow. "The man who killed Arno—he's the double agent I told you about."

55
BERLIN FRIEDRICHSHAIN

"Why are you dragging me into this mess?" Lütten thought I'd gone *pille palle*, bringing Merkur back to the flat like this. I ignored the Rostocker's whining and went to the kitchen to fetch three beers.

"We need your help. We're looking for something in Rostock—and Rostock is your town," I said when I came back.

"I risked head and neck for you today. A bit of shadow theatre is one thing, I don't mind keeping your watcher happy while you go out, but I didn't think you'd be bringing the class enemy home."

Merkur was in the corner, seemingly unaffected by Lütten ranting. In fact, he seemed more interested in the muted television set in the corner. The *Sandmännchen* was about to begin a bedtime story with the aid of a talking duck and a grumpy goblin—not so different to the scene in this flat.

"I should be in Rostock right now, instead of which I'm still here, in contact with an imperialist agent ..."

"So help us out, just this once, and then you can go back to Fishland—it's about defending the security of the Republic."

Lütten stood up and parted the curtains far enough to see a slice of the darkened street below. "Kid's finally gone, he stayed longer today."

I opened the beers and gave Lütten the first one. He took it, frowning with bad grace, but he did wait until we all had a bottle in our hands before taking a sip.

"To unexpected allies," I proposed. Merkur leaned forward to tap his beer against mine, and after a moment's hesitation, so did Lütten.

Hoping the Mecklenburger had decided to get off his high horse, I rummaged in the bag I'd brought back from my trip until I found the street map of Rostock. I opened it out on the table so that Warnemünde was showing. Merkur turned off the television and pulled his chair closer, then both of us stared at Lütten, who was still standing by the window.

"What are you trying to find?" he asked.

"Boathouses," replied Merkur.

"What, any boathouse?" demanded Lütten, still reluctant to help the Westerner.

"I'm looking for a particular boathouse, on a stretch of water with lots of others. I walked all the way along the coast but didn't see anything, and I checked Heiligendamm—I heard that was a resort, thought there might be some boathouses-"

"There's none along the coast—it would compromise the regulation of border affairs."

"So are there any boathouses anywhere?"

"In Warnemünde? The GST keep their sailing dinghies here." Lütten's finger jabbed at a point between the train station and the Alter Strom, but Merkur shook his head.

"No, nothing formal. DIY jobs, sounded like they could be part of an allotment colony, something like that."

Lütten thought for a minute, then turned the map over to show the centre of Rostock. "Angler's club," he muttered, his finger tracing a road that led from the old town towards the south-east. "This is the old river lido—that little island here is covered in boathouses, and there's a few more on the other bank, between the gasworks and the railway yards."

"They're the only ones?" Merkur asked sceptically. I could see why he didn't like what Lütten was showing us—the island was hard by the old town, less than a kilometre from the Ministry's District Administration.

"That's your lot." Lütten stepped away, half turning to the window. "Why are you looking for a boathouse anyway?"

Merkur examined the map for a moment or two longer, then withdrew to his corner, leaving me to negotiate the rest of the conversation. I didn't want to tell Lütten, but he'd been right when he said he'd risked his neck for me, and what's more, he already knew too much. We needed to keep him on side.

"Our friend from the West has access to information that is material to the security of the Republic. There's a cache in Rostock and we're going to retrieve it."

"But you've been suspended," observed Lütten mildly. "You're to wait here until you receive further orders."

Merkur sat up at that, I could feel his eyes on me as I stared at Lütten, wondering how best to ask for the next favour.

"About that house arrest thing ..."

"You want me to stay here? More shadow puppetry for the poor lad who has to watch your flat while his arse freezes to the car seat."

I nodded.

"I'll have to think about that."

"Fine. While you think about it, can we borrow your car?"

56
BERLIN PANKOW

I picked up Merkur in the grey light of pre-dawn. He'd driven over from West Berlin, crossing the border at Bornholmer Strasse as soon as it opened, then parked up in a quiet residential street north of Wisbeyer Strasse to wait for me. Now we were on the motorway feeder in Pankow, heading for the Berlin autobahn ring.

We'd done the small talk, the *any problems at the border?* along with *which passport did you use?* and the jokes about *was it hard to give the rookie the slip?* and now we only had silence left. I was fine with that.

I drove along the motorway, wondering how I'd allowed myself to be drawn into this Westerner's mission. Again and again he'd promised me so much, yet delivered nothing except trouble. In order to escape the consequences of getting too close to this man, I now had to get even closer.

Merkur was my best chance of rehabilitation, it was as simple as that. If he really could provide proof that there was a double agent in our ranks then I could yet be saved from a position in Department M, steaming open letters for the next thirty years.

The motorway divides near Wittstock, one arm heading up to Rostock, the other funnelling Westerners towards Hamburg via Border Crossing Point Zarrentin.

Right at the middle of the junction, a high, square tower draped with mirrored windows and cameras keeps an eye on traffic, making sure the Volkswagens, Mercedes and BMWs don't go the wrong way.

As we drew near, I looked over my shoulder at the back seat, about to tell Merkur to get out of sight, but he was fast asleep, a patterned fleece blanket drawn up to his chin.

Merkur snored so sweetly that I didn't wake him until after Güstrow. When I reached an arm between the front seats to poke him, his snoring turned to grunts and smacking of lips.

I gave him five minutes, then angled the rear view mirror so I could see what he was doing. He was sitting up, staring out of the window at fields blue with snow drifted against fences and gates. I reached into the bag in the passenger footwell and pulled out a thermos flask.

"Here, this'll wake you up," I told him as I passed it over. He grunted again, but I heard him unscrew the top and pour out some coffee. "I could do with a cup when you're done."

He slurped away and I counted down the kilometres until he poured more coffee into the cup and passed it to me.

"I want to get in and out of Rostock as quickly and as painlessly as possible," I told him between sips. "And it's about time you told me exactly what we're looking for." I drained the cup and held it out for Merkur to take. "There's no-one else here, just us two in this car. Nobody listening in—even if somebody thought to plant a bug, it couldn't pick up anything over the noise of this engine." It was true, even though I was keeping within the speed limit, averaging just over 90 kilometres per hour, the pounding of the motor made even conversation difficult.

When there was still no reply from the back seat, I risked a look over my shoulder. Merkur was fiddling with a slim hardback volume with a yellow cover. I squinted in the mirror, trying to see what he was doing. He turned the book over, I got a good view of it, but the writing wasn't clear, even accounting for the fact that I was looking at a mirror image. Then I realised: it was a book of Russian fairy tales, just like the one Source Bruno had been reading on the train during his journey back to Bonn a few weeks earlier—perhaps even the same book.

I checked the road ahead before glancing over my shoulder again, Merkur was using the blade of a penknife to prise a tiny roll of paper from the gap between the spine and the pages. He succeeded in drawing it out, unrolled it and passed it through the seats. Surveying my mirrors for official looking vehicles, I slowed down a little and took the slip of paper from him.

It was smaller than a postage stamp, fine paper that wouldn't take up much room when folded or rolled. Opening it up, I saw it was printed with rows of random letters, each one about a millimetre high.

"A cipher?" I asked.

"Arno brought it back with him." Merkur's voice was scratchy from sleep. "He cached certain material relating to your double agent, and I believe that piece of paper will tell us where to find it."

In my surprise, I took my foot off the accelerator. "Bruno was over here collecting evidence against an officer of the MfS?"

"Keep going, don't stop!" Merkur snapped. I put my foot down again and passed the encrypted message back.

"Let me get this straight—while he was pretending to defect, your Arno Seiffert was actually spying?"

"You want this evidence as much as I do. Let's find it so we can return to Berlin—in and out, just as you said."

I wasn't happy. Every time Merkur changed his story, I had to rethink everything, decide whether and how much I could trust whatever it was he'd just revealed.

So Bruno hadn't come here to offer us his services, he'd actually been doing something else. When I'd been assigned his case last December, I'd read and re-read his file, then I'd spoken to field operatives who'd had operational contact with him, but there was nothing to suggest he'd been more than what he'd claimed to be: a defector. There was no mention, in the file or the interviews, that he'd ever been to Rostock—that fact alone was enough to put everything I knew about him in doubt.

"What exactly was Seiffert doing in Rostock?" I asked.

"I don't know, he never had a chance to tell me. But if I know Arno, he was gathering the material as insurance."

If Bruno was interested in Sachse then that would explain why he'd been to Rostock. Perhaps he'd found the material he was looking for, the kind he didn't want to carry around with him, never mind take back over the border to the West. "You think his cache is in Rostock, in this boathouse?"

"Probably not. All I know is that the key to this cipher is in Rostock."

"Why didn't he take it home with him? Send it by post? Why not use the standard DEIN STAR substitution table?"

"He hid a one-time pad in the boathouse, he said the evidence he'd cached was too important for it to fall into the wrong hands, that's why he didn't post the material or the one-time pad back to Bonn. Presumably he planned to come back and get it."

A blue sign was coming up: Dummerstorf. Only a few more minutes until our exit, Rostock Süd. If we found whatever Bruno had hidden in the boathouse, could I trust Merkur to surrender it to me?

Perhaps not, but I had an advantage: we were in my country. If he made a break for it, I could stop him. And if I couldn't stop him personally, there were nearly a hundred thousand colleagues who would be more than happy to do so.

57
Rostock Mühlendamm

Unsurprisingly, the lock on the river Warnow was frozen solid. But it didn't look like it ever saw much use, even in warmer seasons—the iron bands holding the ancient planking together was itself laminated with rust and age. Icicles dangled from the gates, showing where water would normally rush through the cracks and gaps.

I slowed down once we'd crossed the lock bridge, looking for somewhere to leave the car. The lido Lütten had told us about lay off to the left—a couple of lonely buildings, a few harassed trees and an exposed expanse of snow where the sunbathing happened in summer. The whole complex had an air of dereliction about it, even more than usual for our corner of the world.

I pulled up beneath some scrubby trees. On the other side of the road, a track down the side of a shuttered pub led to the river, the path compacted into ice by all the boots that had gone that way since it had last snowed.

Other than the occasional car heading into the centre of the city, there were no signs of life, human or otherwise.

I opened the door to the back seat and let Merkur out. He pulled his hat further over his ears, and breathed in the cold air.

"Ready for this?" I asked, but he had already set off down the track beyond the trunks of a few mature trees, pausing at the footbridge to an islet.

I caught up with him there, he was eyeing the bridge sceptically. It was a rickety affair, the planks mismatched and uneven, but at least it had a couple of solid looking rails.

"At least we won't get wet if it collapses," I offered.

"Might break a leg on the ice instead."

The bridge spanned the thirty or forty metres of frozen water between bank and islet, which boasted a crop of jerry-built shacks, all of the same school as the bridge: mismatched timber and rough carpentry. At least the huts' bright falun-red paint matched the rusted corrugated iron roofs. They were cantilevered out over the water, rot-laced fringes a mere handspan above the ice.

Off to the right, far beyond the river and shy behind trees, the squat tower of the Nikolai church showed just how close we were to the centre of town.

Merkur took off a glove and opened his coat, pulling a compass out of his inside pocket, the black plastic kind they make in Freiberg, normally used by the army and kids doing pre-military training with the GST. He clapped up the lid and squinted through the sight at the church tower.

"5300 mils," he announced, turning the rose and reading off the bearing. "Give or take."

"If you know the direction, why did we need to ask Lütten for help to find this place?"

"Didn't know which church Arno meant. I tried to work it out that first time I shook off Lütten, but do you know how many churches there are in the whole of Rostock? I couldn't afford to attract any attention, wandering around, taking sightings with a compass." Merkur put the instrument away and set off across the bridge with an air of satisfaction, kicking snow and ice over the edge as he went.

I took another look at the surroundings before I followed. All quiet: no anglers, no crazy ice-bathers. Just the noise and movement from the road.

On the other side of the bridge, Merkur stopped, looking around in bewilderment. I saw the problem as soon as I caught up with him—not only did the boathouses stretch along one side of the islet, they covered the other shore, too. There were far too many of them to search.

A path formed the backbone of the island, winding around wooden fences and gates, leading to ever more boathouses and *Datscheks*. I walked a few paces to a bend where the path took a sharp left.

"I can see at least forty buildings here, and there's more beyond that corner," I told Merkur. He'd been doing the arithmetic too, and was now rubbing his head, his fleece shapka wobbling with each stroke. "Come on, you must have a better description than *a boathouse* with a bearing taken on a church spire? Did Bruno not mention anything else?"

But Merkur was still thinking. I lit a cigarette and handed it to him, hoping it would kick his grey cells into gear. He took the coffin nail and I spiked another for myself.

We stood there for a while, looking for all the world like we had nothing better to do. It's the kind of thing that makes me fretful.

"Have you got that book?" I demanded.

"What book?" Merkur was looking around at the rickety fences and wind-slanted boathouses, probably wondering what the chances were that he could just guess which of them Bruno had chosen as a hidey-hole.

"The yellow book of fairy tales, the one Seiffert gave you."

He put his hand in his pocket and pulled out the book, astonishment written all over his coupon. "How do you know he gave it me?"

I pulled my right glove off and opened the book, my cold fingers fumbling as I tried to turn each page.

"What was that bearing again, the one you checked on the compass?"

"5300 mils."

On the military compass that Merkur had used, 5300 mils is marked as 53, it makes the thing easier to use. Now I flipped through the book, hoping for a page 53. But the stories ran out on page 51. After that came the index and the flyleaf. If you were determined to find page 53 then you'd have to make do with the endpaper, pasted to the flimsy cardboard that made up the cover.

Someone had doodled on it, looked like a child had done a drawing of a bridge with a soft pencil. I turned the book around—now it was a drawing of a monster's head, mouth gaping, showing uneven teeth. Whatever it was, it was in the rough form of a letter C, clumsy patterns that were perhaps meant to be squares dotted the sides.

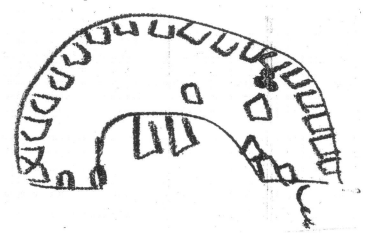

Or, turn it around again and it was an approximate but recognisable representation of the small island we were on. A squiggle at the bottom right-hand corner showed the rickety footbridge we'd just crossed.

"Have a look at this." I turned the book so that the drawing was orientated the way we were standing. It didn't take Merkur long to work it out.

Looking around again, with more purpose this time, I decided the blocks were merely indicative of the many buildings here, they didn't map to the spatial reality of what I could see.

"That just confirms we're in the right place, it doesn't get us any further," said Merkur, brow crinkling under his fleece hat. He went back to brooding, but I was still hopeful about the drawing—after all, we didn't have anything else to go on.

"What about these," I wondered, pointing out a clump of smudges. "Most of the shapes are rectangles, or what could have been rectangles if they'd been drawn more carefully. But these are circles, three of them, they're the only shapes that are shaded in."

Merkur took the book and looked more carefully. The endpaper was crinkled, the pencil marks smeared where they crossed a crease, so it took some goodwill to interpret those blots as three circles. But Merkur wasn't prepared to find enough of that goodwill to go along with my theory.

Rather than argue, I took the book and followed the path to the first sharp curve, keeping an eye out for anything that could be symbolised by three circles.

A block was marked next to the circles, not on the edge of the island, but in the middle. It corresponded to a building in real life, slightly larger than the others, and using that as a reference point, it didn't take me long to find the heap of rubble under the bed of snow—a low pile, dumped on a strip of unclaimed land between two adjoining properties. I knelt down to brush away the snow, noting the friable strands of brown grass wedged between the clay slates, the broken tiles and the bricks made of slag and sand lime.

I didn't have to call Merkur, his curiosity had already brought him along the path, and now he stood by my side, a smile easing his face.

58
ROSTOCK MÜHLENDAMM

There was only enough room for one person in the narrow gap between the fences, so we took turns sifting the broken debris. We worked slowly, lifting every single piece of waste and deposited it gently on a pile behind us.

"Any idea what we're looking for?" I asked the next time we swapped places, trying to rub warmth back into my fingers.

"A small container—film cartridge, matchbox, something like that. I'd say the one-time pad is probably about the same size as the cipher I showed you."

We worked for another fifteen minutes or so, swapping places when our hands became clumsy with cold. The excitement had worn off and more mundane matters were crowding in on me. Like a full bladder.

I walked along the line of buildings and gardens, trying each gate until I found one that was open. Beyond the fence stood a small but well maintained one-room bungalow. But of more interest right now was the outside privy, a rustic affair with a heart cut in the door.

It took a moment or two to find the key, hanging on a proud nail under the eaves at the side of the outhouse, then I let myself in. It was too cold to get comfortable, and I was almost finished when my meditations were interrupted by a shout:

"Halt!"

I pulled up my trousers and ran to the gate. Peering between the slats, I could see two men standing by the stacks of rubble, their dark dederon jackets, beige trousers and leather gloves told me all I needed to know—they were from the same company as me.

"*Is tüddelig worn!*" said one, shaking his head. The other, more inclined to action than commentary, was clambering over the unstable piles. As I watched, he disappeared into the opening between the fences, heading for the water. The commentator, still muttering to himself, decided he should follow.

I didn't wait to see what happened next, I slid through the gate and ran down the path, towards the footbridge.

"He's going over the ice!" The goons were still shouting, but I didn't stop. I'd reached the bridge now, was slowing down to cross the slippery planks. Once off the far end, I picked up speed, ignoring the complaints from my bruised knee and twisted ankle.

A Wartburg stood at the top of the track, a quick glance through the window told me what I'd already suspected: a two-way radio set hung below the dashboard. I took out my clasp knife and stabbed the wall of the tire and, as an afterthought, reached over the roof to bend the aerial. With a sharp click, it snapped off near the socket.

"Halt!" I looked back down the track, towards the river, both of the colleagues were starting up the slope, no more than thirty metres away.

I dashed over the road, got the car door open, key into the ignition, foot pumping the pedal.

"Start you bastard, just start!" I shouted at the dashboard, jiggling the choke in and out, trying to find the sweet spot that would make the engine fire. It caught, blue smoke puffing up outside the rear window. I put my foot down a couple more times to get the petrol flowing and released the clutch—I was on my way, accelerating towards the centre of Rostock, leaving the two goons in the middle of the road.

★

I took the first left, not waiting for an opening in the traffic, but pulling out in front of an oncoming Skoda. Past a bus garage, then another left, hoping to get down to the river. Gasworks to the left, the clump and clatter of railway wagons behind a corrugated fence to the right. The road gave up, leaving only a sandy track with slicks of icy snow and potholes big enough to swallow a Trabant. I could see the river behind a row of trees.

I got out of the car to check, leaving the engine running, and wandered down to the water. I couldn't see the island from there, it was hidden by more shanty-boathouses on this side of the river.

Back at the car, I unfolded the map of Rostock to confirm I was in the right place.

If Merkur had actually made it across the ice and not fallen through a duck hole, he'd pitch up somewhere near here. And unless he wanted to climb that steel fence and cross the railway marshalling yard then he should be arriving up that path at any moment ...

I got into the Shiguli and did a three point turn, sloughing up snow and sand until I was pointing back the way I'd come, then leaned over to open the passenger door.

Merkur was limping up the path, minus one shoe, but with a childlike grin on his lined face.

59
ROSTOCK

I revved the engine to encourage Merkur to move a bit faster, and when he got in, I threw the map of Rostock at him and told him to find us a route out of town. He was still wearing a smirk of the kind I'd last seen on a gingerbread horse, seemingly unbothered by his foot, now blue with cold. He carefully draped his sodden sock over the air vent on the dashboard before unfolding the map.

Despite being the district capital, Rostock isn't that big—it took us less than a quarter of an hour to clear the town and get on a country road heading south.

I filled up with petrol in Schwaan, yet another decayed town, half-timbered houses leaning on neighbours, who in turn shed plaster onto the pavement below. Heavy wooden beams anchored the derelict church and the bridge over the river was restricted to one vehicle at a time.

The road passed a railway station and I was tempted to leave Merkur there, to let him take his chances on getting back to Berlin by himself. But I couldn't do that—I wanted to know whether Merkur had managed to find the key to Bruno's encrypted message.

But Merkur was oblivious to both my impatience and the musty odour rising from his drying sock.

"Did you find it?" I asked after a few more kilometres.

Merkur nodded, looking rather pleased with himself.

"Come on then, let's have a look!"

He put the road atlas on his lap and retrieved an orange ballpoint pen from his pocket, the type kids buy from the stationers at the start of the school year. It was encrusted with dried green slime and something had been nibbling the clip. Unscrewing the tip, he began to scrape at the inside of the barrel with the point of his penknife. Putty crumbled out, and then, with a twist, he hooked a small piece of paper. Unfolding it, he showed me: tiny letters, seemingly printed at random, the almost-identical twin of the cypher Merkur had shown me earlier.

"I'd say that was worth the bother, wouldn't you?" mused Merkur, admiring the one-time pad he'd successfully retrieved.

But I didn't share his smugness. Merkur's rhetorical question, meant as a throw away remark, only aggravated me.

"Worth the bother? Those goons back there, you know the ones who chased you across the ice? They'll have written down the registration number of this car—that's going to put Lütten right in the shit. And what happened to your shoe? You lose it somewhere? Because they're not going to rest until they find it, and it won't take them long to work out it's a Western make. Where did you buy them? Salamander? Deichmann?"

"My gentleman's outfitters, actually."

"Hand made shoes? From the West? That narrows things down nicely." I paused, swallowing my anger. "So before long, they'll be looking for a Westerner in a Shiguli belonging to the Rostock Stasi."

That wiped the smirk off his mug. But spelling out the situation hadn't done anything to help my blood pressure. I could feel a popping in my right temple, and a slow burning somewhere behind my solar plexus.

"Look, just get me back to East Berlin and I'll take myself back over the border. This has gone far enough, I've put you to enough trouble-"

"Shut up!" I snarled. "I only want to hear from you when you're helping with the navigation."

Did he think I'd just let him go? My only hope of getting

out of this mess was to deliver him to Berlin Centre, along with whatever evidence Bruno had cached—assuming it was worth anything.

Actually, I didn't care that much whether I kept hold of Merkur for long enough to hand him over, but until I had Bruno's encrypted message in my hands, I wouldn't let Merkur out of my sight.

"This is the way to the motorway," I pointed to the sign at the side of the road. "I told you: no motorways."

"We go past the motorway junction, it's the way to the trunk road."

"I don't want to go anywhere near any motorway! They may have cops watching the junctions."

"It's OK, we're just going past-"

"No."

There was silence for a minute or two while Merkur bent over the road atlas. "Do a right here, that'll take us across country and we'll pick up the main road north of Güstrow."

I shifted down a gear and did a right, then had to step on the brakes as the concrete surface deteriorated into uneven cobbles patched with sheets of ice where stones had sunk or been washed away. The lane stitched together cottages and old farmhouses for a kilometre or so before conditions improved enough for me to put more pressure on the accelerator.

"Looks like we're not being tailed," said Merkur, testing his sock to see if it had dried.

I glanced in the rear-view mirror. It was true, no-one had followed us onto this lane, but that didn't mean our shadow wasn't racing ahead on parallel roads to pick us up at the other end.

A tractor came the other way, pulling a wagon of silage that was steaming in the frigid air. I pulled into the side of the lane to let it past and used the opportunity to try to rub some feeling back into my face. Merkur was pulling his sock on, and since we'd stopped anyway, I decided to take a break: a cigarette, some coffee and a look at the map, try to work out how I was going to get us both safely back to Berlin.

"Pour me a coffee," I told Merkur before opening the door and getting out.

Wherever we were, it felt like the back of the moon. Endless fields covered in snow, a row of bald trees rimmed the flat horizon. Not exactly Brandenburg levels of interminable blankness, but still pretty lonely.

I rolled my shoulders and kicked at the rime-coated rushes that lined the ditch alongside the road, then, defeated by the punishing cold, got back in the car. Merkur had the cup from the thermos flask in his hand, holding it out for me to take. It was only just half-full, and only just on the right side of lukewarm, but it was still coffee.

I took a sip and placed it carefully on the dashboard while I got a nail going.

"Right, let's have a look at that map." Merkur handed over the road atlas, his finger pointing to our location. "We'll go down past Plau, then head east until we pick up the F96," I decided after checking various routes.

I reached for the coffee again, and that was when I noticed the radio hanging under the dashboard, the microphone on a hook next to it. Stress makes you stupid, that's why the brass back at Berlin Centre are always droning on about cool heads. The whole time I'd been in this company car, frustration and anger bubbling through my veins, worries about possible pursuit clouding my thoughts, and we'd had a radio on board.

Of course, if the Firm in Rostock had kept their proverbially cool heads, they'd also realise we had a radio, so any colleagues involved in the pursuit would be avoiding the usual frequencies.

And if they'd enlisted the help of the cops, then there was the problem of the *Sprechtafel*, a table of common phrases indicated by numbered co-ordinates that changed every day.

Most of the time, cops were too lazy to use the table and just said what they had to say instead of reading off the numbers that codified whatever phrases they needed—this lack of radio discipline meant it may still be worth listening to the radio.

I twisted the volume knob until the radio clicked on, then scanned the frequencies, trying to find the clearest signal.

"Check the road map, see if we're still in District Schwerin," I told Merkur. He stared at the page as if it would tell him what I wanted to know, so I reached over and flipped to the front where the district borders were shown on the overview map. "Still in District Schwerin," I confirmed to myself and returned to the frequency settings on the radio.

I got a good signal on channel 207, control talking to a cop: sounded like he was on traffic duty. Both were using the call-sign *Schwalbe* for District Schwerin—I had the right frequency.

"I've got another job for you, as well as map reading, you're going to listen to every conversation and announcement on the radio. Every time any town gets a mention, find it on the map, and if we've been near it, or are going anywhere near it, you tell me what they've just said. Got that?"

I started up the car, put it in gear and carried on down the lane, the radio squawking every few minutes as messages were passed back and forth over the airwaves.

It took another ten minutes to get back to a proper road, and soon after that we entered Güstrow. A couple of military trucks came the other way, but no signs of cops, nothing to worry about. Through an industrial area, past a sugar refinery, the bitter stench clogging our lungs before we left the town behind us.

The roads were fairly clear of ice and snow, traffic was light and I was gradually beginning to feel more optimistic about getting back to Berlin. Merkur seemed to be enjoying the view —dark forests irregularly punctuated by bodies of water: ponds and meres completely frozen over, small and large lakes still liquid, often with ice drifting across wind-flecked surfaces.

And the whole while the radio talked to itself, but without any mention of place names. It sounded like the dispatcher was keeping track of the location of each unit.

Another lake, more pine forest. Berlin might have bad air, congested roads and too many people, but at least there's some variety, not this endless big nature, long skies and blinding snow.

60
DISTRICT SCHWERIN

We rolled into the next village, a string of ramshackle cottages on one side of the road, a dozen or so railway sidings on the other, the oversized station building looming beyond a couple of low platforms. A heavy, Soviet-built *Taigatrommel* locomotive was pushing out plenty of black smoke as it gathered speed, pulling a rake of flatbeds, each carrying a T-55 tank. I could see Merkur beginning to count them, but then the grey uniforms massing on the platform distracted him.

"Relax, they're not for us, there's an army barracks just up the road."

"You sure?"

I didn't bother answering. The radio was crackling into life again, the signal distorted by the trees:

Schwalbe 127, come in

Schwalbe receiving

Schwalbe 127, table begin 1-5-7-5-3-2 table end, over

Schwalbe copy, out

Another encoded message, leaving us without a clue what had just been reported. Given enough time and material, I'd be able to crack the table—it was just a question of fitting standard phrases to the right numbers. But by the time I'd worked it all out, it would be midnight and they'd change the co-ordinates.

But then, as we left the village and were at a crossroads, another message came in, this time in clear text:

Schwalbe 131, location F103 north of Plau, traffic control established, out

I yanked the steering wheel round to take the left turn, leaving tire tracks in the snow at the side of the road where I'd understeered. Check the mirrors: a delivery truck, a Trabant and a lonely VW Polo. None of them suddenly changing their mind about which way they wanted to go, none stopping to take a closer look at the crazy blue Shiguli that had suddenly turned off without indicating.

"Watch them—see anyone talking into a radio handset?"

Merkur twisted in his seat, checking the following cars, but most of the vehicles that had been near the crossroads when I turned off had already disappeared from sight.

"Nothing," Merkur said. "What was that all about?"

"Weren't you listening? Your job was to glue your ears to that radio! Some idiot out there didn't use the code table—he was talking about a road block straight ahead of us."

Merkur was still looking out of the windows, hoping to catch a driver taking too much interest in us, maybe one that was radioing in to base—anything he could distract me with.

"Listen, I need you to do just three things," I snapped. "One: up ahead, this road splits, we can take it to Waren or Röbel—work out a new route for us. Two: we're about to cross into District Neubrandenburg, retune the radio, see if you can pick up a call sign that begins with N: *Nachtigall, Nerz, Nutria*—some animal name, anything beginning with N." I glanced over to the Westerner, he was focussing intently on the road ahead. "Finally: listen to the damned radio, and listen carefully! I don't want another slip up like that. Have you got all of that, or is it all too complicated for you?"

"I'm not a recruit, I know how to do my job!" The road had lost its appeal now, he was staring at me, looking as angry as I felt.

"You're not a recruit, but you've been behind a desk for too long—you've grown soft! Well, Herr *Polizeirat* Doctor Portz, time to toughen up because so far you've done nothing but drag me into the dreck, and I won't let you pull me in any deeper!"

I turned back to the road and Merkur started fiddling with the radio.

"I've got a dispatcher, call sign *Nander* 12, on channel 215?" he said after a few minutes of listening.

The cops on 215 were disciplined, pretty much all of them using the code table and only speaking in plain language when there was something not covered by the usual stock phrases. That didn't worry me—I was more concerned about the sheer volume of contact on that channel. The dispatcher was checking in with units, one after the other, pretty much non-stop. I'd already counted seven since we'd tuned in.

Merkur had his nose in the map book, flipping pages back and forth to find us a new route. "Main roads only?"

Good question. Sticking to main roads would take twice as long compared to heading straight down the motorway to Berlin. If we wanted to be really careful, we would use minor routes, threading our way through villages and forests—but even then a policeman doing his rounds might think to call in the sighting, curious about the car with Rostock plates being so far from home. "Main roads for the time being, we can use back roads when we get closer to Berlin." A compromise, but hopefully one that would work.

And was I being too careful anyway? It was right to assume my colleagues would be covering the motorway—one message to the tower at Wittstock junction and that route would be covered—but mobilising a search on the main roads through three or four districts? That's a lot of work, a lot of manpower and a lot of responsibility for the duty officer to shoulder.

"I might have overreacted back there," I said to Merkur, warming up to half an apology.

He flipped a few pages back in the map book, still tracing possible routes into Berlin. I didn't think he was going to answer, but then:

"Not surprising after what happened in Rostock. You can't

help but think they were expecting us ..."

I didn't disagree, it was strange. How did they know we were on that island? Could have been a random check, a couple of colleagues from Rostock District, happened to pass and recognised the car, wondered what it was doing parked up next to the river lock? Or a couple of police detectives, too nosy for their own good, as usual?

"And then that roadblock we heard about on the radio ..." Merkur was thinking aloud.

"There for the troop movements—you saw them at the station, going on an exercise. Standard procedure," I was trying for reassuring, but it's not something I have much practice at.

"But those troops, they could have been ordered to search for-"

"Stop being such a *Hausfrau* and concentrate on the radio!"

Despite Merkur's fretting, perhaps because of it, I was coming to the conclusion that I had overreacted. We could still take the motorway, be back in Berlin in a couple of hours, looking for Bruno's cache of evidence. After all, I reasoned, there was an explanation for everything that had happened.

But Merkur was stuck in his rut: "Have you noticed the amount of traffic on this radio channel? Seems to be a lot of radio cars for such a rural area."

61
DISTRICT NEUBRANDENBURG

"Reim?"

"I see them." I'd been checking my mirrors, knew about the two police cars on our tail.

Merkur twisted around in his seat to see the cops just a few hundred metres behind, and gaining fast. No blues and twos, which I was hoping might be a good sign.

I took the pressure off the accelerator as we entered a village—not a good idea to smash the speed limit when you've got the *Volkspolizei* hugging your rear bumper.

As the road widened a little, the first one pulled out to overtake. This was it, they were about to flag us over—one car skewed across the road in front, the other staying behind to make sure we didn't try any fancy U-turns.

I lifted my foot off the accelerator, moving it to the brake pedal, ready to push down hard if it looked like the cop in front might do something daft. The first Wartburg pulled ahead, and as he cleared us, the second followed. Four seconds later, they were far ahead of us, barrelling down the road and round the next bend.

I breathed out and moved my foot back to the accelerator.

"Too many coincidences," muttered Merkur from the passenger seat.

I let him have that. Once someone has decided to be paranoid, you can't stop them, no matter how many rational and reasonable arguments you have up your sleeve—particularly if you're not convinced by your own rational and reasonable arguments.

"Reim?" he said again, as if nothing had just happened. "I need shoes."

He was right, he couldn't cross the border back into West Berlin wearing only one shoe, it would be an invitation to hold him for questioning. But since I wasn't planning on letting him leave anyway, I hadn't been thinking about what to put on his feet.

Still, sorting him out with a new pair might help him relax a little, make him think I was going to let him go home at the end of the day.

The sun set as we came down the hill into Malchow, I could tell because the ashen skies were deepening into blackness.

"Hospital over there, should have parking," Merkur pointed out helpfully, but I ignored him, carrying on down the hill, looking for a quiet back street, somewhere the car wouldn't be an easy find for anyone who was looking.

I turned right just after a cinema, a good landmark in case I got lost later, and the large, barn-like buildings that had dominated the main road gave way to small houses built by merchants hundreds of years before. An unpaved lane opened between two of these buildings, and I took the Shiguli that way, parking in a coal yard. Its stocks had long since been exhausted and were unlikely to be filled again before summer.

"What size are you?" I asked, turning to Merkur.

"Forty-four. Here's some cash."

I looked at the notes he'd given me. Astonishing how little Westerners think household goods cost over here. Just because a bread roll costs five Pfennigs and a loaf of bread seventy, doesn't mean you can buy a pair of shoes for the twenty-five Marks they blackmail out of you on entry to the country. "You might need a little more than that."

"I've only got Deutsche Marks. Here, take this." He pulled out a blue tile—a hundred Westmarks. He probably thought I'd wander into a shop and they'd be happy to take Western money. It might work, but it wouldn't be the most discreet way to buy shoes.

"That'll do. If I'm not back in an hour, start worrying," I told him as I climbed out and shut the car door. I'd buy his shoes with my own money and pocket the blue tile. That way everyone would be happy.

But my plan would only work if they had any shoes in this town.

I found the shoe shop without problems, it was just down the hill from the cinema. But finding suitable shoes was as difficult as I'd feared.

"Size forty-four?" the assistant sucked her teeth for a bit while she cast an eye over the perfectly serviceable shoes on my feet.

She wandered up and down in front of the shelf of boxes that ran along the back wall of the shop, now and again bending over to read a label just to show she was doing something about my request. Standing up again, putting her hands over her kidneys so that her elbows stuck out, she leaned backwards and surveyed the boxes on the top shelves. A ladder stood in the corner, but she didn't feel the need to fetch it.

"That one says forty-four." By now I'd joined her at the wall of boxes, peering up at the labels above head height.

The assistant turned around, elbows still sticking out. "What colour do you want?"

"Don't care. Brown, black, red with gold stars." That earned me a disapproving tut, but at least she mustered the box in question.

"That's a size forty-two," she told me, directing her attention to another column of grey cartons.

"But it says forty-four, look, right there." I pointed at the label.

"*Citizen*, it may say forty-four, but it's actually a size forty-two. And before you ask, I just know. That's why I work in a shoe shop and you're the one needing shoes."

Sometimes I miss not having my clapperboard—a quick flash of the official ID and a secret door would open to reveal a select choice of size forty-fours. Then I remembered I had something nearly as good.

I reached into my jacket pocket and pulled out the folded blue tile, keeping it in my hand, but allowing a corner to show.

"How much does a pair of men's shoes cost anyway?" I asked, allowing the assistant to see what I had in my hand, but making sure it remained hidden from the waiting customers.

She gave no answer to that, but she did pull the step ladder out of the corner, and began making a far more convincing impression of someone searching for a suitable pair of shoes.

After coming up with nothing, she disappeared into the back of the shop. I waited for her, looking out of the window. A *Konsum* grocery was across the road, the queue to get through the door was at least twenty long, snaking down the pavement and impeding the passage of pedestrians struggling up the steep street.

"Dear sir," the assistant was back, wringing her hands at the thought of all those Westmarks, "I'm sorry, but we don't have anything in that size."

"Size forty-five, then?" I asked, hopefully. "Forty-six?"

She shook her head sorrowfully, her face growing even longer as I turned to leave the shop.

"You can try the cobbler's on the island," suggested a middle-aged woman with bottle-black hair. She gave my hand a meaningful look, even though I'd already slipped the blue tile back into the inside pocket of my coat. "Down the main road, over the bridge, can't miss it. Tell him Frau Rupprich sent you."

It wasn't hard to find the island—follow the main road down the hill and over a swing bridge, just like the lady in the queue had said. I had no unrealistic expectations that the cobbler would actually have a pair of men's shoes in the size I was looking for, but the little hope I had soon fizzled when I saw the faded wooden sign pointing down an alleyway lined with shadows. At the far end, a wooden staircase led up to what was presumably the cobbler's workshop, beyond that, the alley dropped down to the lake.

I mounted the steps and knocked on the door. No answer. I gave it a good bang, but still no-one was interested in opening up. That was it, I'd done my best, and I'd failed. Not that it mattered.

Back down the steps, and curiosity took over. I walked the final few paces to the water and lit a cigarette while looking out over the lake. It wasn't frozen solid like the River Warnow at Rostock, or some of the lakes we'd seen today, but it wasn't completely free of ice either.

To the left and right, self-built boathouses lined the shore of the island, much the same as those we'd looked at earlier. Further along, at the end of the island, I could see the causeway that would take us over to the other side of the lake and towards Waren, then on to Berlin.

Traffic was heavy, I could see a steady line of headlamps coming along the causeway from the far shore. But the rear lights of vehicles heading out of Malchow weren't so regular. Or at least, they were regular, just not so closely packed: every twenty seconds or so a pair of red lights would start out over the causeway. Why wasn't the traffic in that direction bunching up like it normally would be?

I could think of only one explanation—a checkpoint.

It could only have been set up a few minutes ago—when I'd walked over the swing bridge onto the island, traffic had been flowing normally in both directions.

A moment's reflection, and I decided we could get round this checkpoint—we'd just take the north route out of town and go along the back roads to Waren.

But what if there was a second checkpoint up the hill, the

way we'd come into Malchow? We'd be trapped.

I flicked my cigarette into the water, eyes on the traffic as it crossed the causeway. Several sets of headlights, wider and higher than those of the cars, had set off from the far bank. A smaller vehicle was in front, blue light flashing, forcing other traffic to the side of the road to make room for the convoy of trucks. *Bereitschaftspolizei?*

Whatever was happening, whether or not it was barracked police troops on those trucks, that convoy probably wasn't good news.

62
MALCHOW

I jogged back towards the car, hearing the lorries rumble along the cobbled road behind me. They came alongside, not the usual lorries used by the *Bereitschaftspolizei*—the flat fronted W50s and LOs, or the tapering nose of the G5—but the heavy snouts of Ural trucks. The red and white circular decals on the doors confirmed the identification: Soviet Army.

I turned off the main road, running down the lane and sliding to a stop as I entered the coal yard. The jeep and military police BAI minibus I'd just seen escorting the convoy were in front of me, hemming in my Shiguli. A handful of soldiers stood around, Kalashnikovs shouldered, a *starshina*, senior sergeant, from the BAI had Merkur pressed against the car.

As far as I could tell, no-one had noticed my arrival, and wanting to keep it that way, I backed into the shadows of the alley. As I did so, something hard poked my spine. The kind of poke that makes you freeze because you know it's been done with the muzzle of a pistol.

It was only a quick jab, enough to let me know what I was dealing with.

I put my hands up and turned slowly to face a tall and thin Russian, his clean-shaven face narrowing into a pointed chin, his mouth as straight and thin as a spent match.

I read his shoulder boards: *leitenant*, one rank above me, with the black flashes of the artillery regiment on the collar of his new-style *afghanka* jacket. The gun he'd used to poke me was a good old Makarov, held in an ungloved hand. I couldn't help but notice the safety was off, so when he gestured for me to undo the buttons on my coat, I did exactly what he wanted, no more and no less.

He reached into my open coat, arm at full length, fingers briskly patting the lining and inside coat pockets, then moving on to my jacket and trousers. At the end of the frisk, he'd collected my Makarov, my civilian *Ausweis* and my pocket knife. Another waggle of the gun barrel, and I started towards the car.

"*Tuda, poshol!*" he barked, even though I was already on the move.

At the sound of his voice, the *starshina* and soldiers stood to attention, thrusting out their chests and lifting their chins the way Russian other ranks do, all the better for an officer to bop them on the schnoz if the mood should take him. Merkur remained where he was, legs wide apart, leaning against the car, but he turned his head to watch me coming towards him, an apologetic smile on his face.

"Find the shoes?" he asked.

I looked at his feet, he was standing on the frozen dirt of the yard, now minus both shoes, socks encrusted with damp coal dust.

"*Moltchat'!*" the junior lieutenant yelled, and it didn't matter whether or not Merkur could understand Russian, the meaning was clear.

With another poke of the Makarov, the Russian guided me around the front of the Shiguli to the open driver's door. As I put one leg inside the car, my foot connected with something hard and long. Without thinking, I reached down to see what was in the footwell, my fingers brushing smooth leather. Another jab in the back made me pull my leg back out of the car and stand up pretty smartish, keeping both hands visible. The lieutenant pushed me out of the way and bent down to see what I'd been reaching for.

He picked up Merkur's abandoned shoe, tapped the heel

against the floor of the car and, reassured there was nothing hidden, tossed it under the seat.

I got behind the wheel and the Russian climbed in the other side, casually throwing another order over his shoulder as he did so: *"Razojdis!"* The squad of soldiers and the sergeant fell back, taking Merkur with them. The UAZ ground its gears and jerked away from my car.

With another gesture of the gun's muzzle, the *leitenant* indicated I should drive out of the yard, back up the alley to the main road.

63
MALCHOW

The Russian junior officer was a man of few words. A sharp *"Tuda,"* and a gesture, either with his finger or the muzzle of the Makarov sufficed to tell me which direction he wanted me to drive.

Over the swing bridge and onto the island, slow down at the red and white trestle blocking the entrance to the causeway. A cop approached, bending down to talk to us, his fingertips already stuck to his forehead in polite salute, and the Russian lieutenant didn't say a word. He rolled down his window and gave the policeman a full-on arrogant stare. The kind that makes uniformed lackeys think they might be in for a recommendation for one of those holidays in Siberia.

The bull's salute quickly turned into a wave, gesturing us on, and I weaved around the roadblock and put my foot down on the long straight of the causeway, sure that no cop was going to pull us for speeding.

Another curt instruction once we hit the south shore of the lake, and I turned the Shiguli towards the motorway.

Forty minutes and very few directions later, we'd left the motorway and were rumbling down the concrete highway that runs south of Lake Müritz, towards the town of Mirow. I stopped for a traffic light on an open stretch of road, wondering what purpose it could possibly have out here in the pampas. The Russian turned to survey the cars that were pulling up behind us, although he could see nothing beyond the glare of their headlights.

A deep hum came from somewhere over to the right, where lights hazed the night sky. The hum lightened in pitch, and at the same time a twin row of lamps switched on. They drew a straight line from the dim lights on the horizon to where we were sitting by the traffic signal.

I leaned forward as the hum turned to a growl, continuing up the scale until rarefied air was roaring and shattering over us. The growl wound itself up to a howl, but it hadn't finished yet—a continuous boom shook the car on its suspension.

I put my hands over my ears as the silhouette of a MiG fighter jet heaved itself over the road, just metres in front of our headlights and low enough to reach up and touch, if anyone were stupid enough to try. As it passed us, the roiling boom was shunted aside by the screaming exhaust burning a bright hole in the night.

"Fuck," I whispered, the incandescent glow from the aft of the plane still scarring my vision. I could barely see the MiG now—it had risen quickly, orange flame dimming as it entered the low clouds. The corrugated groan of the jet still reached us, but was already receding rapidly, leaving an aural sterility that made me doubt I was still able to hear.

The runway lights switched off, the traffic lights turned green and in the headlamps of the oncoming cars, I could see a smile teasing the corners of the lieutenant's mouth.

Before I could put the Shiguli into gear, he pointed out a gate in the fence between the road and the runway. I pulled onto the rough slab track and slowed, aiming to halt in front of the barred opening in the fence, but before I could give the brakes a necessary last dab, unseen hands opened the gate. With a glance at my passenger to confirm, I drove through.

My headlights briefly swept the concrete runway—the cones of light ebbing long before they illuminated even halfway along the piste—then the path took us further to the left, along a line of bare trees. My Russian passenger had no further instructions, seemed content to look out into the night, his head following the dark shapes of low buildings as we passed.

The track was clear of ice and snow, but I took it slowly anyway, not wanting to be surprised by another plane taking off or landing right next to me, so when a soldier stepped into the beams of my headlight, I was ready to bring the car to a rapid halt. He stepped aside, his right arm out, pointing into the trees.

I pulled off the track, my wheels slipping into ruts left by another vehicle, and within a couple of metres we'd passed completely into the trees.

"*Vylaz'! Davay, vylaz'!*" The lieutenant was back to being unfriendly. I followed his orders, stopping the car and climbing out of the Shiguli.

Standing next to the open door, keys in hand, I wondered how much use they'd be as a weapon. The lieutenant was walking around the snout of the car, towards another soldier that stood in the shadows off to one side—in the scattered light from the headlamps, I could just about make out a greatcoat and a wide *teller* cap.

The lieutenant stopped in front of the dark figure, saluted, then reached one arm forward, the naked flesh of his hand glowing dimly in the gloom. The officer—and it must have been an officer, why else would the *leitenant* have saluted?—reached forward and took the offering.

Another salute, and the *leitenant* marched back in the direction we'd come, not bothering to spare me even a sideways look.

The officer remained in the shadows, I couldn't see his face, but his head pointed my way, so I went to see what he might want.

"Burratino." The use of the code name told me who I had in front of me.

"Major Pozdniakov, how nice to see you again."

64
SOVIET AIRBASE LÄRZ

"Did we not have a deal—one hand washes the other?" said Pozdniakov. It wasn't a question, it was an accusation.

"*Usluga za uslugu,*" I mumbled the Russian version of the proverb to myself: *a good turn deserves a good turn.* Perhaps it would have been more sensible to focus on the KGB officer in front of me, wondering what deal he thought I hadn't kept to. But instead I was giving myself grief for not realising Major Pozdniakov would be at the end of this journey.

"Yes. *Usluga za uslugu.* Did you think I gave you the tip-off about your Merkur's booking at the Hotel Neptun out of fraternal feelings for a brother in arms?

"Perhaps you did—perhaps you're naïve enough to think a KGB officer might have your personal interests at heart? Because that was the only explanation I could think of this morning when I found out about your interest in a cell of hostile agitators in the Warnow shipyard. Why did it take three days for this news to reach my ears, I asked myself. Perhaps my good friend Burratino couldn't find a way to reach me? But no, because Burratino is confined to his place of residence, right next to a phone. You'll tell me if I'm boring you, won't you, *tovarishch*?" He broke off for a moment or two, maybe he was glaring at me? Hard to tell in the dark.

"So I send someone to little Burratino, someone to listen to the good reason my friend has for not telling me his news about the cell in the shipyard. But *tovarishch* Burratino is too busy—he's left a colleague in his flat to tell me that Burratino is in the north again. Not only that, Burratino has gone with

Merkur: *an agent of the class enemy!* How I scratched my head!

"Little Burratino, talk to me!"

"You spoke to Lütten? What did you do to him?"

"Talk to me about the *Warnowwerft*," Pozdniakov insisted. He didn't take a step towards me or deepen his voice, he had no need to resort to obvious methods of intimidation.

"The Warnow shipyard? I received information from Codename Merkur regarding *Diversanten* in the shipyard. I took measures to confirm the existence of the people on the list, but engaged in no further action beyond that. There was no indication that Merkur provided the information in an attempt at political-ideological *Diversion*."

"You didn't think to check in with me before you went to the shipyard? You weren't interested in the fact that the Warnow shipyard is building freighters for the Soviet Union? That we necessarily have eyes in that shipyard?"

Good work, Reim, I thought to myself. *Not only do I have Kühn and the rest of Berlin Centre on my case, now I also have to start worrying about the KGB.* I didn't say anything out loud, there was nothing I could say. All I could do was wait and see how pissed off Pozdniakov was, then deal with the consequences.

But it didn't end there, Pozdniakov paused for a moment, before continuing with the bad news:

"The work being done at that shipyard is slow and shoddy, sabotage and *Diversion* is suspected. Months of surveillance, all our patient work, narrowing down suspects—and then you stumble in, like a bear that's smelled honey! Perhaps we have to start from the beginning again, perhaps we will never know." Another pause, just enough to let the information sink in. "So is there anything you'd like to tell me?"

What did Pozdniakov want to hear me say? How much did he know about Secondary Operation Merkur? Lütten had been questioned, so did Pozdniakov know what Merkur and I had hoped to find in Rostock? I imagined the grilling the

Fischkopp must have been subjected to, he'd probably told them everything he knew. Armed with that information, the KGB would merely have had to monitor police and Ministry situation reports to find us.

No time to hold anything back, I told myself. Honesty sometimes being the safest policy, particularly if the person you're talking to probably knows the whole story anyway.

"The imperialist agent Merkur and I went to Rostock this morning to retrieve the co-ordinates of a cache recently hidden by another Western agent. The cache allegedly contains proof that a member of the Ministry is a double agent," I said.

"Did you find this cache?"

"The co-ordinates are encrypted, but we retrieved the key this morning—it is in Merkur's possession."

Pozdniakov's face was still in shadow, I couldn't swear that he reacted, but I'd be prepared to go as far as to say he may have twitched.

"Where is Merkur now?" I risked a question of my own.

"On the way to the border." Pozdniakov reached into his pocket, pulled out an object that, in the darkness, looked about the right size and shape to be a packet of cigarettes. He tapped out something short and slender and put it between his lips. For a moment I was hopeful, I could really use a cigarette, even one of his pungent papirosas, but the packet went back into his pocket.

"Why is everyone always so keen to throw Merkur out of the country?" It was reckless to voice my frustration, I clearly needed that cigarette more than I'd realised.

"The head of your section, Major Kühn, requested Merkur be expelled. You disagree?" Pozdniakov's hand dipped into his coat again, a faint rattling told me he had pulled out a box of matches. He struck one, it flared in the night, the flame imprinting on my retinas, adding to the blur left behind by the ascending MiG.

"Merkur can't be trusted. His story changes by the hour. So far the only solid thing he's provided is that cell in the shipyard. I was hoping to keep him around until I had my hands on the cache," I replied, but I was still thinking about what the KGB major had just said about my boss Kühn. "You told Major Kühn about my trip to Rostock?"

"I did," Pozdniakov took a long drag on his cigarette. "I also told him you were operating under my command."

Perhaps I let out a small sigh, maybe my shoulders slumped a little in relief, because Pozdniakov felt the need to clarify the situation: "Don't think I was protecting you—it is merely a case of protecting my investment." A deep hum started up from the far end of the airfield—there had been noises from that direction the whole time, but this was different, a kind of buzzing. Behind me, the lights on the runway came on, and the humming changed in pitch, I turned back to Pozdniakov, who was still talking, his voice rising to be heard. "I got you into that department, and there's work still to be done—so if I get you off the hook now, don't think it's because I like you."

The MiG-27 thundered down the runway, the air shimmering from snarling turbines, the shriek of the compressor merging into the deep roar as it passed us, wheels no longer touching the runway. This time I wasn't so close, but out here in the open air, the noise was as substantial as a fist in the face. The runway lights and the cars beyond the fence were lost in the glare of the exhaust and in that moment, blinded and deafened, I realised why Pozdniakov had brought me to this Soviet airbase.

The KGB officer was showing me he how easily he could put me on a plane—any time he chose, I could wake up on the other side of the Urals.

65
SOVIET AIRBASE LÄRZ

My orders were simple: find and evaluate Bruno's cache.

Pozdniakov had given me just twenty-four hours to complete my mission—he was thinking along the same lines as Merkur the day we met by the Müggelsee—keep me on the move, acting and reacting rather than plotting and planning.

Problem was, at that moment I had nothing to go on. Merkur had both parts of Bruno's message—even if I had them in my possession, they may not have been enough to find Bruno's cache. Was the cache even where Bruno had left it, or had it been discovered and removed by colleagues of mine or Merkur?

And if I established the location of the cache, there was no guarantee that I could retrieve it in time.

Pozdniakov's only concession had been to agree to keep hold of Merkur and allow me to speak to him the next morning.

I steered the Shiguli back to the road, travelling alone this time. I felt my back loosen as I put some distance between myself and the airbase, but my jaw remained tight, no matter how many cigarettes I used to try to lever my teeth apart. My hand kept dropping from the steering wheel to pat my pockets, feeling the outline of my Makarov and my penknife—which the Russian had returned, along with a bonus surprise: my clapperboard.

I've had the penknife since I was a kid, the only thing I have from my father—a horn handled clasp-knife, the blade tarnished with age—but it was the mass-produced, bound piece of cardboard with badly printed pages that weighed most heavily in my pocket. That little booklet had more power in it than a W50 stuffed with hundred Mark notes—every time I touched it, I felt my sense of self-worth begin to swell to more usual proportions.

Perhaps I should have returned to the motorway, pushed the Shiguli to the speed limit and been at the edge of Berlin within an hour and a half. Instead, I took the scenic route to Neustrelitz, then the F96 south.

Some people get all stirred up about the F96. It starts in the darkest corner of Saxony, where the laws of physics dictate that decadent West-TV is out of reach. From there, it settles on a fairly even trajectory northwards through the Republic— apart from a minor diversion around the Soviet headquarters in Wünsdorf, and a major diversion around the capitalist thorn of West Berlin. After that, it continues on a northern bearing, all the way to the Baltic island of Rügen.

Some travellers on route 96 are in a hurry to get to Berlin for a FDJ youth movement rally, or to dance 'til dawn in an illegal club. Others have their wives in the passenger seat and Peggy and Ronny in the back when they take the Trabant up to the Baltic for the summer holidays. The F96 sees a lot of traffic, but not on a black February night.

It was an hour and a half before I could convince myself there was no-one on my tail. There's never a way to be a hundred per cent about these things, but if anyone was back there, driving without lights on a night like this, then they were pretty much a suicidal case—if they were prepared to take their job that seriously then I was happy to concede the game.

The next town was Gransee, and that was where I decided to have a break. I turned off for the town centre, the road passed between the mediaeval town walls before leading me between dimly lit buildings that were almost as old as the ancient fortifications, but twice as crooked.

The rumble of car wheels on cobbles echoed off the shop windows, and other than the street lamps in their frosted glass skirts, there were no lights to be seen. Gransee closed early, which meant it was perhaps not the best town to find the kind of bar I was looking for.

Ahead of me, a shadow stumbled from the shelter of a wall and stood in the gutter, more lopsided than the surrounding houses. A drunk, struggling to remember his way home. And where there's a drunk, there's drink. I headed in the direction the toper had come.

After that helpful pointer, the bar wasn't hard to find, light from the windows spilled onto the street and I took a good look as I drove slowly past. Steamed up windows: check. Drawn curtains: check. Uninviting exterior: check. This was my kind of place.

I sat in the car, parked as far as possible from any working streetlamps, and peered into the darkness. All seemed quiet, so I reached under the seat and pulled out the shoe that Merkur had left behind.

The Westerner had form when it came to dropping heavy hints—although I'll admit it had taken me too long to pick up on the significance of his repeated requests for directions to Heiligendamm. Now I was wondering about his seemingly innocent question back in Malchow: when a Western agent is arrested by a squad of Soviets, you'd think the last thing on his mind would be whether my shopping trip had been a success.

I pushed my hand inside the shoe, pressing my fingers as far as the toe but finding nothing but lining covering cold leather.

Taking my hand out again, I tried the heel, twisting, pushing and knocking the rubber tipped leather sole, but it remained firmly attached. No secret compartments there.

Finally, I ran my fingernail along the insole, trying to loosen it. One edge lifted a little, allowing me to get better purchase, then I had it out. I angled the shoe and a couple of pieces of paper slid into sight.

"Thank you, *Polizeirat* Portz," I whispered, not bothering to ask why Merkur had left the one time pad and the encrypted message for me to find—that man had played false witness too many times for me to even begin to imagine his real motivations. So I stuck with tactical gratitude and took myself off to the bar for a celebratory drink.

66
GRANSEE

The bar was the usual kind of set-up, not as cosy as some places but good enough for the locals. Wednesday evening isn't the busiest time, nevertheless the usual desperadoes were dotted around the taproom.

The wooden bar itself was old and dark, rubbed shiny by decades of elbows, but the tables placed around the room were standard issue, topped with stained Sprelacart boards, the metal tube seating upholstered with rough, red material.

I set myself in the corner, with a view of both bar and entrance, and when the barman finally saw fit to schlep himself over, ordered a Club Cola.

"Only have Vita," he announced, already heading back to his perch.

"Wait, I'll have a beer," I called, remembering my clapperboard. With that back in my pocket, I could afford to lean on the no drink-driving rule.

The barman took his time finding the bottle of beer, then more time to locate a glass before placing them both on the wooden bar. After that he needed extra time to walk to the front of the bar and fetch the bottle and glass.

I let him have his fun, I was in no rush. I'd waited so long for this drink that another minute or two didn't matter.

When he finally put the bottle on my table, I filled my glass. The first half went down fast. I slowed down after that and took a closer look at the clientele for a while. None of them had anything to do but to keep a watch on their own beers. The barman hunched himself onto a bar stool, ear pressed against the speaker of a valve radio that was older than the town walls.

I decided it was safe enough to decrypt Bruno's message here, and got the necessaries out of various pockets.

On an empty page of my notebook, I copied out the message from the tiny slip of paper. Letter for letter, along the top of a page, turning over when there was no more room and filling the top line of the next page:

W K T R Z L V D O P D I W B H P V Y Y P E E Y P E Y W Y I L
S C X P E J F J V B A H S U G H T O K

I hadn't ever used a one time pad in earnest, although I'd learned how to decrypt them during basic training at the MfS high school near Potsdam. It was a long time ago, but the method is easy enough, I was sure I could still remember how to do it.

Turning back to the first page, I converted each letter into a number, using the basic scheme A=1, B=2 and so on, writing the number beneath each letter as I went.

W K T R Z L V D O P D I W B H P V Y Y P E E Y P E Y W Y I L
S C X P E J F J V B A H S U G H T O K
23 11 20 18 26 12 22 4 26 16 4 9 23 2 13 16 22 21 25 16 5
5 25 16 5 25 23 25 9 12 13 3 24 16 5 10 6 10 22 2 18 19
21 4 8 20 15 24

Beneath that, I copied the key, converting each letter into a number, same as with the cipher.

D Q Z D V N L P S B P O E V U W S Q G U G K V H Q N E H
F D Y O V I G Y N Q S T Y U E B H W A U J
4 17 26 4 22 14 12 16 19 2 16 15 5 22 21 23 19 17 4 21 4
11 22 8 17 14 5 13 6 4 25 15 22 9 4 25 14 17 19 20 25 21
5 2 13 23 1 21 10

Now it was time for the arithmetic: I subtracted the key from the cipher text, adding 26 to any negative numbers so they stayed within the range 1-26:

13 20 20 11 4 24 10 11 7 11 11 20 18 6 18 13 3 8 18 21 24

20 3 8 11 11 18 12 3 8 20 11 2 7 24 11 18 13 3 8 2 13 11 13

20 11 13 20 11

And there it was—once I'd cleaned up the numbers and converted them back to letters, I had Bruno's message:

S T T N D K J N G N N T R F R S C H R U X T C H N K R L C H

T N B G X K R S C H B H N S T K S T N

Trouble was, after all that work, it still didn't make any sense. I copied the message out again, using lower case letters and exchanging each X for a full stop as I went, hoping the meaning would become clear:

sttnd. jnguntrþrschru. tchnkrichtnbg. krschbmustkstn

But it still had me scratching my head. I went back to the top, re-checking my maths, but the numbers added up the same way. Had I misremembered the procedure? Perhaps I should add the code to the cipher instead of the other way round? Or had Merkur mixed up which slip of paper was the message and which was the code?

I started to redo the maths, but the other way round, swapping round the codes on the pieces of paper, starting with the D, subtracting W from it. But when I turned the page to get to the next set of letters, I noticed something about my first attempt at decryption.

There was only one vowel: U followed by a full stop, probably for the word *und*. But what about all the other vowels?

I wrote out the decrypted string of letters again, leaving spaces between every letter that didn't either demand an obvious vowel, or fit into a common combination:

st_t_n_d. jungen_n_t_r_þorsch_r u. techniker Lichtenbg.

k_r_sch_b_m_n_st_k_st_n

It was making more sense now—the first half of the message was easy to understand: *Station der jungen Naturforscher und Techniker Lichtenberg*: the Centre for Young Natural Scientists and Engineers in Lichtenberg.

Each county, and in Berlin, each borough, has one of these institutions, an after-school activity centre, encouraging kids' interest in science. I never bothered with anything like that when I was that age—it was enough that I'd been marshalled into the FDJ, and later on, I'd been more interested in activities organised by the GST, the paramilitary organisation for the youth.

I didn't even know where my local *Station* in Friedrichshain was, never mind the one in Lichtenberg, but that would be easy enough to find out.

Confident that I had the general location, I turned my attention to the second part of the message, which presumably localised the position of Bruno's cache:

K_r_sch_b_m_n_st_K_st_n

I stared at the jumble of letters, wishing I was better at crosswords, but nothing jumped out. Another gulp of beer, light up a fresh coffin nail. Then I started to mentally insert vowels into the spaces, testing what fitted:

Kirsch came out pretty quickly: cherry.

After that, *Baum* was obvious: tree.

Stumped by the next few letters: *Nast* isn't a word, but the next vowel, *e*, gave me *Nest*. A short leap of imagination took me to *Nistkasten*: nesting box.

Centre for Young Natural Scientists and Engineers Lichtenberg. Bird box in cherry tree

I raised my glass to Bruno. Suddenly Pozdniakov's task didn't seem so impossible.

67
BERLIN PANKOW

I noticed the tail as I came off the motorway in Pankow, coming down from the bridge over the S-Bahn tracks.

I'd taken the first side street after the end of the motorway —force of habit rather than any real concern. But if a car follows you into a small housing estate, you think to keep an eye on it.

I was in a good position to do just that—a quiet road, high wall running along one side, rows of housing blocks on the other—some of the early attempts at concrete slab builds. That was when I caught the car in my mirror for the third time, a Berlin registered, light coloured Polski 126.

There are two basic options in these situations: lose the tail or let it stay where it is. There's a school of thought that says you should leave a shadow in place for as long as you can so you can keep track of it, but that night I couldn't be bothered with the usual games. It had been a long day, I'd driven too far and had too much excitement along the way—so you won't be surprised to hear that I began what, in this business, we call an offensive-preventative manoeuvre.

There was a sharp bend halfway along the road, and since the tail was keeping a respectful distance, that curve was just enough to get me out of sight for a few seconds.

As soon as the Polski had disappeared from my mirrors, I turned into a smaller road, switched off my lights and put my foot down hard.

I took my foot off the accelerator before the next junction, dabbing the brake to see what traction I had, then steered into the start of a fishtail skid as I entered the crossroads. The locals hereabouts were clearly good citizens, the kind that don't park cars too close to the junction, so I had some leeway for my next move.

Using the last of the momentum from the fishtail, I steered against the skid and let the back end of the car glide to the side of the road. A sudden stop told me I'd hit one of the heavy concrete flower pots they put around the place to catch idiots like me, but the car didn't complain when I backed up a few metres, so it seemed I hadn't damaged anything essential.

I'd halted on the wrong side of the road, but it wasn't the time to worry about niceties, so I hunched down in the seat and waited to see whether my tail would turn up again.

It took five minutes for the Polski to appear, the driver had obviously missed my sudden turn, had carried on for a while before noticing he was all by himself. Difficult situation—I could sympathise—but the Polski driver had made the right call and had returned to do a sweep of the nearby streets.

He didn't notice the Shiguli parked on the wrong side of the street as he went past. Wasn't even alert enough to clock that my car was the only one not coated with frost.

On the other hand, I didn't manage to get more than an impression of the driver—the streetlamps were directly above the junction, putting the interior of his car in shadow, and I was a little preoccupied with staying out of sight myself.

Once the little car was well out of the way, I started the Shiguli and took myself back to the main road as fast as I could without drawing too much attention.

68
BERLIN FRIEDRICHSHAIN

When I let myself into my flat, the television was on, the after-hours white noise and scrambled screen providing mood music to Lütten's slumber. He was sprawled on the couch, three or four beers and half a bottle of vodka showing the progress he'd made through my provisions.

I sat myself in the armchair and sank a glass or two of the clear stuff. Leaving the television on—the racket would help keep stress levels just where I wanted them—I pulled the car keys out of my pocket and threw them on the table. Hard enough to scratch the veneer, loud enough to wake Lütten.

His head jolted up and he began rubbing his eyes.

"You told the Russian where to find me," I said. I didn't shout, but my voice was stony enough for him to know just how pissed off I was.

Lütten had stopped rubbing his eyes, was now kicking his feet off the couch and levering himself upright. "The Russians came here, asking questions—what did you expect me to do?" He had his elbows on his knees now, was looking at his feet and starting to piece his defence together. "You didn't say anything about the Friends being involved!"

"I let you in on far too much. Who did you tell about today's trip to Rostock?"

"Where's the old man? Merkur?" Lütten reached for the vodka, and I let him. Must have been in the job too long, I was getting soft.

"I asked who else knew about my trip to Rostock?"

"The two Russians who came here ... My department, up at

the District Admin. That's it, nobody else." He sipped his vodka. I glared at him until he felt the need to break the silence: "Thought you might get into difficulties with the car, you know? Turning up in the Administration's vehicle, without your clapperboard—if anyone checked ..." He stumbled to a halt. It must have been obvious that I wasn't in the market for excuses.

"You've been helpful since we first met. Helpful and inquisitive—always nosing around, wondering how you could be of assistance to the man from Berlin." He wasn't going to respond to that, so I asked about something I should have thought to chase up a long time ago.

"What department are you in?"

Lütten hunched over his glass, giving the impression he wasn't about to answer. I stood over him and asked again.

He put his glass down, and without looking up, mumbled, "Department II."

"That's what you told me when we first met, all that time ago in the cutesy tea shop with the funny hat. So, if I phone up Rostock right now, ask for Department II, they'll confirm you're one of their model workers, due back any day now?"

"Department XV," he amended, head still down.

XV, the local level of HV A: foreign intelligence. The same department in Rostock that Sachse was posted to. Department XV, part of the same HV A that sat on the committee overseeing Secondary Operation Merkur, where they lobbied so hard to get Merkur out of the country. The same HV A that, back in the mists of time, had killed Merkur's protégé, Bruno. And if that isn't enough for you, the same HV A that provides the liaison between the KGB and the MfS.

Everything that had happened since before Secondary Operation Merkur even began had been overseen, surveilled and manipulated by HV A.

"The keys to your car are on the table, now fuck off back to fishtown."

69
BERLIN FRIEDRICHSHAIN

I watched from the window as Lütten examined the rear door of the Shiguli, the one that had taken a bash from the flowerpot. He glared up at my flat for a while before driving off.

I remained where I was standing, sipping vodka and staring at the space vacated by the Rostocker's car. Then, instead of refilling my glass, I took myself over to the wall unit, switching off the television as I passed. Opening a drawer, I pulled out the Berlin phone directory and flicked through to S. Ran my finger down the lines until I got to *Station der jungen Naturforscher und Techniker*. It was there alright, but instead of an entry for each of East Berlin's nine boroughs, I found just a single number—the Prenzlauer Berg Station. I flicked backwards until I found *Lichtenberg, Bezirksamt*, but the *Station* wasn't hiding among the libraries and other such borough institutions.

Fine, these places obviously didn't deserve one of the scarce telephone connections, which is why they weren't listed in the telephone book. Still, there were other ways of finding the address of the Lichtenberg Centre for Young Natural Scientists and Engineers. I headed for my coat hanging in the tiny hall.

As I passed my bedroom door, lethargy hit me like the edge of a riot shield.

One more drink, I told myself. It had been a hard day, one more drink would give me the edge I needed to take myself to Berlin Centre in search of the address I needed.

One more drink to get me going, and another wee one after that to celebrate cracking Bruno's code ...

70
BERLIN FRIEDRICHSHAIN

The alarm clock shook me into consciousness at 0530 hours the next morning. My fingers found the catch, pulling the little lever until the bell was silenced, all without having to pull my head from under the pillow. Another moment, long enough to push away the memory of Sanderling, then I folded back the duvet and sat up.

My dreams had been crowded, Sachse was a new guest to my sleep, although he hadn't exactly shown himself. He'd been a shadow in the background, two fingers pointing, thumb cocked like a hammer, aiming at Sanderling, who was too busy staring at me to notice the danger she was in.

I swung my legs out of bed and the shock of the cold lino propelled me onto my feet and towards the bathroom.

As I walked through the living room, a Russian soldier climbed out of the armchair and stood to attention. Even though he was out of uniform, I could tell he was Russian—it was the way he stood there, chest pushed out like a pigeon, chin in the air.

Ignoring him for the moment, I went for a piss, then splashed cold water on my face.

Still not ready to face reality, wondering whether the Russian had somehow escaped my dreams, whether Sanderling and Sachse would be looking for him, I headed for the tiny kitchen and made myself a coffee.

I could see the soldier from my position by the stove, He was still standing at attention. Well, let him—I hadn't asked him in, so I certainly wasn't going to invite him to make himself comfortable. I turned round so I didn't have to look at him, concentrating instead on pouring boiling water from the pan into my mug.

A sip of coffee, and another. OK, let's do this.

"*Dobre utro,*" I mumbled as I sat down opposite the Russian.

He reached into his jacket pocket and pulled out a piece of paper. The usual, grey, coarse kind used in offices throughout our half of the world.

I took it from him, unfolded it and scratched my head a bit. I'm OK on spoken Russian, but reading Cyrillic takes a bit longer, particularly at this time of the morning.

The note was handwritten, printed in neat letters—the kind the technical experts hate because it makes it hard to identify the author: *Subject held at Beelitz, not available for questioning.*

Beelitz, the Soviet Army's central hospital in Germany. Which meant either Merkur had suffered an accident of some sort, or Pozdniakov wanted me to think he had.

"A bit too enthusiastic with the interrogation?" I asked. The soldier thought I was talking to him—maybe I'd spoken in Russian—but I'd actually been addressing the KGB major, who I imagined standing by a bedside forty or fifty kilometres southeast of my flat, in Beelitz.

I dismissed the soldier, but he remained where he was, chest still puffed out, chin up, heels together. The Russians are brutal to their enlisted men, won't let them speak without permission, but I guessed what he wanted without him needing to say a word.

With a sigh I held out Pozdniakov's message, and the Russian pulled a silver Zippo lighter from his pocket and set fire to the note while it was still in my hand.

I dropped the paper into the ashtray and the pair of us watched it burn. When it had been reduced to a fine film of grey ash, the soldier leaned over, using the base of the lighter to mash the remains of the note in with the cigarette butts and bottle caps.

I didn't see my guest out, I returned to the bathroom and started shaving, dragging the blade over my chin and wondering what Pozdniakov's real message had been—why had he given the soldier Merkur's lighter to use?

I shook my head. No point guessing—I'd never understand the way the Russians think.

But Pozdniakov's news didn't matter, neither the written message nor the hidden one—I no longer needed to interview Merkur, I now knew more than him. I'd decrypted Bruno's message and all I had to do was find the Lichtenberg *Station* and then go to retrieve the papers.

Perhaps the only question I had left was whether there would be enough material in Bruno's cache to condemn Sachse. And if so, whether Sachse's downfall would exorcise Sanderling from my nights.

71
STATION DER JUNGEN NATURFORSCHER

Before going to my own office at Berlin Centre, I dropped round to the secretariat at HA XX, the Main Department responsible, among other things, for state institutions. Laying my clapperboard on the desk, I told them what I needed.

"What, *all* of them?"

"Just the ones in Berlin."

One of the secretaries made her way to a filing cabinet while the others eyed me suspiciously. No one asked why I needed the information, but I knew my details would be passed on for scrutiny and further enquiry.

The secretary came back with a file and I sat myself in the corner, perusing the list. It was several pages long, included not only the addresses of each *Station*, but also the responsible persons with their home and work addresses and, where available, phone numbers.

I made a show of examining each page in turn—let the busybodies put that in their report—but I only committed one entry to memory: *Scheffelstrasse 21, 1156 Berlin.*

Despite the heavy traffic typical of this time of the morning, it was only a five-minute drive to Scheffelstrasse, a quiet road that led to a bridge over the railway, just north of the container terminal at Frankfurter Allee.

I drove slowly along the road, counting down the numbers on the unpretentious pre-war flats. The last block ended at 23, after that, a rigid-mesh fence fronted a snow-laden garden dotted with half-standard trees. *A haven for young natural scientists*, I murmured to myself before continuing over the railway bridge and doing a U-turn to park on the other side of the road. While I locked my car, I had a good look around, paying particular attention to the pedestrian traffic—mostly clutches of children making their chattering way to school.

I walked back over the bridge, stopping at the garden fence, next to a gate that allowed access to a cobbled path up to the last house in Lichtenberg: the *Station* mentioned in Bruno's message.

I tried the gate, locked of course, but it was low, no higher than a metre-sixty, so with a brief check up and down the road —just kids intent on organising trips to the recycling shop or whatever it is little snots talk about—I pulled myself up onto the metal gate, rolling over and down the other side, ignoring the inevitable complaint from my still-sore knee.

I wasn't expecting trouble, so I didn't hang around in the cold for long, but followed the cobbled drive up the slight incline, the long and low shape of the *Station* looming behind the bare hedge to my right.

The gate in the hedge was unlocked, I passed through and walked the couple of metres to the *Station*, ignoring, for the moment, the orchard area in front.

I paused at the bottom of the short flight of steps that led to the front door, listening to the cadence of the place: vehicles passed along the road outside, tires humming and crunching over the snow and ice. Sharp clanks and bangs from the container terminal in the railway cutting beyond the garden.

No wind in the trees and bushes, no creak of wood, either from the orchard or the building. I climbed the steps and tried the door. The lock was a simple lever type that needs a heavy key—easy enough to pick, were it not for the padlocked security gate in front. I examined the padlock, no signs that anyone had tried to break it—no scratches around the keyhole

246

or scuffs on the shackle.

I turned my back on the building and stared at the trees as they loitered in the deep snow. I'm no arboricultural expert, couldn't tell a cherry tree from an overgrown asparagus, so I decided to concentrate on locating the bird boxes rather than identifying the make and model of each trunk.

From the road, the snow had looked pretty much undisturbed, but with daylight growing more confident, I could see several sets of footprints. I bent down to examine them, noting the different sizes and vintages.

I followed the traces, my ears picking up the scrape and crunch of snow under my boots and the crashing from the container terminal along with the steady whine of the electric S-Bahn trains as they glided past. A plane banked above, positioning itself to land at the West Berlin airport in Tegel, while down on earth, I circled a tree.

I stopped. Leaning on the trunk of the third tree over was a ladder. There was nobody on it right now, but that didn't mean they weren't still nearby—a ladder isn't something you leave propped against a tree all winter long, it had been placed there recently.

Moving to the nearest trunk, I gave the orchard another sweep, shifting sideways to try to cover the whole area. Life continued beyond the edge of the garden—traffic on the road, trains on the tracks in the cutting, but my attention was focused on the silent building: all windows and doors shut, no lights on.

I squatted in the snow, hoping that by moving closer to the ground I would be shielded from the din coming from the container terminal, making it easier to pick out nearby noises. The grinding of a bus on the road behind me, slap of footsteps on icy pavements, children's voices. Still no birds, no wind in the branches.

I stayed low, listening, watching. The sky was a lighter grey than I'd seen in a long time, maybe it would be the first clear day of the year.

Then the sound I'd hoped I wouldn't hear—the whispered rasp of snow under a boot. Just the once, a single step—not the regular gait of a pedestrian walking along the street outside.

I twisted around, at the same time reaching into my jacket, hand closing around the butt of my *Wamme*. I pulled it out and pointed it at the tall man in a padded buff raincoat and fur hat who had entered the garden from the drive.

He had his hands out to either side, palms showing and elbows crooked, but he didn't stop. He continued towards me, unbothered by the sight of the Makarov aimed at his stomach. I let him come closer—he'd make an easier target if he wasn't so far away.

He was very obliging, he walked slowly, hands always in sight, finally stopping about six metres away. Then he spoke.

"Good morning, Comrade Reim," a Mecklenburg accent. I swore, yet another fish-head.

But he had me scratching my own, non-fishy head. Who knew I was here? I came up with a shortlist of nobody—I hadn't told anyone I was coming, until twenty minutes ago I hadn't even known this place existed.

Another thought: Merkur—I'd left him by himself in the car for about half an hour in Malchow, he could have decrypted Bruno's message then. But who might he have told? Only Pozdniakov.

Perhaps the new arrival could hear the gears working in my head, his right hand crept toward the pocket of his coat. Very, very slowly, so as not to frighten the audience, he pushed the tips of two fingers inside and snagged a green clapperboard, just like mine. This was a colleague.

He flicked the identity card towards me, it landed about a metre away and I put a knee in the snow when I reached for it. With my left hand, I flipped the booklet open to the page showing his photograph: light blonde hair, the irises of his eyes so light they were hardly visible, large ears for someone his age, no glasses, no facial hair, a chin, once strong, but slowly merging with his neck. After comparing him with the mugshot, I read the entry next to it: District Administration Rostock. I flicked the page to look at the name of the *Fischkopp*.

"*Oberleutnant* Gerhard Sachse," he said, in case I had trouble with reading.

72
STATION DER JUNGEN NATURFORSCHER

I closed Sachse's clapperboard and tossed it back. He caught it with one hand.

"I hear you've been looking for me," he said once he'd stowed the clapper. His hands came back to his sides again, palms out.

Now we'd got the excitement of the reveal out of the way, I took another look around the orchard, unsurprised to find it suddenly crowded. Prager, Lütten's big goon from Rostock, had come round the far end of the *Station*, was covering me with his service pistol. A glance over my other shoulder told me that Lütten himself was also present and correct, firearm in hand—although he had the grace to look slightly apologetic about it.

When I got round to looking at Sachse again, he no longer had his hands where I could see them, his right hand was in his pocket, and in the circumstances I felt it best to assume that he was gripping the butt of a pistol.

I kept mine pointing in his direction, but shifted a little to the left, staying low and putting myself in a better position to keep an eye on all three colleagues.

"Sachse—did you kill Comrade Ruth Gericke, who used the legend Gisela Bauer, also known as Codename Sanderling?" I asked. My colleagues at Berlin Centre would have gasped to hear such an indiscreet question in a public place, but what did I have to lose? It was something I wanted to know, and I might not get another chance to ask.

"I want the evidence—I see you've already taken it." Sachse used his chin to point at the ladder and the birdbox above.

"I don't have it. Somebody got here before me," I said, still trying to cover all three men with one pistol.

"Reim, stop wasting my time—I want what you've taken!" This time he used his free hand to gesture at the ladder by my side. "We both know your old friend Holger Fritsch put the material together." The tone of his voice had changed. Until now, it had been neutral, bordering on jovial, but was turning nasty. "You watched him die, didn't you? You saw your friend Captain Fritsch shoot his own brains out. I suppose he didn't have much choice, not after I had a word with him, told him just how much I had on him."

He was actually enjoying himself, I realised as I digested the news that this man had a hand in the death of Holger Fritsch—the only person in the Firm I'd ever called a friend. Sachse had just made things worse for himself, and looking around at the three men, I vowed there would be a time for a reckoning, a time when it was just me and Sachse, one on one.

"To be honest, I'm surprised it took your friend so long to swallow his gun, thought he was more of a man. Tell me, did he mention me? Any last words? Perhaps he made you promise to seek revenge?"

While Sachse was busy congratulating himself, I continued to scan the orchard. I noticed a slight movement in a window of the *Station*, behind Prager—there it was again, a slight refraction of darkness within. Not sure of what I'd just seen, I kept looking back. Prager used the opportunity to edge closer and I flicked my Makarov in the goon's direction, just so he'd know he wasn't being as subtle as he thought.

As I moved my wrist, the window behind Prager moved too, the reflection in the glass shifting as it was silently opened. Just a centimetre or two, perhaps enough to listen in on our conversation.

I turned back to Sachse, threw another question at him: "You don't deny killing Sanderling—but what about Source Bruno, did you kill him too?"

"The only thing you can take from a louse is its life."

"Why? To protect your sources in the Red Army Faction? Is that why you killed them?"

I could see Sachse clearly in the steel light of the morning. He had a smile on his face, big teeth, thin lips. It wasn't pretty.

Before I could throw more questions at him, we were all distracted by the dull shiver of a window pane breaking, followed by the chiming of glass shattering on icy ground.

Four pairs of eyes stared as the rabbit-ears front-sight of a Kalashnikov was pushed through the hole in the window, just behind Prager. Four pairs of ears heard the order: "Drop your weapons!"

It was a woman's voice, accent from the coast. One that had become very familiar over the last week.

73
STATION DER JUNGEN NATURFORSCHER

We all knelt down to deposit our guns on the hard snow.

"Reim, bring the guns to me," ordered Anna Weber. "Take the long way round!"

Checking the safety catches on each Makarov as I picked it up, I brought them to the window. I hadn't needed the dancing instructions, I knew enough not to walk in front of the muzzle of a *Kaschi*, but I still appreciated the sentiment.

"You three, over there!" she shouted towards my colleagues. Lütten and Prager started towards the orchard gate, but Sachse stood his ground.

"You don't expect us to believe you'll fire a machine pistol in the direction of a busy road!"

"Feel free to do something stupid if you want to find out."

I'd reached the window by now, I peered in. Anna Weber was kneeling on the floor, wearing her fancy woollen coat, head wrapped against the cold. She was sighting down the barrel of a kid's model Kalashnikov made of wood and piping.

Weber's eyes flickered in my direction, she gave me a wink.

"I hope you didn't walk through the border with that thing?" I murmured, wondering how sensible it would be to give her one of the Makarovs I'd unexpectedly found in my possession.

"This place is full of junk," she replied, her cheek pressed against the toy gun's stock. "But I thought the front end looked convincing enough."

Deciding it might be wiser to keep hold of the handguns, I distributed three of them around various pockets, keeping my own in my hand.

"What's the plan?" I asked, pressing my back against the roughcast rendering of the outside wall and watching my colleagues, currently regrouping under a tree about thirty metres away.

"Plan? Who said anything about a plan? You're the clever Stasi operative—you come up with a plan." One hand left the toy gun, groping around the floor by her knees, finally appearing again with an oilskin bundle, smaller than I'd expected. She held it up for me to see, but as I gingerly reached in through the broken window to take it, she snatched the package back.

"Is that Seiffert's cache?"

"Go and find a way for us to get out of here," she instructed, her attention back on Sachse, Lütten and Prager.

I slipped along the side of the building, Makarov at the ready, and peered around the corner. Nobody there, no fresh prints in the snow, so I went a bit further.

At the next corner, I stopped. The gardens belonging to the *Station* continued around the back, a couple of other buildings —garages? potting sheds?—were dotted around, the closest at least twenty metres away.

To my right, a couple of mature trees stood between me and a high, rigid-mesh fence lining the edge of the slope down to the container terminal. Another scan of the outbuildings and, detecting no movement, I darted over to the fence, bending low to provide a smaller target to anyone feeling the need to test their marksmanship.

I pulled myself to the top of the fence and took stock of the terrain below: a steep bank, plenty of winter-bare undergrowth poking through the snow. Further down the cutting, two orange gantry cranes at work, heaving containers off the back of articulated trucks. Directly below my position, several railway sidings merged into the mainline track. Beyond that, a flying junction took a spur first over the S-Bahn tracks, then under the road bridge—presumably leading to the central slaughter yard on the other side of Eldenaer Strasse.

I dropped back into a crouch and turned back to the garden, quartering the rows of saplings, snow-blanketed beds and the outbuildings. Beyond those sheds, only a high fence separated us from an isolated corner of Lichtenberg Park. That was our best way out.

I doubled back to the window where Anna Weber was still attempting to marshal my reluctant colleagues: "Keep your hands high, walk slowly through that gate and down the drive —I can see through the hedge, so don't even think of making any silly moves!"

"Time to flit," I whispered, leaning in past the shards of glass that still clung to the window frame. "Across the gardens at the back, into the *Stadtpark*."

"I can still see you! Keep going—nice and slow!" she shouted to the troika moving in single file.

"See you at the back door," I told her, before sidling back around the building.

Feeling overcautious, I dropped to my knees again at the next corner and poked my head out. If I were Sachse, I'd have a couple of men in one of those outbuildings, ready to call on if things didn't go as planned. But if anyone was there, they hadn't taken action while I was scoping out the possibilities a minute or two before, even though they must have heard Weber yelling. Shouting is as reliable a sign as any that a plan's gone wrong, and if they didn't know that already then they were in the wrong job.

So, while it was probably unnecessary, I kept my *Wamme* in my hand while I waited for Weber to appear, and I kept it pointed in the general direction of the nearest building.

I had enough light to work with, the sun hadn't yet crested

the block of flats to the east, but a rose blush was bleeding along the roofs.

The noise of a door clicking open told me that Weber was coming out, but I kept my eyes on the field. Nothing stirred, and that stillness was our signal to move.

We hadn't gone five paces before I heard the chafing of a window opening.

I changed direction, grabbing Weber by the elbow, dragging her towards the fence above the railway cutting.

"Halt!" the shout came from the outbuilding I'd been watching, but we didn't halt, not until we reached the nearest mature tree. Once there, I pushed Weber onwards to the fence and peered from behind the wide trunk, Makarov at the ready.

Would they shoot? Would Sachse and his friends, encouraged by the shout, come to see what was happening?

I glanced to my right, Weber was already over the fence, letting herself down the other side. It was my turn to move, so move I did.

Across the snow, jump at the fence, fingers clawing the bars, feet scrabbling for purchase. The bullet hit me as I swung one leg over the top. Before I even heard the shot, I felt it—a great clout, whipping me round, kicking me over the fence and into darkness.

74
CONTAINER STATION FRANKFURTER ALLEE

I dropped into the shrubbery at the top of the embankment, the dry canes and brambles snagging me, saving me from the worst of the fall. I lay there for a moment—I must have hit my head, I was dazed, unable to see anything, holding my breath and waiting for the pain.

Hearing returned first—they were coming for me, the sawing scrape of movement through the undergrowth, getting closer—here they were, one of them pulling me by the arm. I screamed—the pain had arrived. Sharp, burning spreading through my upper arm, dull throbs in my shoulder and hand.

They pulled me again, this time by the uninjured arm, dragging me through the scrub.

"Come on, Reim—on your feet!" A whisper in my ear, the voice warm, familiar. "You can do it!"

And I could. With Weber's support I struggled to my knees, the darkness lifting. Then a crouch, stumbling through the dry canes and fallen branches, down the bank to the tracks.

As I tumbled, fell and glissaded down the slope, Weber kept me upright. She must have picked up my *Wamme* because she paused, pointing the pistol up the slope and loosing off a shot, then another, the pistol cracking brittle morning air.

As I watched her, I concentrated on ignoring the pain in my arm.

"Don't wait, keep moving!" she pulled at me again.

We reached the bottom of the slope, our feet hitting the

hard but shifting stone ballast.

"Get over that, I'll see you on the other side!" she pointed at a formation of containers on flats, pulled by a crawling Ludmilla locomotive. The driver must have seen us, he let off an angry toot, barely audible above the drumming exhaust and the clicking of wheels over points.

I hauled myself onto the flatbed—steadying myself with only one hand—was on my knees, shuffling to the far side, rocked by the movement of the train, when the container beside me boomed, sparks flashing as a bullet glanced off the metal, centimetres from my head. Diving, rolling across the bed of the wagon, pushing my feet over the far end and dropping onto the tracks, more or less deliberately falling onto my good shoulder.

I levered myself onto my knees, Weber was there again, had me by the shoulders, was pulling me.

"Where now, clever Stasi man?"

Staggering to my feet, stumbling over sleepers and rails. My arm dull, yet somehow still sending needles of pain into my shoulder.

"The flyover," I tried to point, but she had hold of my good arm, was already dragging me in that direction.

I looked behind us, at the long train which still provided some cover from whatever idiot up there had a gun.

"Keep moving, Reim. Your legs are fine, so shift yourself." She turned back and jogged alongside the train, adjusting her pace to stay by the gap between two containers. Raising her arm, she fired into the undergrowth on the bank. She stood still until the next gap came along, aimed and fired again.

I stopped gawping and did as she'd told me, limping towards the ramp up to the flyover.

"More of them that way." Weber had caught up with me again, was gesturing towards a string of blue uniforms advancing along the tracks from the platforms of Frankfurter Allee S-Bahn station, still four or five hundred metres away.

Weber helped me up the low bank and onto the spur leading to the bridge, an S-Bahn rattled and groaned along the tracks beneath, the cold air buffeting us as it passed. Behind us, the container train had rattled and clanked to a stop, blocking the points on the mainline tracks, the containers still giving us cover from our pursuers.

"Come on Reim, run, won't you!" And I did, pushing the pain back to where it came, freeing up enough energy to break into a jog, loping from one decaying wooden sleeper to the next, up the slope until it levelled off beneath the road bridge, then up again and to a sudden halt at a high gate with a red stop sign.

A works security guard, perhaps drawn by the commotion, stood on the other side, watching our approach with suspicion. Weber pulled me around so we faced each other, then unzipped my jacket and reached in to take my Ministry ID card.

She flashed my clapperboard at the guard, and gave him a look I'd have been proud of—he couldn't unchain the gate fast enough.

"Contact the *Volkspolizei*, tell them hostile agents are on the railway! Lock this gate behind us and don't let anyone through, no matter what they say—come on, get that gate closed, *dalli dalli!*"

We passed through, leaving the guard to lock up behind us, Anna Weber almost laughing from the relief of getting ahead of my colleagues.

"Call an ambulance, you can see he's been injured," she called after the security guard who was running for a nearby building to phone the bulls.

She flashed my clapperboard again as we went through the gatehouse and onto the street, looking around continuously. But the road was empty—kids had traipsed into school, shift workers had clocked on and it was too cold for casual pedestrians.

Weber took my hand and pulled me into the road. I didn't know where she was taking me, but I limped along in her wake, finding it harder to ignore the pain now the shock and adrenaline were wearing off. Weber took me down a side street, stopping in front of a grimy, cream-coloured Polski. She propped me against the side as she opened the door, then guided me into the tiny car.

"That was you last night? Following me when I came off the motorway?"

"Shut up, we've no time to chat!"

75
BERLIN FRIEDRICHSHAIN

Weber released the brakes and used the slope of the hill to get the little car rolling before starting the engine.

"Here, use that," she said, tapping the rear-view mirror.

"Nobody there," I said, adjusting the mirror to better see what was coming up behind, then gasping in pain as my left arm hit the side of the seat as Weber turned a sharp corner without indicating.

She didn't apologise or slow down, but continued zig-zagging her way across Friedrichshain in an effort to flush out any pursuit.

After we'd headed west for a while, then south across Frankfurter Allee and into the cobbled side streets beyond, she pulled in at the side of the road.

"Take your jacket off." She reached over to pull a first aid kit out of the glove box.

I couldn't, not in the small car. But I did manage to get out under my own steam, and once on the pavement, Weber peeled off my jacket, easing my clothes away from the wound.

"Wiggle your fingers—good. Nothing serious, just a nick," she reassured me as she cut away the sleeve of my shirt and pullover. I yelped as she poured iodine on, but held steady as she wrapped a bandage around.

"Let's have a look at that head of yours—nasty bang, but you've got a thick skull. Right, back in the car!"

The first aid had taken less than two minutes, then we were on the road again, heading towards Boxhagener Strasse.

★

They picked us up a couple of blocks later: "Sand coloured Wartburg on our tail," I announced as we came up to a crossroads, bracing myself for another sharp turn. The Wartburg was coming up fast behind us, having decided on an aggressive approach.

But instead of the sharp turn I'd been expecting, Weber carried straight on over the junction, twisting the steering wheel when we were half-way across and pulling hard on the handbrake. The back wheels skittered, found purchase for a moment before sliding out again as we hit steel tram tracks. The tyres bit again, and we slithered back onto the side street we'd just come from, passing the Wartburg coming the other way.

Sixty metres later, Weber switched her foot to the brake, and the rear of the car swung out over the slick roadway. The Wartburg had managed to turn around, was on our tail again, but that didn't bother my driver. She hauled the steering wheel around, put her foot down and mounted the curb, a jolt and a scrape as granite stone hit the bottom of the car, then the front wheels were up over the edge and between the trees that lined the road, aiming for a pedestrian passageway that tunnelled beneath a house to join the street on the other side of the block.

There was no time to argue, Weber didn't look like she was in the mood to listen, so I watched the mirrors, preferring what was behind to the wall we were heading for. The Wartburg slid to a stop, four men in it, all eyes on us as we scraped into the alley. I saw the driver's shoulder lurch as he shoved the car into gear again, and they moved off, unwilling to try the same manoeuvre in their wider vehicle.

"Wartburg's gone," I reported.

Weber grunted. We'd come out of the far side, and she was doing another handbrake turn, drifting the rear until we were pointing at the tunnel again. "They'll probably head round the block, try to catch us there—get yourself down the tunnel, signal when you see the Wartburg turn the corner."

I ran down the alleyway, holding my injured arm tight against my body, boots crunching over gritted ice. I slowed at the end and poked my head into the open, in time to see the Wartburg's back end disappear, just as Weber had predicted.

Stepping out of the way, I beckoned Weber on, and she came through the gap, even faster this time, more confident of the car's dimensions. She slowed down to take the bump back onto the roadway, and I pulled the door open and slid in as she went past.

"That way, yeah?" she nodded to the right, the way the Wartburg had gone, and took us in the opposite direction.

Up onto Frankfurter Allee, a right-hand turn, towards my workplace. I wasn't sure that was the best direction to take, but the Western agent seemed to know her way around East Berlin, and she knew what she was doing, so I decided she could take me wherever she wanted.

76
BERLIN LICHTENBERG

I fetched a Bockwurst from the serving hatch and took it back to the table in the underground passageway at Lichtenberg railway station.

"Bockwurst? For breakfast?" But Weber took it anyway and I went back for my own.

When I lifted my roll, biting into the length of protruding sausage, I couldn't taste anything. I was still coming down from the high of being shot and the subsequent car chase. I put the food back on the paper tray, and looked at Weber. She was no ordinary civil servant—she had experience and she'd had training, lots of each.

After we'd lost Sachse and his men in the Wartburg, Weber had brought us here, straight down Frankfurter Allee, past Berlin Centre. Keeping to the speed limit, fitting nicely into the traffic—neither too fast nor too slow. I had to admire her professionalism, but just because I respected her ability and knowledge didn't mean we were on the same side.

"Are you here on a day visa?" I asked.

"Booked into the Berolina." The Interhotel behind the Kino International. Good choice, not as obvious as the Stadt Berlin on Alexanderplatz or the various options around Friedrichstrasse. "But don't worry, I didn't leave anything in my room. I travel light."

"Good, so we can get you back to West Berlin as soon as you've finished your breakfast."

"You look good in that," she changed the subject.

I looked down, grimacing at the lime green and red stripes

of the padded jacket. It had probably been the first item to hand when Weber had walked into the HO clothes shop, but I shouldn't complain, I was at least presentable again, even with my arm in a sling beneath the zipped up jacket.

Still not feeling hungry, I watched the crowds passing us, coming from or going to the mainline platforms, climbing or descending the steps from the U-Bahn platform. A dark blue uniform caught my eye, the only stationary person in the passage. A second glance to check: *Transportpolizei* or the slightly lighter coloured railway workers uniform?

"Time to go," I grabbed Weber's wrist and pulled her from her seat. She came without complaint, didn't even look around. Just left her Bockwurst and neatly twisted her wrist out of my hand as she stood up.

We strode through the tunnel, away from the policeman, up the ramp into wan sunlight, going at a reasonable clip, not quite hurrying, towards the little Polski that we'd left on the station forecourt.

There are always swarms of passengers at Lichtenberg—most long distance trains terminate and start here—Saxon, Thuringian and Mecklenburg accents mingled at the station. As a dense clump of luggage-toting farmers cleared, I saw our car, parked next to a Trabant with a postal horn decal on the door.

I felt for Weber's wrist again, giving it a gentle pull as I changed direction out of the stream of passengers. I put my spare arm around her, pulling her head close as if about to kiss her on the cheek.

"The Trabant next to your car—why would the post office park there?"

Weber leaned in, resting her head on my shoulder, her lips next to my ear. "Post Office employee borrows car, wants to buy train tickets? Or empties postbox?"

She was right, there were so many reasons to park a Post Office vehicle outside the station, but it didn't feel right. I manoeuvred her around until she could see over my shoulder while I watched the car.

"I'm not happy about that aerial on the Post Office car—it's a bit too long," I murmured into her hair. "Man in the driver's seat, looking towards the station main entrance. You see anything?"

"Hang on," she whispered. I could feel her chin nuzzling my jacket as she scanned the crowds. "Yes, got him—another man at the main entrance, taking a little too much interest in the people around him."

She lifted her head, gave me a wide smile, took my hand and started walking towards the road. I fell in step alongside her as we hurried down a side street.

77
KÖNIGS WUSTERHAUSEN

It took nearly four hours to get to Königs Wusterhausen, four hours of winding through Berlin on foot, by bus and tram, then finally, when we were certain we hadn't been followed, the S-Bahn to Königs Wusterhausen.

"I preferred the *Fischerklause*," Weber said as she gave the Seven Steps bar a doubtful once-over. It was the usual sort of place, fluorescent strip-lights, stained Sprelacart tables, hard wooden chairs. Grubby net curtains over the windows. I liked it. "What are we doing here?"

"It's quiet, we can talk." This place and I had history, but I wasn't in the mood to reminisce, pain was making me tired and irritable. "You and me, there's a few things we need to sort out."

Weber took another look around the dive, noting the resident dipsomaniacs, her eyes resting on the barman for a moment or two. "OK, let's talk."

"Start with the basics: what were you doing at the *Station der jungen Naturforscher* this morning?"

Before she answered, the barman came over with a couple of beers. He placed them on the table, was about to turn away when Weber spoke: "I'd like a coffee."

He raised an eyebrow at me, perhaps in reproach for bringing her to his bar, but he nodded and shuffled away.

"*Polizeirat* Portz told me where to go."

That was a surprise. I started my beer, watching her over the rim of the glass. "Merkur knew? So why the trip to Rostock if he already knew where the material was?"

She shrugged, thought about it for a moment. "Perhaps he wanted to test you? Maybe thought he could trust you if you were prepared to risk the trip to Rostock with him? All I know is that he told me to wait twenty-four hours—if I didn't hear from him, I was to retrieve the cache myself. Where is he, anyway?"

"He's safe."

Weber twisted the corner of her mouth up, a slight frown, but she accepted what I'd said. At least for the time being.

"Did he put the one time pad there himself, while he was in Rostock?"

She shrugged again. The possibility didn't seem to interest her, and deciding she probably didn't understand Merkur's contorted way of thinking any better than I did, I moved on:

"Who are you?" I asked, even though I could see who she was. Her coat was over the back of the chair and she'd taken the scarf off, her hair was down, the same as on that first night, in the pub in Warnemünde. Comfortable in her seat, prepared to wait but ready for action—she was a Western agent, and capable with it.

The barman returned, holding a cup and saucer emblazoned with the Mitropa logo. He slid the coffee across the table, gave me another baleful glance then headed back to the sanctuary of his bar.

She didn't lift her cup to drink, didn't even look at it. But she did lift the teaspoon from the saucer and stirred the musty-smelling coffee. The handle of the spoon caught the side of the cup once each rotation: tink, tink, tink.

"My name is Anna Weber, I'm from Lübeck." I decided not to quiz her on the name—Anna Weber was a legend. She'd doubtless given a different name at the Hotel Berolina, if she was staying there at all, and if I insisted, she'd be able to provide me with a third name. Yet I believed her when she said she was from Lübeck—go along the Baltic coast, first town on the other side of the state border is Lübeck, which is probably how she could pretend to be from Mecklenburg—different vocabulary, but no need to change the accent much. "I'm here to support *Polizeirat* Portz in his mission."

"And what is that?"

"Didn't he speak to you about it? *Merkur* you call him, don't you? I thought you two had enjoyed a few cosy chats?"

"You know how it is, we like to have collateral—without corroboration, all material is worthless." I took another sip of beer, then leaned across the sticky table. "This mission, you and Merkur—it's not even official, is it? Merkur has gone off-piste, but what about you? Are you here to drag him back to Bonn, or are you here to help him?"

No answer.

I relaxed back into my chair. Let her take her time, I had a few hours to spare. This evening I would meet Major Pozdniakov, and I would give him the evidence against Sachse, the contents of an oilcloth pouch that Weber still had in her possession. The only question was whether I could get that pouch by using charm, or whether I'd be obliged to resort to force.

"I'm here to make sure Portz is taken back to Bonn, he's got questions to answer." She'd put the spoon down, but still hadn't touched the coffee. Probably not up to the standard she's used to. "But it's not going to happen, is it? I can't see you allowing him to leave."

"Merkur asked to stay, we take care of our guests."

Weber snorted. I gave her a moment longer, just to see if she had anything else she wanted to say, but she used the time to play with her coffee.

"If you're here to take Portz back, why did you help him the other day, all those games we played, the meeting by the Müggelsee?"

She let the teaspoon drop, reached over to take the cigarette out of my fingers and put it to her lips. I watched as she sucked too hard, choking slightly, yet somehow managing to hold the smoke in.

She held the cigarette upright between us, watching the glowing tip.

"I knew Seiffert, the one Portz wants to avenge. What was the codename you gave him?"

"Bruno."

"Right, Bruno. The department had doubts about him—as far back as last summer—so they sent for me. Despite it all, Seiffert was a good man."

"Even though he was about to defect?"

She dipped her head, then handed the cigarette back. I put my lips where hers had been, sucked in, breathed out.

"I'm here to try to get Portz out, take him back to Bonn. But seeing as I'm here, I'm not above getting a little justice for Seiffert—whatever he did, he didn't deserve to go that way."

78
KÖNIGS WUSTERHAUSEN

Weber half-turned in her seat and slid her hand into her coat. When she took it out again, she held a dark-green package.

"Shall we see what we've got?"

"That was in the bird box?" I asked as she unwrapped the oil-cloth.

"Right at the bottom. Underneath all the feathers and bird droppings." She had it open now, the material spread out to reveal a small brown envelope, the kind you find your wages in. Weber ripped open the flap and shook the contents onto the cloth: a strip of 16mm film with four negative exposures and several pieces of microfiche. I took the film strip, held it to the light. A figure, outside a stone building. The next frame showed two men, both wearing suits, shaking hands. The final two frames were blank.

"Can't make much out, what else is there?"

"Documents. Looks like they're from different files," Weber replied, holding the microfiche to the light, just as I'd done with the negatives. "We need a microfilm reader."

And there was our next problem—we couldn't stroll into the local branch of the Firm and ask to use their equipment. I drained my glass and tapped the next coffin nail out of the packet.

"I've got an idea," I told her, heading for the bar.

With the directions given by the barman, it didn't take us long to find the public library. I showed my fake *Kripo* tin and told them what I needed, and they took us down long corridors and through doors marked *No Entry* and *Staff Only*. Finally, the librarian opened the door on a small room with a Pentakta sitting on a desk against the opposite wall. "You'll be able to find your way back again?" she enquired nervously.

I ushered her out while Weber inspected the top-heavy contraption, a doubtful look on her face. Microfiche readers must look different where she comes from, but to me this ungainly chunk of metal was almost as familiar as my *Wamme*.

I fed the strip of negatives into the slot on the side of the hood and plugged the Pentakta in, adjusting the lens once the machine had warmed up. Weber turned the overhead light off, staying by the switch and staring at the projection on the wall as it swam in and out of focus.

Once I'd established that any blurriness was due to the quality of the photograph and not my inability to fine-tune the projecting lens, I stood next to Weber, inspecting the first frame.

Not enough that the picture was slightly fuzzy, it was also over-exposed—but I could make out a figure wearing an overcoat and a brimmed hat, standing in front of a wide doorway faced with dressed stone. The perspective was foreshortened, the shot had been taken with a telescopic lens.

Weber didn't have any comments, so I fed the strip of negatives further in to look at the next frame.

Better quality this time, the picture showed two men in suits. I was interested in the taller of the two men, the one standing to the right. His hair was almost black, a few grey specks giving it texture—allowing for the inversion of colours, this man's hair was very fair, practically white. The eyes, deep in dark sockets, were almost as black as his hair, all except the pupils, tiny discs of light.

I sucked my teeth as my brain, converting the colouring, delivered the identification: Sachse.

The second man, dark hair, glasses, was shorter than

Sachse. Other than a wide desk, nothing of note in the background—no pictures, typewriters or flags to tell us whether we were looking at an office in the East or the West.

"The first picture was taken in Wiesbaden main station," Weber said after standing up to get a closer look at the dark face and the sepia hair of the man on the left. His lips, nostrils and glasses showed up beige, his suit more of a buff shade. The desk was a matt grey, the papers and folders piled on top a deep brown. "This one here," she tapped the library wall where the chest of the shorter man was projected, "looks familiar ... And the taller one—he looks like one of those jokers in the orchard this morning."

I pulled out the negatives and slid the sheet of microfiche into the machine, adjusting the lens again to sharpen the projection on the wall.

We sat next to each other as I shifted the microfiche and the lens around so we could read each document in turn: a typed summar, West German Federal Crime Agency letterhead. A source, referred to only as Codename Dresden, had supplied the information in the report we were looking at—information about Building 74, a debriefing and training centre in the woods east of Berlin.

The next sheet, on the same headed notepaper, provided a précis of the interrogation of Bruno. The next few documents related to Building 74 again, providing the names and dates of visits from members of the West German terrorist group, Red Army Faction.

I watched Weber as she read the reports, but since pointing to the man in the photograph, she'd remained silent.

"Is it true that Bruno was working on identifying second generation members of the Red Army Faction?" I asked when we were finished.

She nodded, looking at the last document, still projected onto the wall.

"Anything you want to tell me?" I pressed.

"The name at the bottom of this file, and this one," she took over navigating around the microfiche, "that's the short man in the second photo."

I looked at the name she was pointing out. "*Polizeidirektor* Jüliger?"

"He's based at the Federal Crime Agency headquarters in Wiesbaden. And as I said, the first picture was taken in Wiesbaden main station."

She pulled the film out of the microfiche reader and I turned it off. We sat for a while in the darkness.

"Do you have any idea who the second man is, this Agent Dresden? Is he the other one in the photograph?" she asked.

"Merkur was looking for this man, he told me he was responsible for Bruno's murder," I answered. I could see his eyes, the almost translucent blue eyes that showed up black on the negative. "His name is Sachse."

"Do we have enough ...?"

Merkur had said that the same person was responsible for the murder of both Bruno and Sanderling—but did I believe him? Not necessarily, although when I'd asked Sachse this morning, he hadn't denied it.

We had enough evidence to open doors, enough to investigate Merkur's claim about Sachse's guilt. I leaned back in my chair, almost feeling at peace with the world, almost feeling I'd be able to sleep that night.

"Enough to avenge Bruno's death?" I said. "It's a start."

79
MITTENWALDE

We caught the next bus out of Königs Wusterhausen. I wasn't fussed about the destination, the point was to keep moving in case Sachse was still searching for us. It also kept Weber occupied while I thought about the next steps.

We sat at the back of the Ikarus bus, both of us aware of what other vehicular traffic was about, although once we'd left Königs Wusterhausen, the roads were practically empty.

The bus was heading to Zossen, but I stood up as we drove up the main road in the small town of Mittenwalde. Weber followed me down the aisle, and we alighted in the centre of the old town. A few citizens moved purposefully along the high street, choosing their queues and planting themselves in the snow and frost, clutching bags while waiting patiently for admission to their chosen shop. A yellow phone box stood beyond the line for household goods, and I found a way through the Omas and mothers with pushchairs and stepped inside.

Leaving Weber outside in the cold, I pushed a twenty Pfennig coin into the slot and dialled the number Pozdniakov had given me—a Berlin number, although for all I knew the call would be redirected to anywhere from here to Moscow.

"Burratino here, I need to make contact," I said in Russian once I had a connection. There was a pause, several clicks, then a voice—male, Russian, but not Pozdniakov himself—came on the line.

"This is Burratino, I am meeting the major in a few hours. I need transport, can you provide?" I was nervous, my Russian coming out slowly, the declensions skewed, but my interlocutor understood.

"What's your position?"

"Mittenwalde, east of Königs Wusterhausen, to the south of Berlin."

"Wait on the bridge over the canal. Twenty minutes."

"There's two of-" But he'd already hung up.

I left the phone box and gestured to Weber to follow.

"What's the plan?"

"I've made contact with someone who can use the material Bruno put together."

"Who? Can we trust them? Will they make sure Sachse gets what he deserves?"

I crossed the road, picking my way between snowdrifts mottled russet and grey with soot.

"What guarantee do we have that your contact will act on the material?" She was persistent, but I wasn't prepared to have this conversation on the high street, no matter how small the town.

We reached the bridge over the canal, and on the far side, I took the steps down to the towpath and walked along a few metres, Weber staying a step or two behind. Once sure we were alone, I turned to her.

"This is the only chance we have—I want Sachse to pay for what he did as much as you do, but I can't do anything by myself."

She listened, hands buried in her pockets, stamping her feet a little against the cold that was creeping up from the ice-bound canal.

"What other options are there? If, somehow, you got this material back over the border, what would you do with it there? You want to wait until Sachse takes a trip to the West so you can arrest him? He's not stupid, he knows what we're up to and he'll make sure never to come your way. No, we have to deal with him over here—and I can't do it and you

276

can't do it, so we need help."

She was thinking about what I'd said, still stamping her feet, and I checked my watch. Ten minutes until rendez-vous.

"You on board?" I asked when it looked like she'd rattled it around her brain for long enough.

She nodded.

"OK, give me the material," I said, holding out my hand.

Weber hesitated, turning slightly to the canal. The low sun picked out each crack and flaw in the ice. Heavy stones were scattered over the surface, thrown from the bridge—I think she was counting them. Then, abruptly, she turned, unbuttoned her coat and reached inside to take out the oilskin pouch.

I took it from her, and we went back up the steps to the bridge.

If anything, it was even colder up there.

The UAZ jeep came from the south, stopped at the curbside and a uniformed Soviet soldier slid out, appearing next to Weber, a hand gripping her upper arm before she could shy away.

She stood there, between the Russian and myself, eyes wide, mouth hanging open, letting the cold air in.

"Sadis' nazad!" the Russian ordered, pulling her towards the vehicle.

I opened the back door, and trapped between us, Weber had little choice but to get in. The soldier closed the door and I went around the vehicle and climbed in the other side.

"Your contact is a Soviet?" Weber whispered, her voice unsteady. I smiled, wondering what fairy tales Westerners told each other about the ferociously ruthless Soviets.

Whatever they said, I doubted it came close to the reality.

80
WÜNSDORF

The driver of the UAZ did a U-turn on the bridge, forcing oncoming traffic to a stop.

"Don't worry." I patted Weber's arm where the soldier had grabbed her. She flinched, but then sat back, recognising there was little she could do about her situation. She spent the journey looking out the window, as if memorising our route.

We were on the old F96 trunk road to Zossen, long since barred to through traffic, leading instead to the headquarters of the Group of Soviet Forces in Germany.

Weber watched silently as the sentries at the main gate first examined the driver's identification, then his written orders. A telephone call was made, then the papers were returned and we were allowed through. Her eyes widened again as we passed along the main road through the camp, women in everyday clothing, stamping and ploughing prams through the snow, surrounded by uniforms and military vehicles of every kind. The bright children's pictures in the windows of a kindergarten, noticeboards cradled in futuristic concrete curves, shops without queues. I had my eyes wide open too, it was the first time I'd been in the Wünsdorf camp, and knowing that this was the biggest base outside the Soviet Union didn't compare with actually seeing the extent of it.

We rumbled past concrete walls, the upper storeys of barracks peeking over the top—the militarist legacy of the Kaiser and Nazi eras repurposed to support the fight for peace and Socialism.

We turned off the main drag, past smaller houses used for

civilian purposes, before pulling up at another gateway. A second inspection of our paperwork, shorter this time, and the gate was opened. Moments later, the UAZ came to a halt outside the Soviet railway station—next to, but separate from the station provided for us Germans.

The driver stayed where he was, but his pal was opening Weber's door before I'd even realised that we'd reached our destination.

He escorted her up the steps to the modern station building and I dutifully followed behind. Ever the polite gentleman, the soldier opened the main door to allow Weber to enter, then a second door off the main corridor. He gave her a not ungentle push into the room beyond and pulled the door shut on her. I briefly saw her face pressed against the peephole before the soldier swung the covering to and latched it.

As I was shown into a more comfortable office opposite, Weber began to hit the cell door, her fists beating dully against the heavy wood. My own door was left ajar and I could see our escort had positioned himself in the corridor.

I could still hear Weber hammering away, but there wasn't much I could do about that, so I looked around my room, trying to work out what kind of trouble I might be in. A couple of desks, several chairs. A mural on the wall, showing Lenin, still holding Marx's bestseller in one hand, the other hooked around his lapel, keeping himself steady while he looked the future in the eye, even though he'd been dead and embalmed for over sixty years.

Other than an out of date copy of the *Izvestia*, there was nothing else to hold my interest. I stood by the window, looking out at a rake of goods wagons, wider and higher than usual for this country—the Moscow express, made up of Russian rolling stock.

My observations were interrupted by a soft footfall behind me. I spun around to find an orderly depositing a glass of tea on the desk.

"The Major will be with you shortly," he informed me.

I drank the tea by the window. Weber had ceased making a din, although the soldier remained in the hallway. Outside, the lamps had been turned on, bathing the platforms and goods yard in anaemic light. As I watched, a small shunter pushed a passenger carriage to the nearest platform. Just seeing the opaque windows, small and high up, was enough for me to guess it was a prison wagon.

"Burratino—you're early!" A warm voice, a smile that didn't reach his one operational eye. Pozdniakov had arrived.

I lifted the oilcloth pouch out of my jacket pocket and put it on the desk between us, but the major ignored the offering, tilting his head towards the doorway he asked: "Who's your friend?"

"She's not a friend. She found the material before I did—thought it best to bring her along."

He nodded, then began pacing along the side of the desk, lighting a papirosa as he went. I lit one of my own coffin nails, and we smoked for a while, doing our bit for German-Soviet friendship.

"Who is she?" he asked after half a cigarette.

"West German. An operative with some experience and good knowledge of East Berlin. Possibly BKA, but her role and skill set indicate *Verfassungsschutz* or BND. First contact in Rostock, she somehow links to Merkur, but I'm not sure whether she's here to support him or to stop him."

Pozdniakov stood still while I said my piece, then went back to measuring the room. I could have saved him the bother—it was five paces one way, six the other.

"Good. You were right to bring her to me," he decided. "And the material? Give me your assessment." He let his eyes drop briefly to the small package on the table.

"Photographic film negatives and microfiches of individual pages from various files. They show operational contact between First Lieutenant Sachse and a senior officer of the imperialist West German Crime Agency, *Polizeidirektor* Jüliger in Wiesbaden. The *Polizeidirektor* handles an agent in the MfS, codename Dresden, and the material indicates that Sachse may be Dresden."

Pozdniakov put out his cigarette. It seemed a little enthusiastic to me, the aluminium ashtray skeetering over the surface of the desk.

"Anything else?"

"Other documents show Comrade Sachse had operational contact with several individuals connected to the West German terrorist organisation RAF, some of whom have settled in the GDR, others who were here for training and debriefing by HV A."

We'd been speaking in Russian, but now Pozdniakov switched to German: "Did you hear all of that, First Lieutenant?"

I stared at the Russian, confused, but then I clocked the figure leaning against the door jamb. Even if he'd worn a wig to cover his fair hair and dark glasses to disguise his translucent eyes, I would have recognised Sachse by the sardonic smile.

81
WÜNSDORF

Sachse strutted into the room. He paused for a moment to smirk at the sling around my arm, visible beneath my open jacket, then stepped around Pozdniakov and reached for the oilskin pouch on the desk. But he wasn't quick enough—the KGB officer's hand was there first, he took hold of Sachse's wrist and jerked his hand down sharply. The rest of Sachse followed, and although he didn't cry out in pain, his grin deserted him.

"You had your chance, and you failed." Pozdniakov released Sachse's wrist, allowing him to stand up. "Go back to Rostock and wait for my orders."

Sachse stood for a moment, rubbing his wrist and glowering at me. "You should take him to Siberia along with the old man and that interfering girl!" he hissed, but Pozdniakov was more interested in examining his watch than listening to Sachse's recommendations.

I watched him leave the room, waiting for the sound of the outside door to open and close before turning back to Pozdniakov. "What's he doing here?"

The Russian didn't feel the need to answer. He picked up the oilskin pouch and dropped it into his tunic pocket.

"You'll use the material against him? Sachse didn't just kill Bruno, he's responsible for Sanderling too—he is, isn't he?" And when I said that, I remembered the airfield in Lärz—how Pozdniakov had shown no reaction when I told him of Merkur's allegation that someone in the Firm was a double.

You only have to whisper the words *Mole* or *Double Agent*

for a hush to descend over Berlin Centre. Tape recorders stop whirring, microphones and lights dim and there's an audible gasp as everyone draws a sharp breath. But Pozdniakov hadn't even paused before moving on to the next question.

Major Pozdniakov left the room, and I followed him into the hall. The sentry had Weber's cell door open, she was standing just inside, her fancy coat, now ripped and dirty, was hanging open, her scarf draped over her shoulders like a shawl. She looked Pozdniakov up and down, her eyes flicking over the blue KGB flashes on his collar, counting the pips and stripes on his shoulders.

"Take her to the train," Pozdniakov instructed.

I didn't know whether Weber could understand Russian, if she didn't, she was about to find out what the KGB officer had said. The soldier took hold of her upper arm, she didn't try to squirm out of his grasp, but she did turn her head to me.

"Where are they taking me?" She pushed her hair back behind her right ear as she asked.

I could have told her: the Moscow Express. But I didn't. I shrugged as she was dragged out of the building and onto the platform.

Pozdniakov had turned, was looking through the window of the office we'd just vacated. Together we watched the guard push Weber up the steep steps of the prison carriage. She struggled briefly, holding onto the sides of the doorway, but the guard swiped the back of her legs and she went down, her knees landing on the sharp edge of the top step.

Only when Weber had been dragged out of sight did Pozdniakov move again.

I tagged along as he headed upstairs, into another corridor, the twin of that on the ground floor. We halted at a heavy, grey painted door, a hinged metal plate in the centre covering a peephole.

"I thought you might like to say goodbye," said Pozdniakov, already turning away.

A uniformed soldier turned a large key in the lock and pulled the door open to allow me in.

Merkur was sitting on a wooden board attached to the wall, he looked up as I entered, but his face didn't lift in recognition or surprise. He was wearing the same clothes I'd seen him in the day before, still no shoes on his feet. His face was grey, except for the pockets under his eyes, which were almost black with fatigue.

"I'm to be taken to Russia," he informed me, his voice flat, his chin slowly dropping until it met his chest.

I didn't reply. I hadn't found any words for Weber, I didn't even bother trying for Merkur.

"I had to tell them about Arno's material, I didn't have a choice ..." He looked up again. "Did you get there before them? Did you find the cache?"

I nodded.

"And you can use the material? Sachse will face the consequences for his actions? Is he done for? Tell me he's finished!" His chin remained high, life briefly returning to his face.

I measured the hope in those eyes, and remembered Bruno, Sanderling and my friend Holger.

"Yes, we have enough evidence," I told him. "Sachse is finished—I'll see to it myself."

Behind me, the guard discreetly cleared his throat. Time up.

"Then it was worth it," said Merkur as I left, his voice almost lost as the cell door slammed.

82
BERLIN FRIEDRICHSHAIN

I caught the next train out of Wünsdorf, but it still took me a long time to get home. I walked back from station, stopping off at every bar to dull the pain.

Once there, I paused at the front door, turning to survey the street. No kid on his first watching mission, no dark blue Shiguli registered in Rostock.

Up the stairs, let myself into my flat and stand by the window, finishing off the bottle of Kümmel that Lütten had brought that night.

Half drunk yet completely sober, I lifted my bag onto the coffee table and started to empty it. The used clothes, the various hats, scarves and other disguises I hadn't bothered with in Warnemünde. And in a side pocket, rolled so tightly it hadn't been crushed, the portrait Anna Weber drew that night in the *Fischerklause*. I unrolled it, clumsy with only one good arm, and stared at myself.

She was right, the charcoal had smudged.

**Reim returns in
Rostock Connection**

List of Main Characters

MfS staff

Eberhard **Dupski**, captain, Reim's immediate superior.

Wolfgang **Koschak**, major general, head of HV A/IX.

Heinrich 'Heinz' **Kühn**, major, head of section II in ZAIG.

Horst **Lütten**, second lieutenant at Rostock District Administration.

Georg **Prager**, corporal at Rostock District Administration.

Hans-Peter **Reim**, second lieutenant based in ZAIG/II, Berlin Centre.

Gerhard **Sachse**, first lieutant in foreign intelligence (HV A/Abt XV Rostock).

Sanderling, code name for **Ruth Gericke**, lieutenant, HA II. Also known under the operational name **Gisela Bauer**.

Walter **Schur**, lieutenant colonel, head of HA II/2

Matthias 'Matse' **Stoyan**, second lieutenant HA VI.

Other characters

Source **Bruno**, codename for **Arnold 'Arno' Seiffert**.

Andreas **Portz**, polizeirat in the BKA, Arnold Seiffert's superior.

Dmitri Alexandrovich **Pozdniakov**, major. KGB liaison with HV A and HA II/5.

Arnold **Seiffert**, officer of the BKA, defected to the GDR in the book *Berlin Centre*.

Werner **Seiffert**, Arnold Seiffert's father.

Anna **Weber**, chambermaid at the Hotel Neptun in Warnemünde.

GLOSSARY

MfS organisation

Abteilung – Department. The *Hauptabteilungen* (HA—main departments) were based in Berlin (most at Berlin Centre in Lichtenberg), responsible for national co-ordination and strategy in their areas of responsibility.
The *Abteilungen* were sub-departments of the HAs, either based in Berlin, (e.g. Abt. M, Abt. 26) or the equivalent departments in the *District Administrations* and *County Offices*. Most local departments kept the number of the Main Department they belonged to (e.g. Abt. II represented HA II), the main exception being Abt. XV, the local level of the HV A.
Main Departments were further divided into Sections.

Abteilung M – Department M, responsible for postal surveillance.

Abteilung 26 – Department 26, responsible for audio and visual surveillance (including telecommunications).

Bezirksverwaltung des MfS, BV – District Administration. Each of the 15 administrative districts in the GDR had a MfS Administration, which co-ordinated operations in that area. The next administrative level down, the counties (*Kreise*), had offices in each county town (**Kreisdienststelle, KD**).

County Office see *Bezirksverwaltung*.

Department see *Abteilung*.

District Administration *see Bezirksverwaltung*.

HA, Hauptabteilung – see *Abteilung*, or the specific Main Departments below.

HA II – Main Department II, counter-intelligence.

HA VI – Main Department VI, passport control, tourism, transit traffic, where Reim was posted until autumn 1983.

HA IX – Main Department IX, investigation, interrogation and prosecution of suspects.

HA XX – Main Department XX, state organs and institutions, culture, church, underground groups; security of military communications infrastructure.

HV A, Hauptverwaltung A – Main Administration A, foreign intelligence. (Many modern German authorities, including the BStU regard the A in HV A as referring to *Aufklärung*, reconnaissance, however none of my primary sources with MfS backgrounds refer to the department as such.)

Main Department see *Abteilung*.

Kreisdienststelle, KD – see *Bezirksverwaltung*.

PKE, Paß- und Kontrolleinheit – Pass and Control Unit at border crossings, part of *HA VI* but wearing border guards uniforms.

ZAIG, Zentrale Auswertungs- und Informationsgruppe – Central Evaluation and Information Group, general staff unit with wide-ranging responsibilities, notably archiving, general reporting and, in Reim's section (ZAIG/II), control and measurement of professional standards.

GDR/German terms

Ausweis – identity card.

ABV, Abschnittsbevollmächtigter – beat policeman with responsibility for a particular neighbourhood or area.

Bereitschaftspolizei der Volkspolizei / Volkspolizei-Bereitschaften, VPB – barracked police troops, used whenever large numbers of police were required, e.g. public order situations or large-scale searches.

Bezirk – the GDR was administratively divided into 15 *Bezirke* (districts), each of which was further divided into *Kreise*, which I've translated as counties (NB some authors and historians translate *Bezirk* as county and *Kreis* as district).

Bino – seasoning sauce, similar to Maggi sauce.

BND, Bundesnachrichtendienst – West German foreign intelligence service.

Bundesbahn, Deutsche Bundesbahn, DB – West German rail.

Bundespost, Deutsche Bundespost, BP – West German post.

Cheka – originally the Bolshevik secret police agency set up by Felix Dzerzhinski in 1917 in the Soviet Union. The secret police agencies in socialist states, and particularly the Stasi, drew on the traditions of the Cheka, seeing themselves as *Chekists*.

Chekist – member of the Cheka.

Comrade, Genosse – member of the Socialist Unity Party (Communist party of the GDR), member of the army and other armed organs of the GDR.

Datsche, Datschek – (plural: Datschen) weekend cottage, hut on an allotment or similar. From the Russian.

Dederon – GDR synthetic material, similar to nylon.

DEIN STAR – substitution (encryption) table commonly used by BND agents in the GDR.

Deutsch-Sowjetische Freundschaft – Society for German-Soviet Friendship.

District see *Bezirk*.

Diversant – (plural: *Diversanten*) person engaged in *Diversion*.

Diversion, politisch-ideologische Diversion – anti-socialist influence or activity, whether in thought or action.

DT64 – youth radio station in the GDR.

Exquisit – expensive boutiques that sold limited edition, GDR produced fashion items not available in the usual shops.

F96 – Fernstraße 96. The Fernstraßen were the equivalent of the Bundesstraßen (the F96 is now the B96): trunk roads, highways.

FDJ, Freie Deutsche Jugend – Free German Youth, Communist Party youth movement.

Feierabend – end of shift, knocking off time, home time.

Fischkopf, Fischkopp – fish-head, derogative term for a resident of the coast.

Groschen – ten Pfennigs.

Grützwurst – type of black sausage.

GST, Gesellschaft für Sport und Technik – Society for Sports and Technology, providing field activities and pre-military training for young people.

GÜST, Grenzübergangsstelle – border crossing point.

Hausbuch – housebook, each residential block kept a *Hausbuch* in which residents' and visitors' details were entered—Westerners on arrival, visitors from within the GDR after three days. The *Hausbuch* was regularly checked by the *ABV*, beat policeman.

Haus des Reisens – central travel agency of the GDR, on Alexanderplatz. A police desk provided registration services for Western tourists to save them the trip to the local police station.

Havarie – technical breakdown, disaster, write-off.

Herein! – come in! Enter!

IM, Inoffizieller Mitarbeiter – unofficial collaborator of the MfS.

Inter-zonal trains, Interzonen Züge – trains crossing the inner-German border, distinct from **transit trains** which served West Berlin.

Interhotel – chain of international standard hotels in the GDR.

Kaschi – Kalashnikov KM-72 / AKM

Kaufhalle – self-service supermarket.

konspirative Wohnung, KW – safe house/flat.

Kripo, Kriminalpolizei, 'K' – Criminal Police, the criminal investigation agency for police forces in German speaking countries. The abbreviation *K* was unique to the GDR.

Lederol – imitation leather.

Ludmilla – Soviet built diesel locomotives hauling passenger and freight trains (Reichsbahn classification 130, 131, 132, 142).

Meschugge – not all there, crazy. From the Yiddish.

Ministerium für Staatssicherheit, MfS, Stasi – Ministry for State Security, secret police and intelligence agency.

Mitropa ran sleeper cars, station buffets and kiosks as well as motorway service stations.

Pentakta L100 – semi-portable microfiche reader, made by VEB Pentacon in Dresden.

Pfeffi – square sweets, originally peppermints, but in later years other flavours were available.

Pille-palle – crazy. Berlin dialect.

Platt – north German dialect, particularly from coastal areas.

Polizeirat – West German police rank, equivalent to Major in the *Volkspolizei*.

Red Army Faction, Rote Armee Fraktion – West German terrorist group, originally formed around Andreas Baader, Ulrike Meinhof and others.

Reichsbahn, Deutsche Reichsbahn – East German railways.

Sandmännchen, Unser Sandmännchen – Our Sandman, children's programme on East German television.

Schlagermusik – German language ballads.

Selters – sparkling water.

Shiguli – car known in Western markets as Lada, manufactured by Zhiguli.

Sprechtafel – radio code table used mostly by the *Volkspolizei* and border guards.

Sprelacart, Sprelakart – decorative laminate sheets, similar to Resopal and Formica.

Starshina – senior sergeant in the Soviet Army.

Station der jungen Naturforscher und Techniker – Centre for Young Naturalists and Engineers, after-school centres encouraging interest in the sciences.

Tacheles – straight talk. From the Yiddish.

Taigatrommel – Soviet built M62 heavy diesel locomotive (*Reichsbahn* classification V200, later 120). Called the Taiga Drum on account of the loud exhausts.

Tote Oma – mashed and heated black sausage, often served with boiled potatoes and sauerkraut.

Transportpolizei, Trapo – East German transport police.

Uffzi, Unteroffizier – the lowest rank of the non-commissioned officers (equivalent to corporal / sergeant), also generally used to cover all NCO ranks.

Verfassungsschutz – West German domestic intelligence agency.

Volkspolizei, Deutsche Volkspolizei, DVP – GDR police force.

Volkssolidarität, VS – mass organisation organising care for elderly and vulnerable people.

W50 – medium sized diesel truck, ubiquitous in the GDR.

Warnowwerft, Warnow shipyard – One of the shipyards in Rostock, based near the mouth of the river Warnow.

Wofasept – disinfectant, used in practically every public building and train in the GDR.

Weiße Flotte – passenger ships plying tourist routes.